HIDDEN VILLAINS

Edited by

ROBYN HUSS

HIDDEN VILLAINS

IN MEMORY OF DAVID FARLAND

A cherished and irreplaceable mentor to a generation.

CONTENTS

INTRODUCTION

Dear Reader,

Welcome to this collection of stories featuring hidden villains. Many of the authors showcased in this anthology have been published and may be names you recognize; others had a story selected as their first publication. I have enjoyed reading, editing, and compiling all of them for you.

As you can see in the table of contents, I have grouped the stories in two sections. Those that feature "the villain in us" are those in which the villains will be revealed in the main characters or someone close to them. Villains in stories that have "the villain in them" are outside the circles of the main characters, in society at large or in alternate societies.

It is my hope that you will see a little bit of yourself in, and therefore identify with, each protagonist — or perhaps their antagonist. The title *Hidden Villains* aptly fits our human nature and our collective intent to conceal the darker sides of ourselves, as portrayed so poignantly in Robert Louis

Stevenson's novella *The Strange Case of Dr. Jekyll and Mr. Hyde*, the tragic tale of my favorite hidden villain. Time will tell if one of these stories will endure as my next favorite.

Wherever these hidden villains may be, I hope you enjoy discovering them!

Robyn Huss, Editor

Robyn Huss is a freelance editor who specializes in heavy developmental and copy editing; she is a thorough grammarian and has a good eye for inconsistencies. She is able to focus on character development, dialogue, paragraphing, sequencing of events and details, theme, and symbolism, in addition to providing a thorough review of grammar, usage, style, and word choice.

Robyn has spent a lifetime analyzing fiction and writing. Her bachelor's degree is in English with teaching certification; she has taught literature and writing for more than thirty years to grades six through college, and she has been editing professionally since 2013. She currently balances editing with teaching at the college level.

You can learn more about Robyn and see samples of her work at www.HussEditing.com.

THE VILLAIN IN US

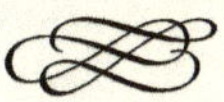

SIREN SONG AT MIDNIGHT

BY DAVID FARLAND

When I was a girl of ten, my father, Stefán Elegante, worked as a paleogeneticist for the Pacific Fisheries Commission, trying to restore extinct tuna and marlin, dolphins, and blue squid. He took me to his lab and showed me how he pulled bits of bone from fossils and dyed the DNA so his computers could read it and build living replicas of the cells: "See, Josephina!" he said, pointing to remnants of a cell under his microscope, rainbow-hued ropes of DNA. "The fishes are still there, waiting for us to bring them back to life, and the DNA is a manual to tell us how." His eyes glowed as he spoke, and I did not understand half of what he said. "This is old DNA. I like the old stuff best. DNA that is a hundred years old is better than that taken from a living cell, for when a creature is living, so many chemical processes happen from moment to moment that sections of DNA often get torn loose and return into place reversed. But a cell that is a million years old is some-times in better shape, because the cells heal themselves. In old dead cells, the chemical bonds between amino acids are so strong that reversed DNA returns to its proper place, you see!"

He watched me with his solemn brown eyes, saw my confusion, and he smiled softly. "Don't worry. Someday, you'll understand all of this, and more," he said, kissing my forehead. "You know, I sometimes wonder: if we destroy our world, do you think God could take this old DNA and rebuild us?" he asked, sincerely awed by this marvel. I saw his fossils and understood only that, like God, he brought creatures to life from the dust of the Earth. On that day, I decided to become a paleogeneticist.

But somehow his hope died. Just as a wasp will lay its eggs in pear blossoms, corrupting their fruit, so despair corrupted him. Once he dared to dream of a restored world with vast rain forests, alive with the cries of macaws.

Wait. I am confused, exhausted to the bone. I'm not sure what to say. I must turn off the recorder for a moment.

[Two seconds of silence.]

* * *

I THINK I began too early. I know I'll live for only another few minutes, and I must record this while I can. Let me begin with the arrest of my father:

Last September, five plankton-harvesting ships exploded in a single evening. From childhood I've seen these Chinese ships off the Chilean coast – floating ceramic cities whose brilliant halogen lights sputter like fallen stars in the evening out on the horizon. During the attack, I was working at El Instituto Paleobiologico in Cartagena, extracting DNA from fossilized dimetrodons. I heard a distant explosion, almost a popping noise, and ran out into the evening. One plankton-harvesting ship had exploded on the horizon, and where it had floated, a great violet curtain of spray was rising into the night, higher and higher, looking almost like a thunderhead. Beside me a small boy cried, "What is that?" and his mother, who perhaps wanted to protect him, said, "It is only angels, washing the curtains of heaven in the ocean."

I thought India must have attacked China, that the Plankton Wars had started again, that they might blow all of the ships. But if the Plankton Wars had begun again, they did so with a twist, for that night the Rio Negro dam blew in Brazil, and two million died as black torrents flooded down the Amazon.

A few hours later, the media revealed that the bombers were chimeras, genetically-engineered men that General Torres had modified to better adapt to life on other planets. They were an aquatic breed and had lived off the coast of Chile for years. By morning the streets were ablaze with news of the attack by "Los Sirenos," the Sirens. The detonation of seven bombs was heralded as if it were a major war, and the Alliance of Nations began to hunt the Sirens. The news fascinated me, not because I longed for vengeance against the chimeras, but because the work of the genetic engineers who created these beings was similar to my own, yet a far greater art.

After the attack, the news showed Brazi mothers mourning for children who had washed out to sea as the Amazon flooded, twisted wreckage, and tiny orphans desperate for food. One commentator told how it could only have been a few Sirens who were gallantly bidding for control of Earth's waterways, trying to stop the plankton harvesters who continually stole food from their mouths. But his voice was drowned by others who decried the Sirens' "crime against humanity." Experts paraded through the media, telling how destruction along the Rio Negro was only the beginning. They said millions in China and India would starve without the plankton harvesters, and they hinted hunger would strike in South America because of the loss of our fisheries.

My father had risen to become Director for the Pacific Fisheries Commission, so I called him on commlink to ask if these reports were accurate. He weighed each word, saying, "The Chinese pay so little for fishing rights, we won't miss it. In three months, they'll be harvesting like always." He sounded harried, tired, and I imagined he was under great pressure.

For a couple of days my friend Rosalinda recorded news holos about the chimeras. We planned to watch the holos for entertainment, but as the holos displayed, I was horrified. Our Marines hooked electronic sniffers to stunners that looked like torpedoes; with these they hunted the Sirens by scent. When they scored a hit, they dragged the stunned Siren from the water, shrieking and flapping its tail. The sirens had pale blue scales covering their bodies, the color of the summer sky on the horizon, icy green eyes, and hair the silver of mountain water. Their women were delicate, with an unearthly beauty, and their cries as they were dragged from the waters sounded like the song of dolphins mingled with a human scream.

Most captured Sirens were women and children who could not swim fast enough to evade the stunners, and the powerful chemical jolt of the stunners was too much for them. Many women and children died. As we watched the children cling to dead mothers wrapped in seaweed, and as we listened to the wails of pain and grief, the horror struck in a way we would not have understood if we had seen the single broadcast of each capture as it happened. We lost our innocence, and Rosalinda ended up hugging me, offering me comfort late into the night. After that, I had no stomach for news. I avoided listening to it, did not think about it. I tried to put it out of mind.

Then, my world changed. Late in the evening on September 15, as I worked alone in my lab, a man crept in – a pale man with an effeminate face, dressed in putrid-smelling street clothes. His was carrying a metal bar, and his hand bled as if he'd cut it while prying the back door open. He stalked toward me nervously, sweat glistening on his brow, swinging the bar into his palm, watching side hallways for signs of others. My co-workers had gone home an hour before. We were alone. The way he looked, I thought I would be lucky if he only raped me.

"Josephina?" he asked quickly. "Josephina Elegante? Daughter to Stefán?" I nodded dumbly and backed away. He lurched toward me. "Here, get these to your father! It is mem-set!" He held out two small gelatin capsules the color of urine.

"What?" I asked, so frightened I did not know what to do.

He looked at me strangely, and smeared the blood from his hand across his shirt. "Mem-set – it is a mind-wiping drug. It keeps one's memories from being scanned. You must give it to your father, for he has secrets that he wants to keep concealed, even beyond the grave."

"What? Are you crazy?" I asked, backing away. And I worried, for it seemed obvious he was crazy.

His eyes suddenly widened. "You don't know?" he asked. "Your father has been arrested for giving explosives to the Sirens. It is on the news even as we speak! He has been charged with high treason and murder. He will surely be executed. As his only relative, you will be allowed to attend the execution. You must give these to him before he dies!" He held out the drugs, watching the halls as if he believed the secret police would burst into the room.

"Wait," I said. I thumbed the subdural presser switch behind my right ear and jacked into a simulcast news holo, keeping it on multitask so I could watch the stranger at the same time. My father, Stefán Elegante, was shown huddling among what must have been twenty Allied Marine troops, all of them in their space-blue armor. They rushed through the streets of Cartagena in a block, and peasants tossed bricks and burning sacks, shouting "Murderer!" The peasants looked confused. They did not know my father's crime and functioned only as a mob. The narrator said, "Now we see Stefán Elegante, alleged traitor to his species, rushing for cover." I stood in shock, as my father boarded a military transport. I jacked out of the newscast, thumbed my comm-link again, and read in my father's code, but he did not answer the call. I jacked back into the newscast: it showed my father on a small boat offshore from our beach home in Concepción, unloading boxes into the waiting arms of the Sirens. The reporter said the boxes held explosives.

I jacked out in shock, for I knew that this was all some magnificent lie, knew my father was innocent despite the holos. What was their evidence? Pictures of boxes?

"Please," the stranger said. "I'm a friend. I'm only one of dozens who helped give your father weapons for the Sirens. Many others like me still hope for a restored world, yet your father knows who we are. His memories will convict us. You see, the Alliance laws forbid the police from scanning the memories of criminals while they live, but once your father is executed, then his right to privacy dies with him, and Alliance surgeons will slice away his cerebral tissue so they can scan his memories at leisure. He knows this. He promised to take the mem-set. We all promised to take mem-set if we were caught. When you go to the execution, hold the capsules between your cheek and teeth until you get them to Stefán, then have him bite them. This is a powerful dose, enough for a dozen people, but you must get it to him at least two minutes before the execution. Once he breaks the capsules, the mem-set will form restriction enzymes. The membranes of his neural cells will harden, and the DNA in his brain will be chopped into pieces, destroying all his memories. Understand?"

The stranger wrapped my fingers around the capsules. "If any of us could hope to get past security to your father, we would gladly take this task upon ourselves. Please, save us! We are desperate!" he said, then he turned and ran.

I stood for a long time, holding the capsules, wondering what to do. I could not believe this stranger, and I wondered if it were some plot to discredit my father. That evening, I began trying to obtain permission to see my father . . .

[Two seconds of silence.]

* * *

I'M SORRY. I had to turn the recorder off. I can't think. This day has exhausted me. I am so angry that they call my father a "traitor to his species." He loved every species. Perhaps he loved them too much. As I record these words, I am sitting in my terrarium at El Instituto Paleobiologico de Colombia – the institute my father funded – feeding my pet euparkeria from a bag of eggs. The euparkeria are a small dinosaur from the early Mesozoic, the earliest age of dinosaurs, and they are a branch of thecodonts, the first true dinosaurs. They are the size of geese, with long graceful necks as delicate as a pianist's fingers, tiny front legs, and forest-green skin. On their backs are yellow-white speckles, the color that the primeval sun must have cast as it burned through fern jungles. One euparkeria licks at an egg with a long olive-green tongue, cleaning the egg yolk from inside a shell, looking for all the world like a small wingless dragon.

My father used to say that euparkeria are an important link in the chain of life. From them sprang many species: birds and pterosaurs, meat-eating carnosaurs, saurischian dinosaurs like the brontosaurus and supersaurus, and the ornithischians, such as the triceratops and ankylosaurus. If each higher animal species were a branch on a tree, the euparkeria would be close to the tree's root. They are one great main trunk from which higher animals evolved, while at the top of the tree would be an insignificant twig, a bud without fruit: mankind.

My father was not a traitor to our species. He only realized that we look on ourselves and think that instead of a twig, we are the whole tree, that we are the crown of creation instead of only another stem.

Anyway, my father was a military prisoner, and despite my pleas, I was forbidden to speak to him before the trial.

My friends disappeared, pretended not to know me. Even Rosalinda, a girl I've known since childhood, closed the door when I tried to speak to her. She shouted at me through the door, told me to go away, and she was crying, saying that the secret police had come to question her. At first I was angry and hurt, but her family had no political connections, and I knew it was better to keep my distance from her.

I accomplished nothing at work and did not eat. I could not ignore the instinct that drove me to believe in my father's innocence. I'd spoken to him at least three times a week for years – knew him better than anyone, and I knew he was incapable of murder. I searched his office, looking for proof of his innocence. His appointment books were gone, and only his computer logs were online. I sat late into the night, reading notes about the various genomes of extinct fishes, trying to extract some clue to prove his innocence.

I imagined that my father had been lured into this. Could it have been that he thought he was giving food to the Sirens? I wondered. That would be like him. He could have handed out boxes, unaware that weapons were stored in them, and now that he'd been caught, he would nobly protect the others with his life, even though they had betrayed him.

I so wanted this scenario to be true that I looked for evidence to support it. I read until my eyes burned from viewing every computer log, until perspiration trickled down my back. Late that night, an orderly came to the office, Mavro Hidalgo, an old man who had worked for my father since before I was born.

"Josephina, what are you doing here?" he asked.

"Looking for something," I said. "I don't know what – anything to prove my father's innocence."

Señor Hidalgo shook his head sadly. "I've already been through all those records," he said. "I've already thought about it. You want proof that don Stefán is innocent, but you won't find the proof in scraps of paper."

I looked at old Señor Hidalgo, my eyes became wet, and I blurted, "Are you saying he is guilty? You believe these lies?"

But Señor Hidalgo shook his head. "You don't need papers. The truth of his innocence is in your heart." He sat next to me, smelling of sweat and beans. He placed his leathery hand on my shoulder. "You know, your father has been sick for many years, suffering from depression." I nodded, for I'd known this. "When he was young, he was worse. For days at a time he would laugh, and his eyes would glow, and he would come to work practically walking on the ceiling! Oh, he was so happy, he did not need wings to fly.

"But then, the smile would fade, and he'd come to work, and you would see him drag as if wrapped in chains, and he'd sit for days and do nothing. We were all afraid for him, thinking he might kill himself, so one day I asked, 'don Stefán, why do you put yourself through this? You could cure this malady with a pill! Then, why do you suffer?' and do you know what he said?"

"No," I answered.

"Your father told me that the time he spent flying through the air more than rewarded him for the time he spent in the abyss. He said, 'Mavro, I know you worry for me, and I know I could take the cure. But I love my illness. You people – how can you appreciate life as I do? How can you live even one moment with passion? It is all so grand, so beautiful. Even when I am lost in the blackest well of midnight, life tastes so sweet to me! Life is so sweet!'"

Señor Hidalgo patted my shoulder, told me to go home, then began to straighten the office. I knew he was right. I didn't need more proof of my father's innocence than the life he'd led. My father could not have given explosives to the Sirens. I'd seen his innocence in the tender way he fed his fish by hand at the aquariums, in the way he kissed the pain away from my childhood injuries, in the way he relished to draw a breath. Life, all life, was too precious to be wasted.

That night, I drove to Concepción, to the sea house, and arrived at dawn. The police had scavenged the house until it was in ruins. My father's papers were strewn everywhere, and the furniture had been ripped apart. I cleaned the mess and walked the beaches in the mornings. I kept the mem-set hidden in my room, and twice the police came to question me, always asking names of my father's friends, of those I'd seen him with. I answered by declaring his innocence.

The details of my father's trial were never publicized. I learned through the news that my father was convicted of treason and accused of stealing a vast fortune through graft. He was found guilty of complicity in the murder of two million Brazis and was sentenced to die. I find it ironic that they convicted him in a secret trial, yet respected his right to privacy so much that they refused to pry his memories from him. Perhaps for them it was just a waiting game, and they believed they would get his accomplices in time.

After that, I learned that a news special would be broadcast by a famous reporter, a gringo cyborg named Todd Bennett who promised to have an "Interview with a Madman." The interview was advertised for days, and I could not sleep because I wanted so badly to see my father, to hear his voice. I watched the holo at home, enlarging the image so it filled the entire living room.

When the interview started, they showed Señor Bennett wearing a smooth white tungsten half-face with six glittering eyes that recorded all he saw in different spectra. The bottom half of his face was still human. He wore a glorious multicolored cape of light, which contrasted with my father's drab attire of prison blue, and it struck me that Señor Bennett knew the effect that his dress would have, for he looked as if he were a beautiful angel of light sent down to torture some damned soul in a tired hell.

"Can I begin by asking a few questions?" Señor Bennett said in flawless Spanish, using over-precise inflections common to those who speak with the aid of a translation chip.

My father wiped sweat from his face and pulled his long hair back over his shoulder, then looked out the window of a small cell. "You can ask," he said.

"Fine," Señor Bennett said. "Then let's establish your guilt. Records show that for months you fed the Sirens. In itself, that was admirable. But what caused you to commit the sin, this crime against humanity, of shipping them explosives?"

My father looked at the cyborg and said, "I am a fantasist, a dreamer. That is my only sin: to dream and hope."

The cyborg smiled placatingly. "Hope is no sin. It's one of the three great abiding virtues. When we die, we take it with us to heaven." I laughed, for I was correct in my assessment of the cyborg. He did want to disguise himself as an angel, and he was too stupid to be subtle about it.

"Hope has done me no good," my father said. "You want to

establish my guilt. It has been established in court. I master-
minded the War of the Sirens – if you can call it a war. I gave
them explosives. It was not a sin."

"Surely," Bennett countered, "you do not expect us to
believe that you acted alone in this act of terrorism? You
have no expertise in explosives. You could not have trained
the Sirens."

My father said calmly, "Believe what you will. If I had
accomplices, I will die before I reveal their names." Then
suddenly his mood changed, and he roared, "I will die!"

"You can't protect them forever," the cyborg affirmed.

My father only shrugged, as if his outburst of a moment
before had never happened.

Bennett asked, "Tell us why you aided the murder of over
two million people?"

"When I was appointed as Director of Pacific Fisheries, I
hoped to save the world," my father said almost casually.
"Ever since we first raped the Sea of Cortes and destroyed
the world's richest oyster beds, we Latin Americans have sold
the spoils of our oceans to the highest bidder. First the
oysters, then the sailfish and tuna, dolphin and manta – 'til
we were left with nothing but algae and plankton."

"One moment," Señor Bennett asked. "These animals you
mention, are they food animals that became extinct?"

"Yes," my father said, "temporarily extinct food animals."

Señor Bennett smiled. "I don't eat flesh, myself," he said.

My father roared, "You eat your own children!" Señor
Bennett lurched back as if my father would strike him. My
father stood and began pacing the cell. "When I was
appointed director, I thought, 'Here I am at last: A man who
can't be corrupted by graft! I can restore the ancient fisheries, rebuild seabeds laid waste by centuries of pollution.
Today, because of continual algae harvests, our atmosphere
has seventeen percent less oxygen than when I was born. You

worry about the poor who have no food – what will you say to those poor in a generation, when the seas are dead and they have no air to breathe?

"When I took office, even the trash fish that used to eat our turds had become extinct." My father paced the floor, moving so fast, speaking so fast, he almost gibbered. "So I committed the sin of hope. As Director of Pacific Fisheries, I sought funds to resurrect extinct fishes and phytozoa, to give the oceans time to rebuild. But I received only promises of money. I tried to reduce the amount of plankton the Chinese could harvest, but Director Nestor de la Luz told me to keep silent. He said the Chinese paid too well and that we would have to let the harvests continue for another year. We were rebuilding after the war with the Socialistas, and he said we needed money for the reconstruction, so money never came to me. It took months and years before I realized I was only paid to be a figurehead – no one really wanted me to restore the fisheries. People had lost their taste for flesh. No one living today cares to eat the fishes our great grandfathers dined upon. So, I realized, I was just fooling myself."

"Is that why you betrayed your species?" Señor Bennett asked in a cutting voice. "Because you were frustrated in your efforts to reduce the harvest? Because you wanted to be more than a figurehead?" He was baiting my father, and I hated him for it.

"No!" my father said. "Emotions had nothing to do with it. For years I enforced the quotas as best I could, but when Nestor died and I took his place, I found that fisheries money hadn't been siphoned off for reconstruction; it had been going into Nestor's pockets all along! He'd stolen from us! And at the same time, I learned that for years Torres' old chimeras out in the ocean had begged us to halt the plankton harvests. These Sirens were starving. Nestor had kept their pleas hidden, fearing that if people knew the truth, they might protect the fisheries, and it would cut into the income he earned from graft.

"But I knew that no one would care. We wouldn't stop the harvests, so I took the bribes from the Chinese, just as all my predecessors had done, but instead of pocketing the money, I bought explosives!"

My father's eyes became wild. I wondered if he'd been drugged for benefit of the viewers. He sat down and then immediately stood up again and paced the room, back and forth, quicker than you would believe possible.

"Truly, I hoped to wake you all, but the explosions only dull your ears! You kill your own children. I pity the poor who will not be able to eat or breathe or escape this planet. Someday they will remember me as a hero for trying to stop this madness while we yet had something to save! We are a diseased branch on the tree of life, and because of us, the whole tree will fall into ruin. I commit the sin of hope no more!" My father began raving, and a curious light shone from his eyes. I don't think he saw the reporter any longer, saw nothing but his own death, for he cursed the world.

Despite his confession, I did not believe he was guilty. I was angry with his accomplices and wondered why the truly guilty party, the person who had trained the Sirens to use explosives, did not step forward.

All that night, I remembered my father's words: "I will die before I reveal their names. I will die!" Was that a plea? I wondered. Did he really want the mem-set so badly that he would almost announce it to the world? I sat in my room and replayed the interview. The man in the holo, the convict, did not look like my father. He did not look like some gentleman, nobly protecting men more wicked than himself. He looked like a killer, eaten by guilt and rage, unrepentant for his murders. As I watched him again and again, pacing his cell like a leopard, I began to consider: my father's illness had made him passionate, a man quickly moved by both joy and despair. He spent so much time walking in that dark abyss that I wondered, could some Siren's song at midnight, sung while my father was deep in despair and at his most vulnerable, have drawn him to his destruction? If, at just the right moment, the Sirens pleaded for weapons instead of food, would my father have succumbed?

* * *

As I RECORD THIS, I've been remembering how when my father put me in charge of El Instituto Paleobiologico, he said, "Once you show people that we paleogeneticists can recreate life from the Mesozoic, they will see that there are no limits to what we can do. The concept of extinction will fall away, and we will be free to rebuild this world, turn it into a Garden of Eden."

Such was my father's hope. But six years ago I recreated the euparkeria, and the world has regarded my work with meagre curiosity and some fear. It was then that I first realized that my father's assessment of the world was wrong. He wanted to recreate rain forests, restore oceans to their pristine conditions, but once people saw my dinosaurs, they did not unite with our cause. In government hearings, bureaucrats decried the cost of such an effort. They said it would take generations to rebuild this world, that such an effort was impractical and would bankrupt nations. My father told them that an effort that took five generations would repay itself for a hundred thousand generations to come. Yet his talk was all for nothing. People eyed my father with the same curiosity and fear that they showed my dinosaurs.

Curiosity and fear. Here in Cartagena, we have a great zoo where they hope in the near future to exhibit some dinosaurs, especially the fierce flesh eaters of the Jurassic.

Many peasants fear I will create such monsters, and that they will stalk the ghettos and eat their children.

Ah well, it is shortly past noon. My father has been dead for more than two hours. I feel tired, and my tongue and mouth are going numb, so I must hurry and record these words:

After the newscast, I sat in my bedroom and pressed the small yellow capsules of mem-set between my fingers, wondering how much pressure it would take to release the liquid inside. I worried that the poisons might escape if the capsules came in contact with my saliva, so I spat on them, then watched to make sure that the capsules did not disintegrate. I remembered a story of an old Socialista general who was captured in Argentina, and he'd poisoned himself with mem-set. I jacked into the computer network and called up the story, learned how he had taken the mem-set and lain paralyzed in his cell. Despite all his captors could do, he died within hours. The article noted that mem-set, because it is catalyzed by uric acid which is a natural byproduct of dying cells, is perhaps the only drug that is more effective in a deceased person than in a living being. Yet mem-set is also a deadly poison – for uric acid is present in small amounts in every human.

In the early morning, I walked the beach and looked out to sea, and among the ghost crabs that scuttled across the beach like something from a dream, I saw a dozen gulls flapping above a heap that looked like a corpse. I ran to it and found a child, a Siren of palest blue, wrapped in red kelp, drowning in the open air. She was gasping, and her eyes were rolled back. I dragged her back to the water and held her under the waves. I watched up and down the beach, afraid someone would see what I was doing, and a moment later a female Siren swam at my ankles in the foam and thrust her head out.

"Thank you," the Siren sang, and I looked into her deep-green eyes and saw gratitude burning there. For days I'd been depressed and frightened, but I looked in her eyes and felt only warmth and peace. The gentleness in that creature's eyes was so convincing, so alien, that I couldn't imagine the Sirens killing humans. I wondered, when the Sirens blew the dam on the Rio Negro, could they have been unaware that so many humans would die? Could creatures of the sea even begin to conceive how vulnerable we humans would be in their element?

Later that day I saw the Allied Marines out in the bay with their black gunships, dropping torpedoes into the water, hunting for the mother and her child.

After less than two months, the authorities declared the War of the Sirens to be over. The Marines imprisoned six hundred of them in secure holding tanks in Jamaica. I suppose the rest of them died. The Alliance slated my father's execution date, making him a single sacrificial lamb. I found nothing to prove either his innocence or guilt.

[Two seconds of silence.]

* * *

THE ALLIANCE DID NOT REVEAL my father's location before his execution. All last night I paced my room, waiting for them to call to tell me where the execution would be held. At dawn, commlink tones sounded in my head. A woman told me to come to camp Bolívar, outside Cartagena. I rode to the Marine camp in a taxi, too nervous to drive, and I found a military shuttle armed with neutron cannons warming its engines just inside the gates. Two police scanned me for weapons and ushered me into the shuttle with a dozen guards. I knew even before we left the coast that we were heading for the desert – the soldiers in the shuttle were adjusting the color settings on their body armor so that it turned an ivory shade, the color of alkali soil. The sun shining through the shuttle windows reflected from their visors as if each helmet were a single white star opal.

We thundered south for fifteen minutes, then plummeted into a desert ghost town high in the Andes. The portals to the shuttle slid open, and my guards scurried like pill bugs from beneath the shadow of an overturned rock. They dropped to the ground and covered the old limestone buildings with their pulse rifles. The cold mountain air hit me, and a cloud of smoky-gray dust and chaff swirled up from the shuttle's landing skids. I stepped out and surveyed the town: the morning sun cast long blue shadows across each fold of the mountains, across each jutting stone. The light was so intense that my eyes could not focus on objects in the shadows. Everything was either black or white in this hard land; there was no room for grays.

From the door of one stone building, a dark little mestizo squinted at the bright sunlight. He wore the space-blue uniform of the Alliance Marines and smoked a thin cigar. He straightened his back, tossed his cigar to the dirt, and ground it under his heel as if it were a locust. "Senorita Elegante," he said, "I am Major Gutierez. The press will be here shortly, and you will not have much time to spend alone with your father before the . . . ceremony."

"Fine," I said, shaking. I held the capsules behind my teeth, hoping he would not search me. He ushered me to the tiny stone building, and my hope rose. The facility was a prison, hundreds of years old with antiquated steel cages for the criminals, though all the cells were empty. I thought that if my father were kept in such a facility, it would be easy to pass the mem-set to him.

We walked down a long corridor to a darkened cell, and I saw my father huddled in a corner, sobbing. He was sweating profusely, as if he had labored in the hot sun, so that his hair hung to the side of his head like a damp black rag, and his jaw was set with fear. A soft orange glow in the air around his cell showed that a repulsion field had been hastily installed. Two armored guards and a priest stood outside the cell. My heart fell as I realized I would not be able to get the mem-set to him through the field.

"Can I go into the cell?" I asked Major Gutierez.

"I am sorry," the major answered, "but no."

"Can I speak with him alone?"

"No," the major answered, but he ordered a guard to follow him as he left, affording a little more privacy. The priest would have left also, but my father beckoned, "No, stay! Please. I want you to hear my confession."

"Father," I said, "I'd have come sooner, but no one would tell me where you were."

"What does it matter?" he said, and he stood and looked out a small window. He placed his palms on the stone wall. His hands shook.

"It matters to me," I answered. "It matters very much. It matters to your friends." My father seemed so despondent that I wanted to see the hopeful fire that had once burned in his eyes, so I said, "I saw a Siren three days ago, a child. She washed up near the beach house. I noticed her only because a flock of gulls had gathered, waiting for her to die. Her skin was purpled, and her gills and fins were chafed. I pulled her to the shallows and held her underwater to breathe. After a moment, her mother swam up and took the child out to sea. The mother thanked me. If she were here, perhaps she would thank you, too."

I do not know why I told my father this in public. Perhaps I was angry with the Alliance and wanted the guards to arrest me – helping the Siren had been an act of treason. I felt that the government was corrupt, and I wanted the guards to prove to me how evil they had become.

"It was the pollution," my father said, as if he were lecturing one of his classes in paleogenetic engineering. "The acidic water makes their gills itch, so the Sirens come to the beach to let the sand wash through their gills and scratch them. Sometimes their gills fill with silt, and as they strangle, they pass out and wash to shore." He fell silent a moment, his voice changed, filling with despair. "You should have let the gulls have that child! You should have let her die! She will starve if the pollution doesn't get her first. Better to let the child die!"

"How can you say that?" I asked. His dark eyes held no hope or solemnity, only crazed despair. He got up and paced across his cell, back and forth, full of frantic energy, and I wondered what had happened to him during the Alliance interrogations, wondered if he were sane. I wanted to ask if he were guilty of treason to his species. I wanted to ask if he had really given the Sirens weapons, just as I had wanted to ask for weeks, but at that moment I was suddenly too afraid to ask.

"Father," I said, "I love you."

He nodded, bobbing his chin with a lunatic grin. "Por supuesto. Of course, of course," he said, as if my love were a given. He was shaking, and he began to cry, then suddenly burst into a fit of laughter. "How is your work? How are the euparkeria?" he asked, not even looking at me, pacing.

"They're fine," I lied. I couldn't tell him that the government had seized our bank accounts. They claimed that, like his little private war, my father had funded my research with graft. I didn't have enough money to feed my dinosaurs for another week, so I'd made arrangements for the zoo to take them.

He continued pacing across the room, licking his lips,

caught in the web of his thoughts. I spoke his name twice, but he did not answer. He swore softly. I'd never seen him like this.

I so wanted him to be happy. I tried to grab at his shirt through the soft orange glow of the repulsion field, and said, "Father, even now, doesn't your life taste sweet?"

My father gazed at me, as if trying to pierce my thoughts, then spat on the floor. I stumbled back a step, and in that moment I realized that he rejected life. Despite my childish faith, my father was guilty of murder.

Gutierez came to escort me from the room, back down the corridors of the old prison to a walled court. In the courtyard stood a dozen dignitaries, as many reporters, and six Alliance Marines with projectile rifles. My father walked into the bright sunlight in company of the priest. My father's hands and feet were shackled, so he took tiny clumsy steps, pulling at his chains.

A hawk was soaring on the thermal updrafts, and my father stopped to watch it sail over a ridge. "My God," my father said, "what does it find to eat here?" He looked across the desert toward the plains, and said to the priest, "Beyond those valleys, there were once rain forests. Great, endless forests."

One marine fidgeted with his rifle. Until that moment, I do not think I believed the execution would take place. I somehow hoped that others would recognize my father's innocence, that the great wise leaders of Earth would stoop to save him. I looked at the rifles, and a thin scream issued from my lips, and I bit it back, tried to control myself. The major escorted my father to a wall and stood with him a moment. Everything was so quiet.

The major said, "Señor, do you want a blindfold?"

My father looked at the ground and shook his head and sighed. Inside his cell he had been sweating, depressed, but the cool morning air dried his sweat, and I imagined that he was almost glad to finally finish it.

"It is traditional to offer a cigar," the major said. My father shook his head, still staring at the ground. "Any last words, Señor Elegante? Last requests?" My father only shook his head. One reporter coughed.

"I have a last request!" I shouted, and the major looked up at me. "Can I speak to my father alone, only for a moment, to say goodbye?"

"I am sorry," the major said, "but no."

"A kiss? Can I kiss my father goodbye?"

The major looked up at me and sighed. "If you wish."

I ran to my father. Everyone was watching, and there was no way to pass the mem-set to him. I was afraid he might swallow the capsules instead of break them, and I had no way to tell him how to use the drug, so I burst the capsules between my teeth, hard. The mem-set tasted bitter, slightly of anise, and I thought I might gag, but I held it on my tongue. And as we kissed, I spat the poison into his mouth, rubbed it onto his lips.

My father lurched backward a step and his eyes widened in horror. "Josephina!" he said, crying out as if begging to know what I had done.

"I don't want to live without you!" I said. "All our work is destroyed. I will always love you! God knows how to read the manuals of our lives. He will put everything back together. For a while – only for a while – the restoration will continue without us!"

My father threw his arms around me and wept. "No, Josephina," he cried. "I did not want this to touch you. I did not want to hurt you."

Major Gutierez pulled at my shoulders. "Do you think you could die, and I would not be hurt by it?" I asked my father. I grabbed him and held, and Gutierez let me hug him for a full minute, weeping, then the major spoke to me softly and escorted me back in line with the reporters. My father watched, his eyes riveted on me. He wept as Major Gutierez read the list of charges and called his troops to ready their arms.

My father shouted, "Someday, we will rebuild this world! The time will come when your children will play in rain-forests, and canaries and hummingbirds will fill the skies! Every beast of the field will be reborn!"

The troops raised their rifles.

"Fishes will swim in your rivers!"

"Aim!" Gutierez ordered.

"Crickets will make music in your pastures, and whales will sing love songs in the seas!" my father cried. "You watch! It will happen!"

"Fire!" Gutierez shouted, and the rifles spat their bullets, filling the bright courtyard with smoke.

My father staggered back, red holes gaping in his shirt. He stared up in the air, beyond the heads of those in the firing squad, and his eyes filled with light, as if he saw salvation hurtling through the sky. The look on his face was so filled with awe, so compelling, that everyone suddenly turned and gazed into the sky also, and then I heard him cry "God," and he spun and staggered against the stone wall, smearing blood on the ash-gray stones.

* * *

I SIT HERE in my terrarium and look at my little euparkeria and stroke his neck. I'm out of eggs to feed him, yet my wingless dragon stands on his back legs, tenderly searching the folds of my dress, expecting an egg to magically appear. It has been nearly three hours since I broke the mem-set between my teeth. Opalescent clouds seem to be forming at the edge of my vision, and everything looks as if it is covered with gauze or silken threads. My feet and fingers are so numb I do not feel them, yet my mouth burns as if it is on fire. I believe the mem-set has begun attacking my DNA, chopping it in pieces so fine that in a million years, even God may not be able to put me back together. I cannot talk into this microphone much longer.

On my way home, I jacked into a news broadcast. The reporter said that the Alliance of Earth Nations is considering plans to exile the Sirens to Darius Four, a water planet without human occupants. So, the pollution will continue unabated. I could not help thinking that though the Sirens lost their brief battle, they have won themselves a world, while day by day we are losing ours.

Also on the news, I heard a reporter say that as my father died, he shouted "¡Vivan los Sirenos!" Long live the Sirens!

But that is not true. I was there. He shouted only one last word, crying with a thrill of hope in his voice: "¡Vivamos!" Let us live!

[Uninterrupted silence to end of tape.]

DAVID FARLAND (DAVE WOLVERTON) began writing during college and entered short stories into various contests, but his career began in 1987 when he won the top award in the Writers of the Future Contest. Farland published several science fiction and fantasy novels including On My Way to Paradise, Star Wars: The Courtship of Princess Leia, *and several bestselling fantasy series including* The Runelords *and* Of Mice and Magic. *He was nominated for the Nebula Award and the Hugo Award. Farland became a Writers of the Future Contest judge in 1991 and served as an instructor at the annual WotF workshop for several years.*

To read more about David Farland and his work, visit his website at www.davidfarland.com.

ACCOMPLICE

BY TIM LEWIS

Copper

The stringent metallic taste of copper in blood can make a person retch, but I've gotten used to it over the years. I lay sprawled on the ground and could feel the warm liquid pool in my mouth that contrasted with my cheek pressed against the cold marble. I spat, and blood smeared across the floor in a macabre Rorschach design.

I was really going to pay to earn the money for this second job.

I rolled over and started to prop myself up, and the room spun as my head went vertical, then a searing pain went through my side as I was kicked. I felt ribs strain almost to the breaking point.

"I said stay down," came a hoarse voice from above me. "You were told not to come here anymore."

I coughed as I tried to spit out a little more blood and absorb the searing pain in my gut. "Look, I thought this was a chic after-hours speakeasy. The darkened windows. The goofy-looking bouncer outside. I just tried to sneak in because I didn't think I could afford the cover."

I grunted at another point of a cowboy boot in my side as the goofy-looking bouncer took another strike.

"Easy," a voice said from the other side of the room. "She's not one of your sparring partners."

I look tough. My long dark hair is usually tied back in tight bun. I wear no makeup. A scar across my cheek looks like a knife cut but was really from a fall off a jungle gym. My thick leather jacket gives the impression that I have some bulk. And of course, there's my proclivity toward witty banter. But underneath it all, I'm still human and still fragile. One of these days my smart mouth is going to get me killed.

"I'll collect that cover now." He leaned down and grabbed a fist full of my jacket with a club-like hand. He lifted my head and shoulders off the ground and brought his other fist back.

"Hold it," came the same voice from the side of the room. "I want to talk to her for a second, before she squares the debt."

Without hesitation the brute let go, my head smacked the marble, and once again the room swam. I think the bouncer was actually holding back a little because I was a woman, but it sure didn't feel like it in that moment.

"So, Ms. Douglas. Why are you coming by my place again?"

I started to right myself once more, much slower this time. Maybe a smart-ass remark wasn't the right strategy. "I'm just looking for information about a kid who was here two nights ago," I said, still not able to focus on the person across the room. My head swayed, I was nauseous, and I realized my bones actually ached for the first time in my life; it's a very peculiar sensation.

"We have lots of people that stop by," he said with a scoff.

"What woman are you referring to?" he asked nonchalantly, as if a missing person was nothing for him to be concerned about.

I turned my lips into a knowing grin. "Oopsy, I never said woman." Then everything went black.

* * *

MY NAME IS CHARLIE DOUGLAS. My mom thought it would be cute to have a girl with two boys' names. My entire life I've been called everything from Chuck, Chucky, Doug, Dougy, C-Dog, and a dozen other versions of the names from so many people who each knew a different side of me, to the point that I didn't even know myself. Oddly enough, most people who know me best just call me Fred, but that's another story.

My job is a private detective, which is why some call me Dick, for added irony. I don't have an actual license for the private business, so I'm more of a cleaner. The clientele I support don't care much about licenses or pedigree. The people I'm working for and the people I support don't want a record. They don't want to be known by the police. Whether they work in a gray area or don't want the publicity to impair their social standing, they need someone who can delve for information, clean up messes, and above all, do the work discreetly. That's what got me here; a rich guy had a friend of a friend who heard of me.

Fly Strips

Yesterday I stood on the side of Paint Rock River in the hot June air as the lingering smell of the body wafted up the bank. It reminded me of the fly strips we had growing up. My dad would hang them off the veranda to keep the bugs out of the house. They contained an odor that attracted the pests, something that appealed to their scavenger nature. To most, their scent was too subtle to notice, but to those who have been around death, like me, there was no mistaking the putrid stench.

The police tape still quartered off an area around the bank, but the cops and the coroner — and the body — had left twenty minutes ago. I had to watch from a distance to glean what I could through a cheap pair of Walmart binoculars I picked up on the way. With the trees and rolling land, there was no way to get close enough to see anything, and I couldn't risk the cops seeing me at the scene, so I had to come in on my own after they left.

Standing at the edge of the crime scene, I looked for any clue that the police might have missed, and any clues they already found, so I wouldn't have to *acquire* them later.

The person they found washed up on the bank turned out to be Sharne McAllister. She was last seen at a local club two nights prior, who witnesses said was seen leaving out the back with a woman.

Her dad reached out to me the following morning to locate his daughter, after her dorm roommate told him she didn't come home. Apparently, there was some shindig that morning and the family freaked. I had times as a kid when I didn't show up to family events, or didn't even come home for a week, and no one looked for me, but I guess the well-off are a little more paranoid.

The dad called the cops, but he knew they weren't going to look hard for a twenty-something woman who was only missing for a night. So, he wanted someone a little more motivated, and little motivates better than money. I had finished a job the previous night providing some support for a little extortion, so I thought I might as well put a little more cash in my pocket. It's all about money, and ethics cloud earnings.

I went to the club to quietly ask around about the daughter, but was confronted by the bouncer who told me he never saw her there. He was pretty insistent and dismissive, telling me to quit wasting his time and not to come back.

I awoke to a text from my source: *Police investigating washed up body.* The text included a pinned location, and that had brought me to the riverbank.

I paced off the area in a grid, looking for any missed clue that might point to the assailant. The place had been beaten down with dozens of footprints in the soft earth. The cops in New Hope didn't deal with homicide very often, so the whole precinct came out to gawk. They could have used some better protocol; I could tell their sloppy work destroyed or missed any potential evidence that pointed to the killer. As I walked around, I twisted each foot in the soft earth so as not to leave additional marks that might implicate me.

The river was covered on each side with tall ash tree canopies over the water, blackberry bushes creating a thicket, and long grass patches dotting the banks. I squatted down and could still see the indention where they pried the body out of the silt.

There was nothing leading to the area that would indicate the body had been dragged there, so the rain over the past two days must have built up the current until it washed up the bank and settled in the muck. There was no telling where it could have been dumped unless someone was willing to walk more than twenty miles of creek to check every bank. The cops wouldn't have the resources to bushwhack through bramble-covered wilderness to possibly find a clue, so there was no point for me to check either.

"Hey!" A voice yelled from up the hill. "This is private property."

I sighed and slowly stood. "Well, I don't mean to be a bother, just having a gander." I laid on the thick Alabama accent I had worked so hard to rid since I was a teenager.

"Y'all police?" The man seemed to settle down after he realized I was a woman. Misogyny has some benefits.

"Just followin' up, makin' sure I didn't miss a thang." Technically, I never said I was the police. I pulled out my bun and let the hair obscure my face. I wasn't memorable, but the scar made me stand out more than I needed.

"Well, a'ight. Jus' don't hang out there too long. Don't want no cottonmouth latchin' on to those pretty little ankles."

I looked down and realized my jeans had ridden up from squatting, exposing a scandalous few inches of skin between cuff and ankle socks. *Good ol' boys.*

"Thank you kindly," I pandered. "Before I move along, can I ask ya somethin'?"

He didn't respond, just raised his eyebrows and chin to say okay. "Are you the one that found the girl?"

"Naw, I'm the one that done called the police when I figured out what them boaters were screamin' about durin' one of them floatin' trips."

"Anything seem off about 'er?"

"Well of course. Unless everyone is now going canoeing in sparkly dresses." He chuckled to himself, then went solemn realizing his joke was about a dead girl. He didn't strike me as a person who paid attention to detail.

"Well, I won't keep ya. Thank ya kindly." I made my way up the hill, taking a less worn path to avoid the trail where he was standing.

"Since I helped you, maybe you'd be so kind to do a little sumpin' fer me?" he asked, and started making his way over to intersect. *Fuck.*

He approached me and held out his hand. There was a small purse with a wrist strap just big enough to hold a few cards and some cash.

"This washed up with her. I took it up to the house when I called so I could give the police her name," he said, and held up a small brown knit bag with embroidered daisies.

"I gave the cops the IDs I took out, but done left the bag at the house when I met them down here. They asked me to bring it back down to them, but I guess they already left." He handed over the small clutch. "Please and thank you."

"No problem," I said.

"Well, the missus is fixin' dinner." He stretched his back and scratched his belly.

I could still smell death in the air, and my stomach turned trying to imagine how anyone could think about food. "Then I'll let ya get at it." I started up the trail toward my car.

"It's not a far walk out, but you be safe out there. Holler and I'll come a runnin'." He turned and called over his shoulder, "Got daughters of my own. Some *bad* people runnin' around, so good people need to look out fer each other." He headed up an opposite trail and was lost in the thick forest after a few moments.

That was almost chivalrous. I might have to rethink my stereotype of the good ol' boy. There are apparently still some good people in the world, though I know I'm not one of them. It was a shame; it looked like Sharne could have used a few good people on her side.

Clutch

I drove up the back roads over the mountain and to my

apartment in downtown Huntsville. Oscar greeted me as I opened the door, and the smell told me he was still a puppy that I left alone for too long. I cleaned up the mess, then took Oscar outside to make sure he was completely empty.

We came back in, and he started jumping around for his after-walk-treat. I emptied my pockets on a small coffee table. Car keys, pocket wallet, Swiss Army knife, some change, and Sharne's clutch. I opened it to see good ol' boy had pulled out every card and given them to the cops, leaving it empty. I tossed it back on the table.

Oscar jumped up and put his paws on the edge, thinking it might be his treat or something to eat. *Yeah, I probably need to feed him.* Sniffing around, he knocked the clutch back to the floor.

"Oscar, you're a dork. There's no food." Looking down at the wallet, I noticed a subtle line along the back side.

I picked it up, after wrestling Oscar for it, and along the face was a seam to a small outside pocket for easy access. I dug my fingers in and pulled out a small damp Post-It note with bleeding blue ink: *Sharne, guy called — Voodoo Lounge 10pm. Can't make it. Call me in the morning at my parents. — Jen 768-9035*

The place was the same club on the city square in Huntsville that my source had texted was the last place the police said Sharne was seen. Her roommate knew she went there, and the note meant others probably knew why she was there.

Looks like I'll have to make a late-night visit.

Voodoo

The place was only a few blocks from my apartment. I walked past the courthouse down Franklin Street and could see the faint outline of the neon sign on the south side of the square.

It was five in the morning, and just a few lamps lit the rain-soaked streets. The sun would be up soon, but it was still dark enough that no one was awake yet, and the bar crowd was at home sleeping it off. I kept moving along Franklin until I got to the alley that backed up to the strip of stores on the square.

The smell of old trash tossed out by the Commerce Kitchen and the distant sound of scurrying paws made the darkened alley feel like this was a stupid idea. I paced along the rear of various businesses until I reached the familiar back entrance of Voodoo.

A bottle rolled across the asphalt, and I jumped — and maybe peed myself a little. A tabby appeared and leaped over a fence to a lot on the other side. I checked the alley again to make sure the cat was the only other one out for a crepuscular jaunt.

The plan was to sneak in and acquire some surveillance footage. I noticed the cameras inside the other times I was there, so I figured they kept a copy for legal reasons. I needed to see who they had on tape talking to Sharne that night.

Along the back of the building was an industrial fire escape from the top floor continuing with steps below ground level. I made my way down to the basement door, being cautious so my footfalls didn't echo on the cement steps. I knelt on the stoop, grateful for the darkness, so I couldn't see what I hoped was rain runoff soaking into my jeans. I pulled out a leather pouch with various metal tools I've started carrying as habit. I'm no expert, but I am persistent when it comes to picking a lock. After about five minutes of tumbling various pins, I felt the satisfying slip as the torsion bar rotated the cylinder.

I turned it until I heard the satisfying click of the deadbolt reach its stop, then fell forward as the door was yanked open from the inside. I hit the marble floor face first, sprawled along the entryway, feeling the blood pool in my mouth. The only thing in front of me was a pair of snake-skin cowboy boots with steel tips, with which I would soon become intimately familiar.

Belted

The feeling of bracing water splashed across your face is a great way to exhilarate the senses and get the day started. Having a leftover rum and Coke with ice tossed from a plastic tumbler — not so much.

"Hey, she's awake," said the bouncer, followed by the hollow clank of plastic from the empty cup he dropped to the floor.

"Damn you fucking oaf. You didn't have to punch her so hard." This voice came from the man in the corner.

My senses started to coalesce as I remembered getting cold-cocked and dragged around the room by the bouncer for a smart-ass comment about the woman, and I found myself strapped to a chair. I sputtered and coughed, trying to exfiltrate a little bit of the stale cocktail intent on making a home in some deep part of my lungs. It was difficult to properly inhale with a leather belt tightened around my arms and chest and woven through the back of the chair. I guess clubs don't keep a good stock of nylon rope lying around for these situations.

"So, where did we leave off?" I coughed the words.

This time the person from the corner of the room stepped forward. He seemed so ominous as a voice in the shadows, but standing in front of me was a scrawny man in his forties, desperately trying to style a comb-over of thinning hair to look like he was in his thirties, dressed in fashion attempting to make people believe he was in his twenties.

"Mike sent you, didn't he? You were gonna do a little damage to encourage me to pay the money my ex-wife owes. She stopped by the other night asking for cash and I didn't give her any. So you tell Mike that's on her, not me. That's what this is about. He sent you, didn't he?"

I heard the words, but they didn't register. *Did they think I was here to wreck the place?*

"Ya best answer Mr. Bartowski," said the bouncer, now coming into focus. He stood there in a bulking mass with one hand in a fist and the other cinching the side of his pants to hold them up.

"Ew, it's *your* belt?" I asked, genuinely skeeved, as I strained against the leather.

Bouncer reared back his free hand before Bartowski put up his to stop him. "Easy. I don't want to have to wait for her to wake up again." He turned back to me, "We tied you up so you won't run off while we get some answers."

I turned my head to look around the bare room. I was in a parlor that used to be a formal meeting area with marble floors, rich dark wood-paneled walls, and thick crown molding. Now it had worn, paint-blistered walls, the perpetual stench of cheap beer and club kid, cracked marble tiles with stained grout, and abstract art of my blood from earlier. One wall had a window that had been painted over to keep the club dark, but a few places, where people had scratched their initials into the paint, let through the first light of day.

"So again, Charlie Douglas of 204 Greene Street," he drew out my name and address while holding up my ID as a weak veiled threat. "Why did you come here?"

There was no point grandstanding any longer. These chuckle-heads had no clue what was going on, and the threats were pretenses. Everything was staged theatrics they probably gleaned from bad television to intimidate me, although Bouncer's kicks were pretty real. I exaggerated crossing my legs and was able to rest my hands on my lap, despite the restraint, trying to appear like I was sitting comfortably in a meeting.

"Well, Mr. Bartowski, I'm not here about money your ex-wife owes. I was hired by Mr. McAllister to find his missing daughter. The police evidence pointed to this as the last place she was seen, so I came here to acquire your security video and confirm her last whereabouts and who she might have left with as a potential suspect. My missing person case has turned into finding who may have caused her death."

This brought him up short. "Wait, she's dead?"

"Screw this," said Bouncer. "I'm out of here — I'm not getting mixed up with murder."

"Glad to know your threshold stops at aggravated assault against a woman." *Damn*, I really have to learn when to shut up.

He turned and stood directly in front of me, but my statement appeared to make him reconsider whether he'd up the ante on his current list of charges.

"Easy, Ton-of-fun," I said. "It was a misunderstanding. You were just doing your job. Nothing permanent, and no hard feelings."

His shoulders relaxed, and he looked relieved.

I quickly raised my foot using my instep, like Coach Wilmok taught me in high school soccer, and connected with his balls. The unexpected hit caused him to collapse to the floor in a whimpering pile as he made his own Rorschach next to mine, but with vomit. "And now we're even."

Mr. Bartowski, like most men, was easily entertained by the kick to the nuts. He hovered over the bouncer, laughing as he writhed in agony then slowly recovered and made his way to his feet. In the commotion, neither noticed I had pulled a knife from my front pocket and worked the blade up through the leather belt. Gotta love Swiss engineering.

I stood up and held the knife in front of me, pointed at Bartowski. With his muscle barely standing, and who I thought might be crying a little, Bartowski's demeanor dropped.

"Whoa, take it easy," he said, hands up.

"I think it's your turn to tell your side," I said, trying hard not to sway as cramped and sore muscles loosened up.

"Look, I'm just doing a job. Guy paid me to call another guy when the girl showed up. She's a regular here. I gave her a call to come out that night in exchange for free drinks for her and a few friends. Told her we had the band playing at ten and needed those influencer skills these kids have to draw a crowd. She shows up, they drop ecstasy, dance all night, snap-filter it or whatever it's called, and the followers show up. It was a win-win for me."

Bouncer groaned and shifted a little bit, but he was done playing the heavy now that the ante had gone up.

"And?" I pushed, jabbing the knife toward him a little. It was only a three-inch blade, but apparently this guy had little threshold for bodily harm.

"They said something about Daddy being in government contracts and needing a little leverage. So the guy showed up, and his friend got her to go out to the balcony in the back," he said, palms still up with complete focus on my little red knife.

"Tell me about the friend," I said.

"I don't know, just some woman with long dark hair he brought along. Only saw her from the back on the video." He looked me up and down. "About your size. I guess he hired her to help him because it's easier for a girl to coax another girl out of the bar."

"Where are the videos?" I pressed.

"Gone. Deleted. Don't want no liability. After I heard she

fell, we watched them, and I erased all records of them ever being here."

"So you saw her fall?"

"Looked like they got into an argument," said the bouncer in a strained voice, still cradling his boys. "A little struggle over something, and she freakin' Peter Pan'd right off the balcony."

"Peter Pan was a boy." I played it off with snark, but the image of her falling off the balcony and hitting the ground turned my stomach.

"Sandy Duncan, *a woman*," Bouncer said, a little haughty, "popularized the role during her Broadway musical perfor-mance, not to mention fourteen other —"

"Enough," chided Bartowski.

It appears Bouncer had a little bit of culture. He was still a douchebag, but he did go up a point.

"Look," continued Bartowski, "she fell, but she was alive. Just bumped and bruised. The guy told me. Saw on the video the two lift her up, take her to the car, and they drove her off down the alley."

His adrenaline was wearing off, and he was starting to calm down. I needed to wrap it up and get out of there before he got a little brave or Bouncer figured out how to exhume his testicles from his abdomen.

* * *

I WAS outside in the alley, with the sun beating down on my face. I could see the spot where Sharne would have fallen. There was no evidence of the fall, but I knew this was the spot. She must have had some hidden wounds and died during the drive, and then the guy dumped the body. Bartowski told me they guessed they were going to use her as leverage against her father —snap some video of her accepting a drug deal and use that to coerce Dad to do anything to protect his little girl.

I do my research when I take new clients. Dad worked proposals for large companies and had the reputation of making and breaking deals. Seems petty, but some government contracts are in the hundreds of millions, and executives stake their careers on a win. Desperate men; desperate actions.

The goons said the girl must have figured out what was going on, gone for the phone, and, in the tussle, fell. They had that much right.

I had my answers, but I was beat, literally, and just needed some sleep. I should probably have gone to the hospital, but I've been through worse. I wanted nothing more than to get home and get to bed, probably after I cleaned some more puppy poop off the carpet.

Envelope

I woke up that afternoon to a tongue running up my face. "Hey, Oscar."

I slowly pulled myself out of bed. It still hurt to breathe from the pummeling early that morning, but it was not going to compare to the pain of what I had to do next.

Oscar and I took a short walk from my place to an area of town called Five Points; Huntsville was not a big city. The area was the historical district, which was just a euphemism for very expensive old houses.

I made way past several million-dollar homes before coming up to one residence surrounded by a wrought iron fence enclosing a perfectly trimmed lawn. There was a long cobblestone walkway that led to a gray brick house with vines crawling up the sides in a style that was carefully manicured to look natural.

We walked up the path to the porch, and I tied Oscar's leash to the stair rail. I knelt down to scratch his ears. "Be good; I'll be right back."

I took a deep breath and swung the antique brass knocker several times. After a few moments, Nathan McAllister, Sharne's father, opened the door, and his look of disappointment soon mirrored mine. He ushered me in to a formal parlor where we sat across from each other. It reminded me of the room at the Voodoo lounge with similar marble floors and wood paneled walls, and I felt just as uneasy.

"Can I get you anything?" he asked absently.

"No, I'm good," I said, which was the expected response. I was left with no choice but to tear off the Band-Aid. "I'm sorry, Mr. McAllister, I failed you. Your daughter got into the middle of something with some bad people looking for a little leverage."

"What happened?" he asked. His hands clenched a crystal highball with the remnants of some whiskey, and his eyes focused on the floor. He was in pants and a button-down, probably his usual work attire without the jacket, but he looked completely run down. His hair was combed, but disheveled. His shirt buttoned, but wrinkled. His shoes on, but untied. He was numb with a mix of grief and anger.

"She was targeted and brought to the club under pretense. A woman lured her onto the balcony. The guy they hired was going to sell her some drugs, and his accomplice was going to film it. They were going to use the video as blackmail against you to keep her out of jail."

He looked up at me with a sense of recognition, as if he'd heard this before, but dropped his head again. "Go on."

"Your daughter was smart. She figured out what was going on and tried to grab the phone from the woman. The two of them struggled, and she fell. It was quick; she didn't feel anything."

I saw McAllister shudder, but he didn't look up or respond, so I pressed on. "The man and the woman put her in the car, then drove her to the river where they tried to hide the body to cover up the accident. The storm surged the river and she washed up where the police found her."

I took a deep breath, trying to make sure I stayed calm and matter-of-fact. "I followed up at the club, and there was no evidence of the people involved. The owner said he just called her up to watch a band that night, and he was clueless about what was really going on. The number he called to tell the pair she was there was to a burner, so nothing to chase there."

I took another deep breath, the image of her body on the shore etched in my head. "I followed up with the police investigation and the, uh, location, but they botched the job and there won't be any solid information that could point to the people responsible."

McAllister didn't say anything or look at me. In an instant, the highball flew across the room and shattered against the wall. I jumped back into the couch expecting him to come at me, but he just hung his head again.

He had his answer, but not the one he wanted. He wanted a name, retribution: revenge. The best I could provide was a little closure. I was sure his lawyers would go after the club to try and locate the guy and make someone suffer, but it would be a difficult case without witnesses.

"I'll get your money." He stood and left the room, still without making eye contact.

He came back a little later holding a small manila envelope with a few bills, the amount previously agreed to, stuffed inside.

I stood, and he handed me the envelope. "I'm sorry for your loss." I showed myself out.

Oscar and I were walking along the sidewalks heading home when my phone chimed that I got a text from my source: *Is it done?*

I looked around, without a reason other than general paranoia, and replied. *Leaving now. We're clear.*

I pulled the SIM card out of the burner, snapped it in half, and tossed both down a storm drain along the sidewalk.

I take on jobs as they come, from either side. The job for McAllister was simple: find the person responsible for his daughter's death. The most difficult part of the assignment was that I had to fail and ensure her murderer couldn't be found with the clues left behind; because of my prior job, I was the accomplice who led Sharne to the balcony and took the video.

TIM LEWIS MANAGES rocket programs by day and collects hobbies by night. Writing has been his longest running hobby, going back to middle school and first place in a Halloween story contest. He took creative writing at Purdue, but his public works have all been scholastic and technical. In the years following, there has been an accumulation of short stories and scenes brewing that few have seen beyond his laptop. Tim leans toward science fiction, urban fantasy, and noir, where each contain an element of humor from a life spent as a smart ass. He published his first fiction work, "Switch," in 2019 and continues to write and submit as he aspires to his favorite quote by Benjamin Franklin: "If you wou'd not be forgotten / As soon as you are dead and rotten, / Either write things worth reading / Or do things worth the writing."

To read more about Tim and his work, visit his website at lewisventure.com.

THE ACQUISITION OF VIDALIA SOMERSET

BY SARA JORDAN-HEINTZ

I was working in my garden, pruning the last of the roses; it was so late in the season for them still to be in bloom, but ever so fortunate, I thought to myself.

It wasn't much, but my family and I were quite content in our little cottage in Cohoes. I paint. A little. Enough that autograph hounds stop me at the local deli on occasion. It was a comfortable Upstate New York existence in a modern age — 1958.

Suddenly, she was standing over me, a petite woman with freckle-kissed arms, her hands protected from the sun by her cranberry-hued gloves. I looked up, slightly startled at the sight of her silhouette looming over my frame. She extended a hand that looked suspended in time as she waited for me to collect my bearings.

"The name's Coreen Denton. I just moved into the cottage next door. Guess that makes us neighbors," she said in a firm, clipped tone. A New England accent?

"Vidalia Somerset," I replied. "Pleased to make your acquaintance," I uttered as I removed the gardening glove from my right hand.

Her grin was infectious and playful, with those peach-hued lips, cat-eye sunglasses, and freckly face. So many freckles. I haven't a clue as to why I remembered the freckles so vividly. Her appearance was not unlike my own, save for my darker hair, and I didn't have as many freckles despite all the time I spent outdoors. She drew me into an embrace, those delicate hands on my upper arms. Then she leaned in and kissed me square on the lips before sauntering away.

She passed me on her bike riding into the village that afternoon. She returned with a tall, brown paper bag filled with what-nots. I remained planted in my garden until nearly twilight.

Later in the evening, her windows were open, so I could hear the notes of her modern jazz music humming from her record player. She danced barefoot as I watched from my study, paintbrush in one hand and palette in the other, working on my latest masterpiece, the bowl of half-rotting bananas, apples, and pears sitting on a table across from me as some sort of pseudo-inspiration.

I went to her house that next evening, just to drop off some veal cutlets and a bottle of wine. I didn't expect Ryan and Susan back for another six days from their fishing trip to Maine. I rather preferred the silent sounds of the house over their raucous laughter from private jokes whose meanings were only known to them. You see, Susan is really my step-daughter.

Coreen and I must have gabbed half the night, telling tales out of school, regaling each other with stories of our college days. She had attended an elite all-girls academy too. I even told her about my sexual relationships with women and the greatest loss of my life — the death of a sister I never had the chance to know.

What hadn't we seemed to have in common? I suppose we had begun a bit of an affair.

It was that same way the next night, familiar camaraderie, and the night after, and the one after that.

On the eve before my family's return from Down East, I decided to phone Coreen to invite myself over to her house for one last quiet night together before my homemaking obligations resumed. The shrill, rapid bleeping sound told me she was either on the other line or had deliberately taken her phone off the hook. I decided to walk the short way to her cottage and let myself in through her back screen door.

I don't know what got into me, but I decided to glance at the mail on her kitchen counter. I was struck by the oddity of so much mail for a woman who hadn't even lived there a week. It was strange. I noticed one letter addressed to me. A card and package for me as well. Even a few bills were in my name.

I spotted my gardening shears tossed haphazardly at the front door.

"There you are," she called to me. "So glad you dropped by, but I'm afraid I have to break our dinner date. There are so many of those feminine touches to do before my daughter and husband arrive home late morning."

Daughter and husband? Coreen never mentioned having a family. I had the strangest feeling of foreboding — that she was going to announce some rather bizarre revelation or start levitating or something.

I looked around her cottage. Pictures of Ryan and Susan had been placed on the fireplace mantle. An image of Susan, demure in her First Holy Communion gown; Coreen by their side in a photo taken on last summer's fishing trip out West. I spotted a painting propped on an easel; I'd know my brushstrokes anywhere. I pivoted around and caught a glimpse of my bedraggled frame in a white, oval mirror hung above a secretary's desk.

"Coreen, you look rather pale. Are you all right, Dear?"

she asked, her voice saccharine, her eyes rimmed in far too much charcoal. "Here, drink this, my darling," and she thrust a highball glass under my nose. Its acidic scent bespoke of gin, yet . . . She pushed, pushed, pushed, and before I knew it, I'd drunk half the glass' contents.

* * *

"THEN IT ALL WENT FUZZY. Not black, just murky. Sort of a dark, greenish gray color. Then I woke up here, where the smell of antiseptic burns my nostrils, the light so bright and white it stings my retinas, and I'm dressed in whatever passes for proper attire in a place like this.

"I don't know how she did it — how she turned you all against me. I don't know why, either. I don't know where she came from. Nothing. I really know nothing about Coreen beyond all those tales she told me, and the nights we spent in her loft bedroom overlooking the bay."

"Well, Miss, all I can do is pass along your inquiry to the doctor on duty, but he's tied up now with a delivery of twins. Here, I brought you some magazines to help while away the hours before you're re-examined."

The fresh-faced nurse leaves the room. She has lots of freckles on her face, too. I can tell she made a concerted effort not to refer to me as Miss Denton, as it says in all of my paperwork. I never did reach Ryan. I'm sure he and his daughter are back from their trip by now. What time is it anyway? There's no clock on the wall. I sort through the pile of magazines the nurse left for me. As expected, most issues are dated six months or older, several have pages torn out, and someone let their kid color all over them and create his own illustrations. I select an art magazine and casually flip through its colorful pages. It appears to be somewhat current in its material. I hear the notes of voices coming down the

48

hall — that freckle-faced nurse and a doctor. "Delusions" I hear him say after she mutters just the very basic points about my case.

I whip through the pages faster, becoming bored and distracted by noise in the hallway. The cover spread catches my eye. Is that Coreen? I say out loud to myself. I scan the article. It's a human-interest profile on a local artist. I choke on my breath as I read the title: "Vidalia Somerset seeks the meaning of life in her paintings."

Coreen is wearing my gold charm bracelet in the photo shoot. I could see the little dangly charms: a paintbrush, palette, tube of paint, ruler, and beret. It was a gift from Mother upon my graduating from college in 1948 when I was a very mature twenty-two years old.

I glance around my drab hospital room. Where are my belongings? I hop out of bed and go to the closet. There on the floor is a simple, cotton laundry bag. I find my clothes, a jacket, and wallet. My driver's license! I undo the snap closure and pull out — it's my face, but Coreen's name and address are clearly labeled. How did she . . . ?

I quickly dress, collect the rest of my things, slip out my room, run down three flights of stairs, and go out a side door. I hail a taxi and slide into its back seat.

"Could you drop me at 1862 Reed Avenue? Yes, I know it's a bit of a trek out there," I say to the driver.

I have to find her before my family sees her first. It's as though . . . Grandma Maggie used to talk about it in her later years, after dementia had set in. What was the word? Double gang . . . ?

Doppelgänger.

But Coreen isn't my double. Not exactly . . .

The cab pulls up alongside her cottage. My chest constricts. She's in my garden, resting on bent knees. Her hair is dyed a shade similar to mine.

I spot my gardening shears off to the side, pick them up, and conceal them behind my back just as she turns to face me.

"Who are you and what do you want?" I growl.

"You bitch! I'm not gonna let you ruin this! With your fraternal twin sister having died at birth, I lost my chance to enter your world and take over her life. I got rid of your doppelgänger and made my way here to even the score. It took me thirty-two years to travel to you in this dimension, and now I'm claiming what's rightfully mine.

"It's all falling neatly into place. Except you, my darling neighbor — psychotic fool. You shouldn't have left the hospital. Pity, the sheriff will have to be the one to find your bruised, broken body at the base of that cliff."

She dusts the dirt off her slacks and wipes the sweat from her brow. That toothy grin would look perfect in an advertisement for Colgate Dental Cream toothpaste. She grabs me by the elbow and tosses the gardening shears off to one side.

My sister never had a chance for a life. Even if she had, I'd have never let this spook get within an inch of her. I drag my feet in the ground, forcing her to pull me along.

Coreen leans over me, ready to push me off that craggy slope, when I reach into my jacket pocket and pull out the syringe I swiped from the nurse's station. I thrust it into the side of her neck, the shock of it giving me the precious few seconds needed to shove her down that incline. I cringe as I hear the sound of her body land on the boulders below. I carefully make my way down to ensure she's truly dead. But she's disappeared, leaving a faint trail of bluish smoke and debris.

Gold glistens in the ashes. My charm bracelet. I flip over the palette charm to locate the inscription: "To V, Love Ma."

I place the empty syringe back in my pocket, then wipe my forehead and cheeks. I could use a drink. I clasp the bracelet onto my wrist and walk back in a daze to my cottage.

A "for rent" sign still looms on Coreen's front lawn.

SARA JORDAN-HEINTZ IS A WRITER, editor, feminist, and 20th century historian. She has written hundreds of articles for newspapers and magazines, many republished through the Associated Press and USA Today Network. She is a recipient of the Genevieve Mauck Stoufer Outstanding Young Iowa Journalists Award from the Iowa Newspaper Association. She is published regularly in Antique Trader *magazine. Her novella* A Day Saved is a Day Earned *was published in Rod Serling Books' inaugural anthology* Submitted For Your Approval *edited by Anne Serling. Her flash fiction has appeared in* 101 Words, Red Planet, 365 Tomorrows, Friday Flash Fiction, The Mambo Academy of Kitty Wang, *and in the* Brilliant Flash Fiction *print anthology* Branching Out. *She is the author of the classic cinema book* Going Hollywood: Midwesterners in Movieland *and the author of the new true crime mystery* Who Killed Dorothy Kilgallen? *based on the contents of her 2007* Midwest Today *magazine article of the same title. She most enjoys writing speculative fiction, human interest stories, and pieces meant to provoke deep feelings and opinions in their readers. She lives in Iowa with her husband Andy Heintz, also a writer.*

You can follow Sara on Twitter @SaraEliz90 or on Facebook at https://www.facebook.com/sara.e.jordan, and her books are available for purchase at https://pageturner-books-international.myshopify.com/

CATALYST: ORIGIN

BY VAIL HENRY

Part 1

Many people would decry me as a monster if they saw me for what I have become. Typically, though, they've not been able to see even themselves. That's the real problem — what's hidden inside people; what each individual secrets behind excuses while they betray it in their actions.

I've been learning to read people's inner natures for twenty years. It started involuntarily; I was seven.

—

Jingle, jingle: I have money in my pockets, little girl. *Jingle, jingle*: shiny, shiny coins.

I had just finished second grade. I quickened my pace at the sound of the *jingle, jingle* of leather-faced men shaking their pocketed hands at my passing. I comprehended the invitation vaguely and with distress.

One or two of these men always stood in front of a cramped liquor store with windows stained yellow from cigarette tar. They'd stop their tinkering as soon as I passed without heeding them.

In spite of the walk to get to the donut shop, I loved its syrupy, vanilla aromas, and I spent my meagre allowance there. The shop's sign idolized a rosy-cheeked blonde winking over her cartoon cleavage. After scaling a chrome-plated barstool with both hands and one knee, I'd straighten my flower-print skirt and wait.

"What can I get you, Honey?"

"An apple fritter, please." Lumpy, brown, and sometimes extending over the edge of the waxed paper, those biggest but ugliest donuts secreted pockets of fruity delight covered in a shine of glaze. I'd always been a person more interested in what's on the inside — even of donuts. I'd tear the pastry apart to uncover its secret, doughy caverns and then devour it by the mouthful.

"What's your name, Sweetie?"

"Lyst."

"Are you here alone, Honey?"

Ar-are-y-you-ou-h-hhe-heerre-al-alo-ooone? And there it started. An insidious voice had fractured the waitress' words, breathing them directly into my mind. Confused, I sat still and focused on the ruffled, pink gingham of her uniform. I held on to the counter. As moments passed, the waitress grew more concerned — but so did I.

"Honey? Are you okay? Are you here all alone?" *Aar-re-yy-ou-hhee-eere-alll-all-lone?* The discorporate, broken words conveyed a strange insight: Sometimes the pocket jinglers asked the same questions the waitress did, but from the donut staff, those words meant something different. They meant protection, nearly the opposite of what the pocket jinglers meant. The contrast came from something inside the people, not from the words themselves.

The inner nature of people determined what would happen around me and to me. I learned that the important things to notice never occurred on the outside. For the first time, I saw a divergence between what they were trying to make happen and what they wanted to appear to make happen. It broke human action down the way that the voice in my head cracked apart words.

I felt what, at the time, I called a *double-pull,* like two violin strings connected to the center of my torso. Vibrations and tension changes flowed through each. The inner nature of the waitress — kindness, concern — activated in that double-pull. I saw how two things could happen: a *reaction* or a *not-reaction.*

"Okay, Sweetie. Let me get your donut, and I'll check in with you when you're done. Maybe I can call someone for you then? We've got a phone in the back." She slid the pastry in front of me with a long look of concern. I still said nothing.

"Ma'am, I'm done here; thank you," said the only other person in the shop. He tapped the counter twice and set an old fedora back on his head. At that moment he paused, looking down, and *th-thann-kyyo-you* ran through my head. The reaction side of the double-pull vibrated more and seemed to connect Mr. Fedora with that moment. In my mind, I leaned toward *reaction* because it seemed warm and sweet. In that instant, Mr. Fedora seemed to make a decision. He indicated me with a nod and told the waitress, "You keep being the kind type you are. Need more like you." He handed her a bill large enough to pay for ten or twenty apple fritters, tilted his hat to her, and exited before she could make change.

Th-the-k-kin-nd-t-typ-ype-yyou-aa-are, the voice inside me concluded, and faded out. The double-pull had ended: reaction had occurred. The waitress said the same thing as the pocket jinglers, but she said those words in an honorable way — and someone honored her for it.

I liked that the world worked that way.

Even though the voice unnerved me with its slow, halting brokenness, I found myself intrigued by how it seemed to know what things could react with each other in each situation.

Walking back home took me past the same liquor store. As the familiar tones of a pocket jingler sounded, the disjointed voice tried to emulate the rattle of the coins. Again, I felt a double-pull, and out of seven-year-old curiosity, I leaned-without-leaning toward reaction.

The door of the adjacent tool shop slid open, and an officer walked out. Still staring at me, the jingler failed to notice.

"Hey, what's this?" The officer looked as tall, solid, and dark as an oak tree. "What's going on here?" His focus shifted to me. "Little girl, are you okay? Do you know this man?"

I shook my head no, wide-eyed, and then continued walking home — but faster. When I was a few steps farther away, the officer began to address the pocket jingler. "Do you know her?"

"No, no, I —"

"What were your hands doing in your pockets?"

"My keys. I need my keys."

"For what?"

I turned at the next intersection to cut through the neighborhood. I altered my course partly to get away from the attention, but partly so nobody would see me smile. The double-pulls were fun. Watching things react to each other felt good.

—

Such lessons began my ability and interest in reading the inherent nature of different people. Multiply this experience by two decades, and perhaps my strange abilities make sense. I developed the most natural of superpowers. I didn't encounter toxic sludge or issue from an alien race; I just grew more perceptive from people's attention.

Attention is magical, after all; make any two people pay attention to each other, and they will start to produce an emotional reaction. Endothermic, exothermic, it could be anything. They could fall in love, they could want to destroy each other, or maybe both. It depends on how their innate personalities are shaped. It depends on what else in their environment they can react or not-react with.

—

By the time I was nine, I knew human patterns so intuitively that I began playing along; I enjoyed watching people make things happen to themselves. If someone followed me, I changed my direction in a big, comical fuss. This forced them to commit to their inner nature: had they really been following a little girl, or was their direction and timing a coincidence?

All of the pocket jinglers had been thinking about following a little girl. I knew that. Put on the spot to demonstrate it, though, most of them chose to deny their nature: *I wasn't really going to follow her, I'm just keeping an eye on her. For safety.* They'd come away from such moments with a dissonance that would break up their thoughts and slowly eat at them. I found this delicious. After jingling their pockets at me enough times, most of the men outside the liquor store faced a choice to end their inner conflict: Either they had to stop shaking their change at girls, or they had to admit to themselves that they were trying to solicit children.

A few of them eventually became people who would look out for me — not because they ever wanted to, but because they were too ashamed of themselves to admit the opposite.

When I was nine, I learned that others' shame is useful and can taste as sweet as apple fritters. I sensed where people aimed themselves, got out of the way of their choices, and watched their consequences meet them.

I've eaten a lot of apple fritters without ever coming to harm.

Part 2

TWENTY YEARS after I'd learned the patterns of pocket jinglers, I stalked into the VIP lounge of a waterfront wine club. My curtain of hair had turned prematurely silver, perhaps from too much anticipation of others' futures. Its reflective luster shone back everything the world threw at me. I wore clothes to match. I strode amid the magic of people's attention, yet reflected their intention back at them.

Inside that upscale wine lounge, my nose met cedarwood and lime — inexpensive aromas that catered to a masculine sensitivity and bore no relevance to winemaking. A backlit, granite bar showcased the wines and separated a third of the cavernous room. The sparse décor reflected a geometric concept of haute couture mixed with Scandinavian hang-overs. It was exactly the sort of place to get my next so-called apple fritter.

In green heels and cutoffs, my friend Dorma breezed ahead of me, past the room's empty bar tables and full-height windows, which offered panoramic views of industrial rooftops. Per the nature I've always adored in her, Dorma whirled into a conversation like a wild schizocarp dropping off a maple tree.

"Miniature poodle in a purse: yes or no?" Dorma hit the lounge's bar counter with one palm. It took a moment for the clerk and two gentlemen customers to find their bearings regarding her statement. I hung back to watch their reactions.

"Excuse me?" the one on the left replied first.

The one on the right responded more playfully: "Where else would you put a miniature poodle? That's why they make them miniature! For your purse." *Aha*, I smiled.

There's a luscious moment when someone reveals what they value. In three tiny sentences, Right Customer had showed us that he was cool with Dorma's unpredictable, strange conversation. He saw something worthwhile in speaking to her. I started fitting him into a pattern, anticipating how this would play out for him.

"That's what I'm saying!" Dorma cooed, then looked at the clerk. "I'll have whatever's on tap." Stifling my chuckle, I inserted myself between Dorma and the other customer to block him from intruding.

"Ah, so, apologies, but at this wine club, our vintages are all in bottl—"

"I'm kidding! I'll have whatever he's paying for." Without giving anyone a chance to object, Dorma continued to her new friend, "I have this idea. Photo shoot. Miniature poodle." From behind her, I knew exactly the warmth and joy that would be in her eyes. She'd sincerely wanted to do this photo shoot for a long time. "But there's a catch. The purse is . . ." Dorma gestured at the center of her bikini top and deepened her voice, ". . . *my purrrrse!*"

Right Customer laughed — a sound of two-thirds social obligation and one-third amusement. *Ah*, I thought. *He is polite.* He shifted weight over his khaki shorts and crisp, button-down shirt.

I faced the other customer and blew out a chuckle. I whispered as an excuse to stand closer to him. "Do you think she can get a small dog to stay there?"

"I'd check out that possibility all day if you could convince her to face me, instead." *Aha, less polite.* Raising his left elbow off the counter, he stroked a bit of hair already perfectly in place. His oversized gold watch caught light; so did his eyes, which darted around, making sure I was paying attention. He wanted to flaunt his wealth. Here came the card-reveal of his nature: he craved attention for things he bought, not things he was.

It sounded like fun already.

"Well, *I'm* facing you." Hundreds of bits of mirror decorated my sleeveless top, picking spotlights across his face.

"She actually gonna go through with the dog-n-tits shoot?"

"I guess we'll see." I wouldn't have bothered telling an egotistical man that I knew things he didn't. Effervescent with glee, Dorma had previously selected three different cosplays to purse a small dog amid her breasts. Her photo shoot would happen. Whenever it did, I intended to celebrate whatever inspiration or disaster it turned into — even if she'd have to humanely stick the dog to her boobs the same way she stuck on her bras.

"Is that what you two are doing today?" He stopped looking at me to feign disinterest, but I'd already clocked him. He had something to invite us to.

"We're just wasting time today."

He thumbed his nose as a scanty cover for looking me up and down. Even while looking at my body, he paid attention only to himself, so I knew what he'd see: Skinny slacks with metallic threads running through the verticals; a wide, nickel-plated belt poking beyond the bottom hem of my mirrored shirt. I caught light everywhere. I made dazzling scenery for someone's ego. I served up obvious curves and less obvious curveballs.

"I'm here to pick up three cases of champagne for my yacht." He paused too long, watching my unchanged expression. "If you two ladies want to join in the fun on the water? I have a whole group going. Actually, there are two yachts. We have a flotilla."

His bragging continued like a river babbling along its predictable course. And, like a river, I wanted to throw a rock at it. A rock would eventually connect. It wouldn't be mine, but I wouldn't help when it hit: I am not some hero hiding in this story. And I am not some passive piece of scenery.

I am also not the villain. Yes, I absorbed the selective attention he offered, but I hadn't forced him to offer it. He wanted me to help him see himself as a person so attractive that beautiful strangers would instantly go on trips with him. He wanted me to flatter him, to make him look better to himself like a carefully concaved mirror. This was foolish: nobody gets to control what mirrors show them.

"I think I've got you all squared away, Sirs." The round, polite words of the clerk preceded him and an assistant rounding the corner with two hand trucks. Three cases of champagne were stacked on one; two cases of wine occupied the other. "And I have these all set to be hand-delivered to your respective boats."

Mr. Join My Flotilla perked up like someone else in the room actually existed. "Boats! You're sailing out of here too? Are you the owner? Where are you docked?"

Right Customer looked past Dorma and smiled briefly. "Yes. Just outside for now."

"Join us! We've already got two yachts going! Food, drinks, the whole party. What's your name? I'm Beau!"

"Hi Beau; I'm Remmond. A pleasure." As I watched the approach and hearty handshake between two people who had bothered to learn each other's name, I heard those same vocalizations repeated in the broken, dissonant voice I'd come to enjoy quite a lot.

B-B-Bea-Beau-eau-eau-u-u. R-Re-Rem-emmon-mon-ond-d.

I stopped and dropped into the sound.

—

What I first experienced as a double-pull had grown over the years. It developed into a triple-pull, then a quadruple-pull, and eventually a multitude of connections all to different possible effects. I experienced it as an itchy web of magnetic affinity among things. The halting voice still cued my attention to break down the patterns in people's behavior. Meanwhile, it broke down their words, drooling phonemes like sugary sap dripping down lines in the web.

There in the wine club's lounge, I recognized the reactivity of Beau's egotism. I wanted to watch it play out for what it was, so I leaned toward the charged, thrumming surface of his pride and listened along the line that connected him to everything else.

B-Bea-Beau-eauu-u, the voice cooed. My friend Dorma and I were going on a boat ride.

—

"Try this." The voice of Mr. Beau Join My Flotilla snapped me back to attention. Dorma's flamboyance still engrossed Remmond. A stem of bubbling liquid stood before me. "This is what I'm getting for Flotilla Day."

Flo-flooat-till-la-Day-ay. I felt the slack of unused potential: The captain of the boat had already downed three glasses of champagne. I clinked with him. As I raised the effervescent fluid to my lips, he lowered his gaze down my body again.

Jingle, jingle: have some champagne. *Jingle, jingle:* sparkly, sparkly wine.

Beau wouldn't have enjoyed knowing he shared a pattern with pocket jinglers from twenty years ago — not that I had any motivation to tell him so. I would not interfere with what he chose to be.

I savored the itchy thrum of energy down that part of the

web. I wished Beau to receive exactly the experience he aimed himself toward.

Someone else was speaking. I blinked back into my mundane existence. "—guess I can join you for a few hours, sure," Dorma's new friend Remmond had accepted Beau's invitation to take part in the flotilla. His brow furrowed, though. "But I've got to get going now, so I can reschedule some conference calls."

Gu-Guess-I-ca-can-jo-joi-oin-you-ou. I would have wondered what Remmond had gotten himself into if I hadn't already known: Remmond had signed up to be Remmond. I'd signed up to watch the play.

"Great!" The two men clapped into a big handshake with unequal enthusiasm. Remmond left, leaving Beau glancing around for me and Dorma to entertain him while the clerks were away. A swank, crooked smile rolled over his dimpled chin. A tiny play of his tongue touched his upper teeth like a freshly washed siracha pepper. "And you two ladies are joining us."

It wasn't a question, but it needn't have been. I wasn't going to miss watching his consequences.

I'm not the villain in this story; I'm hardly part of this story. I walked into a wine lounge asking for nothing, and I'd leave the same way. I'd walk onto a boat ride, freely offered, and later I'd disembark — neither adding nor subtracting anything from Beau's life. He comprised most of the pieces of his own story.

Part 3

DORMA DREW circles in the air with her backside aimed at Remmond. Well, that was Dorma. Remmond leaned away, but stayed trapped in his seat by her proximity. He glanced a look of long suffering at two other guests in what I thought of as the living room of his yacht. A central, oval table offered space for four chairs and supported a handsfree speaker for his cell phone. Sofa benches in off-white leather lined the room.

Remmond seemed as sober as Dorma wasn't. As she encroached, he pushed his back further into his seat and turned his face aside from her undulations, appearing embarrassed. I knew his pattern then: he'd do no harm.

I took Dorma's cup and refilled it, then sat on the opposite side of the room, hoping to lure her over and give Remmond space to be himself.

It worked. "Did you fill my champagne for me?" The word sounded more like *shhhram-par-aiiin* because of her slurring. "You are always the best. Did you know I made a catnip mojito? It was purple. I used food dye." Dorma had wanted to study the effects of radioactivity on catnip. In pursuit of her education, she'd bought four books about atomic energy; one had come from the graphic novels section. She sat down heavily on the bench beside me, spilling the drink, and threw her arms around me. "I love you so much, Lyst."

"I love you, too." I could never aspire to be like Dorma. She bumbled happily through situations by charm and ignorance. I, on the other hand, saw too much about people to feel such glee. I brushed hair out of her lovely face and cupped her cheek. I could sense delight in her, whereas my emotions felt chemically stripped, as though they'd been broken open and left scratchy and dry. This is why Dorma's chaotic nature appealed to me so much: she could revel in things because she didn't know what would happen. I could keep her safe by reading the pattern of things.

I needed her. Emotionally, I could feel more through her than through myself.

Remmond, however, had tired of her intensity. He got out a book and alternated glances: longing toward the book; forlorn toward the noise coming from the other boats.

I left Dorma slumping across a bench in Remmond's yacht, fading asleep with her feet dangling, then went outside and dove into the water to watch consequences play out elsewhere.

—

The proud, white angles of three boats drifted across the bay in perfect range for jealousy by the traffic crawling over a nearby bridge. Ropes with fluorescent floats extended between each vessel, tying them together as a few dozen party guests uncorked, disrobed, and splashed. Tinny, electronic-style remakes of classic rock songs thumped from outdoor speakers mounted near the third boat's roof. Angular supports on Remmond's and Beau's boats offered different deck levels for outdoor party space. The quieter hull of Remmond's yacht reached up in a dynamic, horizonal sweep that closed in his living space. It didn't seem to belong.

I boarded the low, back deck of Beau's vessel, then wandered through in my own disconnected way. Women in sunglasses took pictures of each other from high angles that would feature their cleavage. Older men talked with each other while the bored, pretty twenty-somethings beside them stared at their drinks. Red solo cups with remnants of poorly mixed rum cocktails littered the seats. Piles of wet towels competed for space with trays of overheated cheese and crackers.

"LUST!" Beau called at me. "Where've you been?" At some point, he'd learned my name, but Beau liked easy jokes. Surrounded by people dancing in their swimwear, he ground on each in turn and drank double-fisted. One of his companions had settled his toned rear against the steering wheel of the anchored boat. The thong of his suit had disappeared from the known universe, and he laughed and wiggled, pretending to butt-steer the ship port and starboard in the wide, placid water.

I looked on at their joy, unmoved. I missed Dorma.

Captain Beau broke free from the thong throng. "Pouring more drinks! Hang on!" I watched him retrieve the last two bottles of champagne from the second box, which he then kicked to the side. Beau dumped champagne across a mess of hastily assembled, plastic flutes. Where it missed the cups, the liquid ran down the table and across the sticky deck. After pouring both bottles out, the flutes sat only half-full, and Beau frowned — then smiled.

I leaned back on the railing to observe. Instead of opening the third case of sun-warmed champagne, he drew a bottle of vodka from the compartment under a seat and, more careful this time, filled the flutes the rest of the way up.

Vodka in the champagne. Captain Beau was watering the wine. Vodka, which I've heard translates as *little water*, is my alcohol of choice. I like to see what people do with it. Sneaky, almost undetectable, it lets you make any decision and then hands you your backside for making it. Vodka is liquid consequence. You can make a martini clean, dirty, very dirty, or however you like to take it, but you'll get exactly what you chose to pour.

"Fresh champagne! Who is celebrating?"

Who here is celebrating? I wondered, instead, who was *responsible*.

"Have some champagne. Hey, do you have a glass?" Beau called to his guests. He never mentioned the added vodka. Sun beat down on the crowd, and guests handed flutes even to the swimmers, who managed to tread water and drink without life vests. Of course; it is the nature of the drunk to celebrate being drunk.

But it is the nature of boating to require a sober, able captain.

Wh-who-oo-her-ere-is-ss-ce-cele-elebrat-t-ting?

Beau called to a guest, "Take the float tray. Swim some of this out to Remmond! Tell him come out!"

"Oh, he said he has to go soon," replied some guest still wet from the swim back. "But he can take anyone back to shore who's done for the day."

"Who would be done? Where's your drink?" Beau noticed me. "Lust! I haven't seen your tits yet. Drink more!"

I smiled and remembered the pocket jinglers of my past. I took the proffered flute of champ-odka and raised it to him and his consequences, but I did not drink.

Wh-who-oo-her-ere-is-ss-ce-cele-elebrat-t-ting?

"Where's your friend?" he demanded.

Her name was Dorma, but he'd probably forgotten. "Drunk. Sleeping on Remmond's. I should get back over there and babysit her back to shore."

"What? The party isn't even started!" He scowled at me, which changed nothing. I could feel a magnetic affinity building in the way things connected.

Waving me off, Beau continued, "Eh, you weren't that fun anyway. Get out of here and babysit. But tell Dorma I'm gonna call her. She's a party girl. I'd like to take her out sometime just her and me." Beau smiled with plenty of teeth.

I knew that pattern, too: isolate a pretty woman who likes fun, and there won't be any witnesses, there won't be any help, there won't be so much risk of encountering consequences or cognitive dissonance for wanting to be a stand-up yacht owner and a pocket jingler all at once. In no version of my future would Dorma ride Beau's yacht without me.

"Sure. I'll tell her to expect your call. Sorry I'm not more fun. Thanks for the party."

He turned his back on me without answering.

"Bottoms up!" someone yelled.

"Bottoms off!" another voice laughed.

"Bottoms!" cried a third, in a happy but unstable tone.

Wh-who-oo-her-ere-is-ss-ce-cele-elebrat-t-ting?

I'm not the villain. I didn't plan the flotilla party. I didn't make Beau drink. But I didn't mind it all coming together: at some point, on some trip, these factors were going to crash into each other. You couldn't be Drunk Captain Beau without running into some sort of consequence eventually. Yet the delicious pause as conditions clicked together lacked some vital component. I puzzled at that missing factor as I dumped out my cup and swam back to Remmond's soon-to-depart boat.

The discordance was me. Something within me got involved. After his comments about Dorma, I wanted Beau to meet his consequences soon, not eventually. The itching of the way things connected to each other touched upon my desire to protect the one person I love.

By the time I climbed out of the water, my own inner nature felt changed, and I couldn't wait to see what was inside.

—

I could still hear the music, but I was waiting for the bass drop.

Dorma's sleeping head lay safely in my lap, purring her quiet snore. I'd levered open a window of Remmond's boat to better hear as he slowly motored away from the party.

The other two yachts took off with more speed once all the guests limbed and flopped back on board. They approached the bridge crossing the bay when I first heard the drop in engine noise as the other two boats cut acceleration.

Wh-who-oo-her-ere-is-ss-ce-cele-elebrat-t-ting?

I felt the final component this situation needed click into

place: the bridge. Yet the boats looked as though they'd clear it just fine. *It's a shame,* I thought, *to have all this setup and not the conclusion. This could have been so much more satisfying.*

Jingle, jingle. Something in me activated. It didn't make sound, but the shiver of it danced over my skin the way tones disturb the surface of water. The inside of my skull itched.

Beau's boat swerved, threatening to intersect with the other, which tried to dodge. A few guests spilled into the water. Beau's boat, steered either by a drunk captain or the butt of a guest, overcompensated. With an ugly, metal crunch, its starboard side scraped and tore open against the concrete of the bridge. That part — only that part — was me leaning hard into a reaction.

Guests dog-paddled to the intact vessel, which had stopped. From the look of things, Beau's yacht would host no more flotilla parties — not that he stood much chance of keeping his boating license or, when the charges followed the rescue workers and news crews, his wealth and freedom.

Searching my emotions for guilt, I found none. I'm not the villain hiding in this or any of the many stories I watch play out. People have their own inner natures. They bring what they want into their lives. I'm just the catalyst.

I don't fight crime; I fight stagnancy. I usher in conse-quence for what people have already chosen. I'm the world's least welcome superhero: the one who hastens them to see the villainous natures they've hidden within themselves.

Vail Henry's debut novel World One *was featured in 2018 by NYC-based Bookstr. At the same time, she was serving as the lead illustrator for the award-winning humor series* The Allmoods Cookbook. *In 2019, she created the weekly webcomic* 70% Love *and has been its sole author-illustrator since. As an MBA and creative director, Vail Henry's works have appeared on* Times

Square and in a monument permanently installed near the White House. She resides in Washington, DC.

FEAR OF MONSTERS

BY MARK BEARD

hy had she taken him? Why had she abandoned reason? How could she get away with such a crime? The boy should be dead. She knew it. She knew and she ran.

The clouds across the horizon blocked the setting sun, bringing an early gloom. Sambiria's dark gray dress pulled against her shins, her boots spattering mud from the dirt road. She couldn't sprint, not with the boy in tow, his hand in hers. She couldn't defend herself. She couldn't do anything. She could only move as fast as the boy could go, and she had already carried him as far as she could.

Sambiria stole a glance down at him. His thick and healthy blondish-brown hair fell in a bowl around his head, and his large brown eyes were compelling and frightened. Cheeks round with baby fat led to pouting lips. Fur that smelled like wolf wrapped the collar of his coat. His legs protruded beneath, running with clomping steps in child-sized boots.

She saw the man behind them again, moving through the edge of the trees. She hadn't expected to outrun him. The fact that he had not overtaken them gave her brief hope. The nature of her crime flashed in front of her, and she grimaced. No, Odolf would not give up his pursuit.

She recalled their first meeting. He had come to the village four years before, a minstrel, singing the news of a savior from the distant foreign lands of the Mediterranean. She had initially seen him on one of her rare visits to town. He had singled her out for the same reason she shied away from entering the village: her golden-brown skin and hazel eyes. Her skin tone and dark plume of hair did not match the rest of the villagers, or the rest of the region. When she went into the settlement, some looked the other way, some offered expressions of scorn, and a few would call out insults. Her father had experienced the same, despite having pale skin. The village folk accepted their trade and their denars, however.

Sambiria's complexion had intrigued Odolf. He had later told her that her tones reminded him of the colorings of bears. No wonder he had felt an attraction.

Why had Odolf allowed them to get that far down the road? What was he waiting for? Did he hope she would come to her senses? Did he hope to share the reward if she did?

Sambiria no longer lived in the village of her birth. How could she? She recalled the stone-wrought walls, the woven roof, the soft threshing on the floor. She had spent her first fourteen years there with her mother and father, then four with her father. Those memories occurred only as images, unattached to emotions.

Her father had died, and his dairy farm had burned. The cows had disappeared shortly after. She had observed the deterioration of the farm on fleeting return visits, spying on the destroyed home and the surrounding pens from the bushes at the edge of the forest. Only the old grave of her mother had escaped damage. The sight of her former home, destroyed and abandoned, soaked into her; the smells of burned wood and the iron tinge of blood swirled in her nostrils. A distant ache threatened. She forced the grief away. She had buried it deep. She had killed it. She had had to.

She kept track of the edge of the forest where it ran along the road. That way led uphill. On the other side of the road, the land sloped downward, toward open fields and winding brooks, and beyond that, the terrain curved upward into mountains. Her current life didn't allow her to visit those towns where the road led. She had anyway; foolish, but she had. She brushed at a spot of dirt on her dress. She had preserved the outfit for such journeys.

At last, she spied the tree that marked her territory. From the road it appeared typical, so as not to alert passersby who journeyed down the empty stretch between distant towns. The forest side had scratches in the bark to mark it as hers.

She pressed her eyes closed at the recent image of her foray into the town of Brzegrzeki. That's where she had met Wars, the boy. She had only visited his farm four times, but she had encountered him on each. His bright smile and his exuberant health had charmed her. She could never go back to that town. She glanced down at Wars. Neither could he. His family was no longer there to take him back. That farm, on the outskirts of Brzegrzeki, had offered too tantalizing a target, too remote and secluded. She recalled the blood splashed across the walls, the offal spilling from the dead. She remembered the feasting. She remembered her crime.

She left the road, pulling the boy toward the woods.

"Sambiria, no," Wars protested. "We can't go in there. The monsters are in there."

She gave the little hand an extra tug. "The monsters are everywhere. This is the only place I can keep them at bay."

She rushed across the space between road and the trees. Odolf would see. She knew he would. They had to hurry.

They passed amid the trunks, the anticipation of night hanging heavy beneath the canopy of green. Odolf knew where she headed. Would he cut them off? He could. Did he hold back to offer her more time to reconsider her terrible choice? Would he stop her and demand an answer, or would he rush them, feral and murderous?

Wars cried, tears streaming, his pout accentuated. How great would his horror be if he had seen his family? Sambiria could never tell him. She could never watch that reality manifest on his innocent face. She bared her teeth in a snarl, pushing the regret and the angst away. Why had she done it? She had broken the sacred code. And Odolf. Did he suspect? The warmth of Wars' hand soaked into her like an accusation. She could smell his fear and his sweat; she imagined the softness of his flesh. How great a prize had she stolen away?

She directed them into a ravine, the dark of night descending. Wars stumbled, but Sambiria could see. She aimed them up a rocky incline, a natural stair of uneven slate protruding from thick green mosses. The incline ended in a steep but short cliff face where an opening waited, devoid of light and surrounded by ferns. Sambiria ducked to enter, hauling Wars along. The little boy gasped with fear when the darkness enveloped them.

A rustling outside the cave mouth alerted Sambiria. She hastened Wars forward, lifting him from his feet for the last stretch. She put him down against the back wall. He wouldn't see the bones, and she had no intention of starting a fire.

"Stay here no matter what you hear," she said. "I have taken you to the only place I can defend, but you must remain back here."

"I'm scared," Wars said.

In the blackness of the cave, she could just make out his eyes, the eyes that held the beckoning in them that she had failed to resist; so easy for a creature like him; so dangerous for her.

"Sambiria," Odolf called from outside the cave.

She closed her eyes. How would she explain? Odolf had seen the boy. He would smell him.

"Do not move," she repeated to Wars. "You cannot escape this cave. Do not try."

Wars pulled his knees to his chest, his cheeks sinking against the fur on his collar. Tears welled in his round eyes, so large on his youthful face.

She stood, straightening her dress and raising her chin. With determined steps, she marched to the fore of the cave. "Odolf."

"I don't recall inviting you to Brzegrzeki."

She could lie, tell him she hadn't been there. He had smelled her presence at the farmhouse, surely. How else had he tracked her with such swiftness back to her home?

"I'm concerned, Sambi." He hovered just outside, a hand resting amid the ferns over the entrance.

He had a long straight nose, skin as pale as her father's; she supposed some considered him handsome. She did not. Her introduction to him had erased any hope of attraction. It had not erased his. Loose clothes that might have fit a bigger man hinted at wealth, or at least they had once. He had over-worn them, and Sambiria could smell a hint of blood. Odolf would have to wash them or steal a new set for any future ventures into civilized areas.

"Bring him out."

"No."

Odolf looked to the ground and back up, reflected light from the disks at the back of his eyes flashing. "What do you intend to do?" He waived a hand as if to draw the answer from her. "That little boy should be dead, if not by us then by you. What do you have in mind?" He tilted his head as if concerned. "I fear you might endanger yourself."

"I don't know what you mean," she replied. She knew the lie held no power.

"The Code of Claw," he said.

She had to hold him off, but bitterness turned her words haughty. "Explain."

"Have you lost your appetite?" he asked. "Has the lust of the feast eluded you?"

A pang of fear trickled down her center. None of them could resist such desires. Yet, she had been there. She had stood in the adjoining room listening to the rending, the crying moans of the dying, the gurgle of opened lungs, and the slap of wet flesh upon the floorboards. Her lust had not won her over but rather another force, one more horrible, one against which they had warned her. It ate at her insides, consuming and overwhelming. It would turn her. It would make her an enemy.

Odolf did know.

"Tell me where you found him," Odolf said. "I could smell him in that bedroom, but that doesn't mean you met him there. Tell me where he was."

Odolf extended a means of escape. He handed her a way out. All she had to do was tell him she had found the boy in the farm fields or wandering down the road. However, if she did, that would end their debate and Odolf would expect what came next. He would demand it.

It reminded her of their earliest encounters. For a long while, she hadn't admitted to herself that he had been the one, the one who had brought about her new life. Even when her sense of smell improved to its height and she found his scent in her memories, she dismissed the connection. She hadn't wanted to know that he had been the beast at the edge of the woods. Her brown skin and hazel eyes had bothered the inhabitants of her birth village. Odolf had hungered for those differences. To have a woman who appeared much like a bear, as he saw her, pleased him.

She tugged at her hair, and it sprang back stiffly. She had to admit the similarities did exist, at least to those intimately involved with bears, to those who saw the world through the eyes of such creatures.

Odolf had allowed Sambiria's changes to ensue without his interference after she had crawled back to her father's farm, torn and bleeding. Terrified at first, she had managed to successfully hide her developing feral nature from her father. That she remained on the farm did not please Odolf. He beckoned her away. He showed her that others shared her new gifts. He had taught her the ways of the wilds, taken her into deep woods and onto the sides of high mountains. They had roamed, wild and savage, free. Her old life called to her, however, and she told Odolf that she would return to her farm.

A day before her arrival, her father had died in a fire that burned the home. She had refused to grieve, looking from the bushes at the ruined homestead. She had smelled the blood. She could not deny what her senses described to her, that her father had not died in a fire but rather from something bloodier.

She knew anger, but she kept her calm. Her father had meant something to her once, but the Code of the Claw forbade such connections. It forbade such affinities. Sambiria had pushed away the pain and buried the grief. She was no longer human and could no longer behave as though she were. Being a monster dulled the pain, and once she pushed it away, it had not returned to bother her again.

Odolf ducked his head inside the cave, and his foot followed. Sambiria swelled her chest with a deep breath, staring at the scuffed boot with indignation. Odolf slid the foot back, his head retreating. "Let me share your feast," he said.

"I do not wish to share."

His voice lowered, threatening. "Let me share it."

"It is not for you."

His eyes widened, the light catching the disks at the back again. "I did not go to Brzegrzeki to dine on old men and women and then have the best of the gorging whisked away." Frustration raised his voice. "I want what I'm due."

Sambiria drew a fierce breath through her nostrils. "What you are due." Her fists clenched at her sides, and she trembled. "What you are due? Where have I heard you say that before? You seem to think the whole world and everything in it is due to you. Did you think my company due to you? Did you think my place among the feral kind due to you?" She pounded fists into her thighs. "Did you think, once I joined the wilds, I would then be due to you?"

He stepped back, the pleading in his demeanor replaced by a cold accusation. "You needed me. You wanted me. What we shared, you enjoyed." He scoffed. "And what if it was due? I might well have eaten you instead. You owe me for your very life."

"I owe you nothing."

His palms pounded onto the upper rim of the cave mouth. "Let me in." His head jutted from between his shoulders and his teeth protruded too far forward. Odolf's control had slipped. "You have violated the Code of Claw. I can see no other justification for your actions. I will have what belongs to me. I will have what I want."

"What you want?" Sambiria snapped. She felt the adrenaline surge, the burst of energy that would make her lose control. "What you want? What you need? What you lust for?" She bared her teeth. "What you desire?"

His eyes widened, alarmed. His voice burst, deep and

gravelly, hairs bristling on his previously shaven face. "Do not dare."

"Dare to say it? Dare to speak what I have suspected for so long?" She stepped back, into the darkness. "I will say it, Odolf. I will. You let the sin against the code inside you long ago. Yes, I might have fallen to that villain today, but you, you fell long ago. You have walked in guilt and treason against our kind for years before this. When we ran off into the wilderness, you had already broken the Code of the Claw. When you attacked me and transformed me into this creature, you had already broken the code. You broke it when we first met, when I was still human walking the streets of my village. You fell when you first saw me."

Odolf roared, allowing the beast within to emerge. She knew he would kill her. He had no choice. She had given him no way out.

Sambiria shuffled back, slipping from her dress and throwing it aside. She accepted the tingling burn of her adrenaline. Her muscles burst with mass, her bones shifting, cartilage popping.

The bear that Odolf had become entered the cave, the cave that belonged to Sambiria. The savage roars of two bears filled the stony space and, at the rear, Wars screamed in fear.

* * *

Wars' hand warmed hers. She smiled at him. She didn't bother to deny the sensation.

"Will you be all right?" Wars asked her. "Should we get help in the town?"

The mountain winds buffeted her hair and his. On the slope of a valley below, gray stone walls and rooftops with a dusting of snow supported chimneys purling smoke. "We can't go down there, but don't worry. This limp of mine will go away faster than you think." She touched the bandages hidden beneath her dress, wrapping the battered ribs on one side. "For now, we have to run away. We have to flee for a terribly long distance."

"But we already have," he replied, his high-pitched voice innocent.

"We must run so much farther," Sambiria said. "We must pass through these mountains and then cross the sea to the northwest, to the lands of the Norse peoples. Then we will go farther. They say that beyond the northern seas, a hidden land waits in the west where no one goes and no one lives."

Wars frowned.

Sambiria smiled. "The monsters will not forgive me for saving you. They're afraid of me because I am no longer one of them. My crime could lead to chaos among them." She stroked his hair. "You showed me what I forgot about myself. You broke the part of me that made me a monster like them."

"Because you killed that man to save me?" he asked.

"No," she answered, giving his hand a squeeze. "Because I love you."

Mark Beard enjoys writing stories that take place in the wilds, with characters outside their zones of comfort, but he flipped this concept for his Hidden Villains *story to instead make the characters themselves the embodiment of savagery and unpredictability. You can find Mark's debut heroic fantasy series,* The Jeweler of Tirravon, *on his author website at https://www.lanthanor.com/*

INHERITANCE

BY SHERRY ROSSMAN

I shot up in bed, my mind's eye projecting my dream into the night as a brilliant light receded from within the cracks of the doorframe. I rubbed my eyes and looked at the door again, only to find nothing but darkness and the smell of the holiday potpourri Aunt Viola loved so much.

The grandfather clock continued its tick-tock in the hall, a pendulum of the family blood-line, according to my aunt. The clock had marked the births of the Olden clan for over two hundred years. *Shall I inherit that, too?*

I lay down again, this time facing away from the door, my pill bottle on the nightstand staring me right in the face. The letter Aunt Viola had sent me three weeks ago was still secure between the pages of my novel. I brought it with me in case Viola needed proof — in case she had made a mistake in sending the summons to the wrong family member. After all, I hadn't seen her since I was a child. My own father can't even remember how many times removed we are; we just know she is his aunt, my aunt, and my cousins' aunt. Of some sorts.

So here I am, a distant niece, wide awake in her third floor north-facing bedroom. All because I was the only living relative to ever use the family china.

It was a necessity. After graduating college, a large portion of my teacher's salary went toward paying back school loans. And the medical bills. What I really wanted was to start my own school with more hands-on learning than traditional classrooms offered, but my debt cancelled those plans and any hope to have a nice place of my own in the near future. My apartment isn't bad, it just isn't good.

The only dishes I owned were the set Mom and Dad had given me — antique bone china from the endless collection of family heirlooms. Mom prefers a contemporary table setting, one where she can easily replace broken plates and chipped cups, so she passed the old collection on to me.

I not only needed dishes, I loved running my fingers along the scalloped edges of the plates, over the hand-painted roses and the melodic edges of crystal goblets that served my ancestors through more than a few generations. I liked to think that mac'n'cheese tasted better on antique service, but all it offered me was a sense of unease. And then came the whispers and the panic attacks. Was it the out-of-place luxury?

Mom thinks I just needed a break after college, but in truth, the financial strain was too much. Three times when I went shopping and stood in front of the cashier — my face beet-red — my credit card was declined, and I had "forgotten" my pin number.

At least I had plates to eat from.

My cousin Lizzie sold her Revolutionary War-era jewelry to cover her college education. She now has the latest trend in flatware and no debt.

My sister Eva placed her first-edition set of classic novels in a box where they will sit in the dark of her attic until being passed on to her own children when they reach the age of eighteen.

Cousin Michael, Lizzie's brother — maybe the best one of us all, sold his Queen Anne desk and a gold pocket watch that once belonged to an ancestor who signed the Declaration of Independence to help pay the medical bills of his gravely ill best friend. He should be here accepting the inheritance, not me.

Eleven. That's how old I was when I visited Aunt Viola with Michael, Lizzie, and Eva, when we had ice cream served to us in crystal goblets and swam in the nearby creek for two weeks of idyllic fun until the evening before we went back home. Viola sat us down in the parlor and told us we would all inherit a portion of the Olden heirlooms. "They belong to the family bloodline," she said, her silvery crimped hair a mold of perfection against her wrinkled cheeks. She clasped her hands together on her lap and all six of her rings caught the light of the lamp next to her. "Your parents will give you an allotment when you turn eighteen. In time, one of you will inherit a little more." I can still smell the lily of the valley perfume she wore when she said that, wondering why only one of us would collect an additional portion of her beautiful things. It haunts me, just like her last words before we left that summer. "Remember, it would dishonor the family if our treasures should fall outside the Olden line."

It would be a dishonor. The words that decided my debt and my studio apartment.

How did she know Michael and Lizzie sold their heirlooms? I was sure my sister and I were the only ones who knew.

But I got to eat like royalty. Well, not the meals so much. I suppose that's okay — those plates have seen rations before. But for some reason, they didn't feel like mine.

At least I'll have *something* to pass on to my children,

should I have any. If they honor the family name, they'll have accumulated enough antiques to remind them our family has put a firm fingerprint on this world.

I snuggled into my pillow and listened to the clock tick away the night. *The very clock Elisbeth Olden, your great-great-great grandmother, died in front of while in childbirth,* said Viola when I turned in for the night. As if I could forget that story. And then she actually told me to sleep well.

Tick tock.

If I inherit this clock, I will ask Mom and Dad if I can store it in their basement.

I pulled the blanket over my head, but the clock kept beating its ghostly pulse.

Forget it. I threw on my robe and crept downstairs, staying close to the wall so the creaks wouldn't wake Viola. I eased the back door open, slipped outside, and made my way through the trees, thanking the moonlight for showing me the old trail that led to the creek and for the breeze that would stir up a lullaby.

I walked along the bank, feeling overgrown. I took up more of the space between the water and the foliage than I had as a child. At regular intervals I had to slip into the trees to avoid walking into the creek itself. Within twenty minutes, I was delighted to have found what I was looking for.

I crawled onto a large, flat rock and reclined near a symphony of homemade beer chimes. *Church bells,* sweet Minnie called them. She chuckled when she told me, Eva, and our cousins about them when we played in this creek so many years ago. Daily she brought us chocolate chip cookies and lemonade, stating that a person should give out of the bounty they had. "Don't got much, but I always got treats." The corners of her eyes crinkled like a swatch of thin pine needles when she spoke. I liked her. Summer days were happiness in that creek with Minnie watching over us after she'd cleaned Viola's house, dusting all those antiques and scrubbing floors.

I peered through the dark where the moon grazed the back of her old trailer. Beer bottles swayed underneath grand trees like mismatched lace edging debutante gowns. The keys and spoons strung below them chimed an enchanted melody. The memory of her words came to me as if the bottles preserved them like lost treasure.

"Jake drank as if his life depended on it. All's he did, to tell the truth." At that, Minnie turned her head away to flick a calloused finger across her cheeks. She then looked at me and pointed to her chimes. "I saved every single one o' them beer bottles and made m'self a choir. Something good had to come out o' them. Remember that, children. Holy ground is where sins've been made clean."

Jake only appeared one time while we were there, in late afternoon while we enjoyed a snack underneath the growing bottle choir. His face, unshaven and dirty, resembled a burned-out fire pit; his gait an unsteady aggression. His eyes, though. That's where the beer bore its rotten fruit. Through them, Minnie was prey.

Michael understood before the rest of us. He was four-teen and, to us, well-established in the ranks of teenage-hood. He had developed a dark veneer above his upper lip and had an inborn passion for justice that earned him a few early scars on his knuckles.

Jake ignored us as he stumbled toward Minnie. He clutched a bottle in one hand and all of his anger in the other, his fist already swollen and red from an earlier attempt at expelling his demons. Minnie shook her head and pleaded with Jake to go, but he kept advancing, slurring threats. Michael shooed us back to Viola's, but the three of us didn't want to leave him behind. When we had run far enough to convince him we were gone, we bunched together behind an ash tree and watched Michael yank a bottle from the branch above him and smash it against a rock. As he held up the remainder of it, the sun caught the sharp, fragmented edges like a golden crown. Minnie grabbed a bottle of her own when she saw Jake whip his head toward Michael. But she didn't need it. Michael didn't budge; in fact, all he did was speak.

"No."

No. Just that one word. Jake, his hand clutching Minnie's shoulder, stared at Michael with his dead-coal eyes, and his face shed the rest of its color. I don't know what he saw — if it was the way the light hit that bottle or Michael's willingness to use it, but Jake released Minnie and wobbled down the creek bank.

Viola beamed when we poured into her house and told her what happened. "It's the Olden honor running through Michael's veins. Aren't we proud of him the way he defended our Minnie?" she said.

"Is Minnie blood, Aunt Viola?"

"Of course not, why do you ask?"

"She acts like one of us. And she was going to try to protect Michael even though she was in more danger."

Viola lifted her head for a moment, staring past me to the top of the stairs where the clock stood, but said nothing more.

Three days after I returned home, I received a phone call from Viola, telling us Jake had drowned.

"Don't worry about Minnie, dear Niece; I will make sure she has all she needs."

I scooted higher on my rock and rested against an old gnarly tree, listening to Minnie's holy chorus where the worst could have happened, but instead, something mysterious shielded Minnie and Michael that day. It sure wasn't me. Minnie, of course, said it was the holy ground that protected them.

I reluctantly left my rock when I found myself fighting sleep, noting the peaceful atmosphere Minnie's chimes offered in comparison to Viola's clock.

My shoulders tightened when I climbed the porch stairs. I caught the scent of coffee and let it draw me into the kitchen. Viola perched on her window seat, hair waved to perfection as if she had just begun her day, and lowered her cup to its delicate saucer. "Trouble sleeping, Dear?" She smiled as proper as the gold script branding her teacup.

"Yes. I'm comfortable enough — I just don't sleep well when I'm away from home." I filled a pale green cup to the brim and joined her near the window. "I'm sorry if I woke you."

"You didn't wake me, Dear; I'm often up at this hour."

"Where's Minnie, Aunt Vi? Doesn't she work for you anymore?"

"Dear Minnie has dropped down to part time. The years have been rough on her I'm afraid, first living with Jake, and then living with one less paycheck. You'll see her in the morning." Viola raised up and placed her tea set on the counter, then sat down again. I set mine next to hers when she held out her hands for mine. "Minnie's not the only one who needs to retire. I'm sure you know why I invited you to come."

"Your letter said I was to inherit the bulk of your estate. I don't understand, Aunt Viola. I would gladly share it with Eva and my cousins. With Michael."

"Ah, but the estate comes with a job. One that belongs to the only descendent of mine who hasn't either become greedy or forgotten to honor the Olden name."

"But Michael —"

"I know what that dear boy has done. He has a generous

heart and all that, but you see — *he* doesn't know what he's done. Michael thought he knew the true value behind the family heirlooms. In any other family, I would agree that he did an honorable thing, but our things are *special*."

I shifted in my seat, unease running laps along my legs. Viola pulled a ruby ring off her finger and handed it to me. I turned it back and forth, noting the engraved "O" on either side of the square-cut gem. Although the top of the ring framed the stone in ornate, gold curls, the band was worn smooth and thin, like it might disintegrate with one more generation.

"The ring comes with the job. One I'm ready to pass on to you." She let out a sigh and settled lower into the seat.

"What do you mean? I thought you were . . . retired."

Aunt Viola chuckled. "You thought I sat in this grand house and twiddled my thumbs, did you?" She rose. "Try on the ring."

I slipped the thing on my finger, immediately anxious as to what would happen should I ever lose it. Strangely, it fit. I looked at Vi's slim fingers and back at my thicker, working woman's hands and raised a brow.

"It's not just any ring." She smiled at me and glanced at the cups on the table in front of us, pulling my gaze to them. I leaned forward to spot the object of her interest. I didn't finish my coffee. Should I have? It was so easy to forget the etiquette of the old ways Viola clings to. Just as I reached for my cup, the ring began to vibrate, ever so slightly. I pulled it off and rubbed my hand. "My fingers are shaking . . . must be the coffee." I tried laughing it off, but that's what crazy people do, isn't it? I lowered my head and took a few deep breaths.

"Put it back on and follow me. You'll see."

I slid the ring back on and as we entered the hall, I felt someone watching me — a presence, just like in my room last night. I glanced at the portraits. Great-Greats, so many of them. A drop of sweat slid down the center of my back. I must have forgotten to take my pills this morning.

The parlor reeked of holiday potpourri. Vi glided to the baby grand opposite the fireplace and settled on the bench, her long fingers over the keys. "Just relax, Dear, and let me play for you," she said. "My father taught me this song."

Relaxing on an antique couch is not easy, but I managed to situate myself in the sunken end closest to the fireplace. I rested my hands on my lap and closed my eyes as Viola's soft chords flowed through the room. The music reminded me of full ball gowns and white gloves; it matched perfectly with the décor of the house.

The ring began to vibrate and grow warm. I rubbed my hand as tingles flowed up the length of my arm. The piano was submerged in a deep glow, pulsing brighter in rhythm to Viola's song. I sat up, my eyes opened so wide they hurt.

She lifted her hands from the keys and laid them in her lap. "Do you see, now?"

I tugged off the ring, letting out a breath when the strange sensations left me. The piano darkened to its polished brown state. Viola lowered the lid over the keys and caught me in her gaze.

"I'm so very tired." She touched her forehead and blinked twice. "As I indicated in my letter, you will inherit the estate. You will also become this home's host, a most honorable position."

"What do you mean? I mean, I would gladly welcome visitors . . . "

Viola's lips twitched. "Did you know I've been playing that song since it first became popular?"

"That's impossible, that song was writ—"

She smiled, and the corners of her mouth twitched like

holding aside too many rings on a tree. "Time is as special to our family as the old pendulum that keeps it."

I inhaled deeply and stared at the ring, turned it around, and thought of my dishes back home. Could it be? "How old are you, Aunt Vi?"

She rose from the bench and sat near me on the hearth as the clock upstairs counted the seconds to her answer. When her eyes met mine, my father's voice echoed in my mind. *No one can remember how many times removed we are. We just call her Aunt Viola.*

I slowly slid the ring on again, instantly feeling a connection to the house. The piano appeared to be inanimate, but I swear it was breathing. I kept my head in one direction, not daring to look at any of the portraits. A chill turned my bones to icicles.

Viola continued, "What Michael didn't know is that he sold a lot more than antiques. *He sold the family.*"

I sprang from the couch and stuffed the ring in my pocket. "That can't be. It's impossible." But I knew it was true.

This house was some sort of limbo.

"It's my turn to move on, dear Niece, and with that ring on, you'll be able to escort me to where my heart belongs." She gazed at the piano, a soft longing in her eyes. "I'll be with Father and Mother again. And any time you need to feel me near you, you just come sit at this piano and put your fingers on the keys. I'll help you play my song."

This is why my antiques didn't really feel like *mine*. They were coffins, already spoken for. How I wished she had summoned Michael. I had to dig deep to find my voice. "And that's what my job is? To keep the family trapped in these *things*? How is that honorable?"

I stretched my arms to the sides to indicate the wood and glue, the paint and porcelain that chained my ancestors' spirits to this world. My heart pounded, yet I could still hear that clock ticking upstairs. I curled my fingers around the ring and squeezed.

Vi stood, her face sunken and weary as if melting. "We influence future generations. Our wisdom gets handed down, year after year, but very few use the heirlooms anymore. How can we honor all our ancestors have accomplished; how can we learn from them when we put them away in attics, or worse? But *you*. You use them. You *knew* not to discard them."

"I felt no influence other than not belonging."

"Think! Did you not hear a whisper, or feel an idea impressed upon you? Were you not able to make decisions you weren't able to make before, when you used your china?"

"I decided to go into debt to get what I wanted! I thought I was losing my mind — that's not wisdom, it's a curse!"

"A decision that earned you an education."

"I could have had one without the debt." I held the ring up.

Viola buried her face in her hands, her shoulders shook. I crept forward and laid a hand on her arm, but she lifted her face and pushed me away. "We don't know where they'll go after, don't you see? They're safe here, as long as the house stays as it is."

Is that why she held on so long? Vi's crumpled face melted me. I moved toward her again and knelt at her knees. "But don't you sense it? It feels heavy here. Anxious. That's not good." Immediately, a memory surfaced of Minnie and her bottle choir. *Holy ground is where sins've been washed clean.* Whether that was a triggered memory or the cry of an imprisoned soul, I didn't know, but I knew what I had to do.

"I'm sorry, Aunt Viola. I think my new responsibility has overwhelmed me. I'll take care of the house, I promise." I put the ring back on and held my hands out to her.

She grasped them in her own and said, "Walk me to the bench."

She sat down and laid her head over the enclosed keys. As her eyes dimmed, she whispered, "I release to my niece the duty as host." My ring grew hot. With a flash, Viola illuminated as the sun, then dimmed as a blue-white orb separated from her body and dissolved into the piano.

"It'll be okay, sweet Aunt. I have an idea." I jogged up the stairs, cast in the first rays of morning, and stood in front of the clock, its face level with mine. A keyhole nestled to the left of the glass that covered it. Dang it.

"It's right here, Honey."

I jumped at the sound of Minnie's voice. She stood garbed in overalls, gray hair tied in a red handkerchief. Her smile brought in the rest of the morning light. I pounced and hugged her tight.

She patted my back and laughed. "I'll be honest, I didn't think you had it in you. I thought if anyone'd figure it out and be willing to stop it, it'd be Michael. I'm so proud of you." She handed me a weathered gold key. "Found this on top of the clock when I dusted it, shortly after Vi hired me. I left it there until I understood what was going on.

"Fifteen years ago, I came back late one night when I realized I left my earnings in the upstairs bathroom. There was Viola, ushering a spirit into a silver punch bowl. No body to go with it. I guess the family souls are drawn here. Thought Jake'd laced my iced tea with one of his beers. This clock lit up like a pumpkin on Halloween, all glowing through the seams, ticking like it managed Time itself. I slipped out before Vi saw me. I desperately needed the job." She crossed her arms and stared at the clock. "I always thought there was something strange about it. Do you know it keeps perfect time?"

"No, I guess I hadn't thought about it."

"Saw your aunt talk to that piano more than once. It didn't take too many years of watching her that I figured out why I always felt eyes on me in this house. I stole the key so she wouldn't be able to wind the clock, hoping the souls could be free once the clock stopped. But it hasn't stopped, in all these years. I kept the key after I realized that, so —"

"So Vi wouldn't get rid of it forever!" I was uncertain about the afterlife, but Minnie had discernment far beyond mine. I certainly didn't want to end up in a punch bowl. I placed the key in the lock and turned it. It was stiff, and I had to wriggle it to get it to turn, but when I did, I pulled aside the glass, held the pendulum still with one hand, and wrapped the fingers of my other hand around the clock's hands to keep them from progressing.

I could feel the strain of the clock as it tried to maintain its pulse. Suddenly, an explosion of light filled the house. I crouched down, covering my eyes. I felt Minnie kneel next to me, murmuring to herself or to God, I don't know. My hair lifted from my shoulders, then whipped across my face, pulling in the scent of Vi's perfume. Hundreds of voices fluttered through the halls as if we were in the midst of a muffled dinner party. Silver utensils clanked crystal bowls. Silent Night played on the piano.

Minnie giggled, her shoulders bumping into mine. "Holy sounds, like my bottles. You freed 'em, honey. You made a chorus out of the captives."

The breeze swirled into a zephyr, and with a final whoosh, the house fell dark and silent.

We stood, arm in arm, and walked through the rooms. The paintings on the walls were nothing more than beautiful memories brushed with paint, the teacups mere vessels waiting for guests. The house stood bright and lovely, its burden gone.

I turned to Minnie and slipped the ruby ring on her finger.

She slid it off and handed it back to me. "It's still a family heirloom."

"There wasn't a drop of blood that left this house a few minutes ago. It was all souls, and there's nothing wrong with yours. Take it. Do whatever you want with it."

She put it back on and spun it around. "I'll be thinking on that. Thank you kindly." Her eyes roamed around the parlor, coming to rest on the piano. "This will make a nice home now."

"Perhaps." I turned around, eyed the wide hall, the spacious rooms, the acres of land so beautiful through the windows. I smiled as an unfettered idea came to me. "Maybe a school."

SHERRY ROSSMAN IS the author of the bestselling novel Faith Seekers; *the* City of Light *series; and* Welcome to Velvet, AZ. *She loves exploring fantastical ideas and discovering how our world is more magical than we give it credit for. In her experience working with young adults and, more recently, the elderly, she has learned that life is interlaced with beautiful stories forged from adversity and perseverance. These observations inspired "The Water Man," which appeared in the anthology* Mythic Orbits 2016: Best Speculative Fiction by Christian Authors, *and her recent short stories.*

Sherry makes her home in the high desert of Arizona with her family and boxador, Bella. You can read more about Sherry and her works on her website at https://sherryrossman.com/. She can also be found on Instagram at https://www.instagram.com/ sherryrossmanauthor/, and you can visit her Facebook page at https://www.facebook.com/Sherry-Rossman-155850011109024.

THE LAST NECROMANCER

BY A.R.R. ASH

Atop his mount, Knight Commander Ashtar ascended the slope to the crest of the escarpment. Alighting, he removed his falcon-shaped helm, its burnished steel coated in thick black gore, and tucked it beneath his mailed arm. The chain coif underneath had already begun to cool against his nape. Despite the chill, sweat beaded upon his forehead beneath the heavy helm, and he felt the biting winter air against his copper-complexioned brow. Without the helm, the bracing air filled his lungs, invigorating him. He fancied that his escaping breath resembled some of the ethereal abominations they'd battled.

Ashtar surveyed the vista before him. At the start of the day, the canyon floor had been blinding in the reflected light of Glorious Ra from a pristine carpet of unbroken snow. Now, in the failing light, the ground of the canyon was churned brown, red, and white and dotted with the bodies of mounts, his brother knights, and the remains of the twice dead. The bronze-armored forms of lesser-ranked knights flitted among the corpses of fallen paladins and bestowed benisons that would prevent the deceased from rising from their deserved rest and raising arms against their erstwhile brothers of Ra. At the northeastern end of the canyon stood a massive, stepped tower, like a circular ziggurat, that was the last refuge of the Necrolatrists, that Ra-damned group of Black Necromancers. Beyond that, beginning just before the mouth of the canyon, was a pine forest blanketed in white.

"Commander!"

At the stentorian call, like rumbling thunder through a still night, Ashtar turned to face the approaching form and stood at attention. With eyes toward but not focused upon the imposing paladin, he said, "Lord High Commander."

"Well fought, Commander." Hakor stood straight and tall, his full plate of golden ceremonial armor exchanged for one of blue steel, his peregrine helm held in the same manner as Ashtar's own. "Report."

"The abominations were destroyed, and the tower is besieged. Tomorrow, Ra's light will see the tower fall." Ashtar clenched his jaw and ground his teeth at the insidious pride that found outlet in his voice. A knight of Ra should not cling to pride. His actions were irrelevant. All happened by Ra's will alone.

"Well done, Commander. Ensure final preparations are made. I will lead the assault on the tower myself."

Beneath his gore-splattered plate, Ashtar felt a moment's pang in his chest. Again, he chided himself for his pride and vanity. Such reactions were beneath the dignity of a paladin of Ra. As Lord High Commander, it was Hakor's prerogative — indeed, it was only fitting — that he lead the Knights to victory. "It will be done, Lord High Commander!"

"May Ra's light shine upon you, Commander." With that, Hakor turned and strode away, the sun setting behind him and the clank of azure armor fading as he went.

The remainder of Ashtar's night was spent in a frenzy of inspections, strategy meetings, and tactical planning, reviewing troop placements and company assignments. Nevertheless, before Ra's light crested the escarpment above the canyon the following morning, Knight Commander Ashtar sat upon his destrier at the fore of the amassed force of plated knights and barded mounts. Before him was Lord High Commander Hakor, gauntleted hand raised in a fist.

The bodies of the fallen knights had been gathered and would be set upon carts once victory was attained. The bodies of the twice dead fed a great fire that still blazed, sending ash falling like black snow.

Ashtar held his helm in hand to feel the dual sensations of Ra's light and the stinging breeze upon his face. The breaths of hundreds of knights wafted and dissipated in the current. Between excitement and final planning, he hadn't slept, yet he felt no fatigue, as if Ra's light infused him and gave him strength.

In the momentary lull before the start of battle, Ashtar's mind strayed to recent, fond memories . . .

* * *

Just a sennight earlier, Ashtar had knelt, a knight crusader, in the courtyard of the bastille before Lord High Commander Hakor and Defender of the Faith Kashta, the former in his brilliant golden panoply, and the latter in gleaming platinum plate that seemingly caught every bit of Ra's light and shone like a small sun within the bailey. Hundreds of liveried knights encircled the trio and watched in respectful silence. He'd spent the previous day in prayer within the Paned Chamber — so named because the plates of the glass dome were so lensed and situated that, wherever the sun shone, at any time of year, the light would be focused upon the large golden disk of Ra. Then, the morning of the ceremony, he had been anointed in sanctified oil, which smelled of oranges and roses, and donned naught but a tabard depicting Ra's symbol, a yellow sun disk.

Ashtar had spoken his part of the Rite of Ascension with an earnestness and eagerness that caused his whole body to tremble: "Glorious Ra, under Your shining light do i kneel, Your faithful servant upon the earth; my sword, my life, is Yours to command. For myself, i seek no glory, i crave no renown. i desire only to serve. Humbly, i entreat You, if You deign me worthy, raise me up that i might better see Your will be done."

Defender Kashta had dubbed him with a knightly sword of a luster that matched his armor — the pommel in the form of a golden sun — and spoken the remainder of the words of the rite: "Glorious Ra, under Your shining light do we stand, Your faithful servants upon the earth. Hear the entreaty of Your suppliant and, if You deign him worthy, raise him up that he might better serve Your will."

When Ashtar stood, he did so as a knight commander. The tear that had clouded his vision gave testimony to that as the proudest day of his life, save, perhaps, for the day he'd been admitted to the Knights of the Righteous Light.

A fortnight before that ceremony, Ashtar had partaken in an assault against a covert of the Necromancers they'd uncovered within Photopolis itself, the center of Ra's worship. The existence of the Necrolatrists in the heart of Ra's own city was an affront, an embarrassment that necessitated immediate, overwhelming retaliation. During the battle, Ashtar's superior, the previous Knight Commander, had been killed. Ashtar himself had been forced to put down his erstwhile commander when he rose again in arms against the Knights, and Ashtar had been instrumental in capturing one of the Necromancers for interrogation, from whom they'd learned of the tower.

The day after the Rite of Ascension, Ashtar had stood

behind the Lord High Commander and the Defender of the Faith, upon the platform within the square of Photopolis, before the cheering throng of the city's populace. Defender Kashta had announced their intention of marching upon the tower of the blasphemers and eliminating their scourge from the earth. The citizens had seen them off with cheers and shouts of acclimation, invocations to Ra, and thrown roses.

Riding out on his destrier, Ashtar had grinned beneath his tercel helm, the roar of the crowd infecting him and imbuing him with a sense of immortality.

* * *

. . . No! Such thoughts were impious. As he swore in his oath, his reward and his life were of no moment. All that mattered was the holy mission given the Knights of the Righteous Light by Glorious Ra.

The Lord High Commander's azure fist lowered in the direction of the tower, and that simple motion banished all other thoughts and memories from Ashtar's mind. Breathing deeply of the bracing air, Ashtar donned his again-gleaming helm.

With a benediction to Ra upon their lips, a band of bronze-armored knights surged forth, a steel-capped ram between them. At ground level, only two brazen doors, reliefed with the image of a skeletal hand gripping a scepter, allowed entrance into the tower. The steel point of the ram impacted the doors with a booming clang that resounded through the winter air. With each impact, the brazen doors screeched and shuddered. That no enemies came to defend seemed an ominous sign to Ashtar, though he did not know what to make of it.

With a booming crash, the brazen doors gave, and a cheer went up from the besiegers. Dropping the engine, the rammers were the first through the opening. Others flooded in after them, Ashtar and Hakor dismounting to join the fray themselves. In a commanding baritone, the Lord High Commander ordered a contingent of knights to remain behind and guard the doorway to prevent enemies from circling behind them. From their momentarily slouching posture, Ashtar knew that those assigned resented not participating in the infiltration. Yet they were paladins of Ra, again standing straight and acknowledging the order in sure unison, and he was confident they would carry out their duty.

Like the exterior, the interior walls were built of thick blocks of limestone, forming a maze of passages and corridors. At the first fork, not far into the tower, Hakor ordered Ashtar and a contingent of knights to follow one branch, while he and another troop followed the other.

Progress was slow and costly. Multiple passages branched, and countless chambers, prime locations for ambushes, lined the corridors. The sheer number of remaining enemies surprised Ashtar, and he realized the reason for the earlier lack of resistance: the Necromancers had wanted the knights to enter the tower, where the confining space allowed for attacks of surprise by the twice living and limited the knights' range of movement. Yet, of course, the craven Necromancers would not come themselves.

The close halls reeked of death and putrefaction, made worse by the lack of ventilation. The passages became crowded with bodies, and the walls and floor slick with the blood of knights. More than one paladin tripped over a fallen comrade, only to be set upon by a vile abomination.

Those abominations with physical form often resembled their living selves, yet their flesh, where it still clung to the bones visible beneath, was blackened and decayed. Indeed, some still wore the holy armor of Ra in which they'd been killed. Blood did not flow through the veins of the twice living, yet the offal and ichor of their corrupt forms joined with the spilled crimson of fallen knights, creating a foul black mixture that smelled of copper and decay.

Ashtar dispatched runners to maintain lines of communication with troops sent down branching passages. Some failed to return to make their reports. He could be sure his men cleared the rooms and corridors of corporeal enemies, though the insubstantial ones, the ones that could surprise from above or below, through solid stone, were an ever-present threat. Such foes had the forms of shapeless shadow, gray mist, or even the hazy, shimmering reflection of their living selves.

Ichor from a cleft, rotting form splashed through Ashtar's visor, forcing him to remove his helm. Unencumbered by the heaume, he breathed fully the noisome air. Gagging and nearly retching, he coughed and spat to clear the palpable taste of butchery and carrion from his mouth.

From some distance ahead, a scream echoed around a corner and down the corridor: a raw, primal scream only heard when faced with the horror and pain inflicted by the twice living.

Ashtar replaced his helm and moved to investigate. The screaming stopped, yet before the cause had come into view, a chill worse than the winter air outside settled over him. A shapeless shadow, black as void, descended through the stone above and contacted a nearby knight. At its touch, the knight gave a strangled cry and fell forward, stiff and cold, his countenance frozen in an eternal scream.

Ashtar swung his knightly sword — blessed with the power of Ra, it glowed with a fiery yellow radiance in the presence of the ethereal — and rent the shadow as if it possessed physical substance. The umbral form dispersed into fading wisps like tendrils of black smoke, and the unnatural chill left the passage.

Ashtar and his contingent, fully a quarter less than its original complement, reached the stairs leading to the second level. There, he enjoyed a brief respite and held the knights until, with the coming of the Lord High Commander and his men, the securing of the first floor was reasonably assured.

Each successive floor went much the same as the first, though fewer knights remained after each, despite subsequent levels being smaller than the preceding. Finally, when they had reached the seventh and uppermost floor, only Ashtar, Hakor, and fewer than a dozen knights remained. Ashtar lamented the overwhelming losses, though they had died in service to Ra's holy mission — a mission near completion — and nothing could have been a more worthy cause. Indeed, he almost envied them their sacrifice in service to Glorious Ra.

Doors of brass, smaller than those on the first level leading to the exterior but with an identical design, were barred at the seventh-floor landing, preventing entrance to the level proper. Lord High Commander Hakor stared in still silence at the doors for some time.

Ashtar cleared his throat. "We could fetch the ram from below, Lord High Commander."

His only response was a distracted grunt.

Finally, he shook his head. "The door is likely warded, and the ram is too heavy and will take too long to trudge through the tower and up six flights. I can bypass the magic on the door."

Without being ordered, but all of a singular mind, Ashtar and the other knights stepped backward, Ashtar to the edge of the landing and the others upon the stairs.

Hakor removed his gauntlet and reached beneath his

cuirass to pull forth a golden disk on an argent chain. Holding the symbol toward the doors with an outstretched arm, he uttered the benison that would bring forth the needed magic: "Glorious Ra, through Your light, all in darkness is made visible. All that is corrupt is cleansed. All profane, sanctified. i, Your humble servant, beseech You, grant me use of Your Power."

The disk flared and cast a blazing white light upon the doors, which flashed in response. A click, and the doors swung outward, revealing an antechamber.

Ashtar, sword in hand, surged forward to intercept any enemies. The periphery of his awareness registered that his blade glowed with yellow light a moment before the sight before him forced Ashtar to an abrupt halt. The insubstantial creature floating toward him appeared as a pale, amorphous collection of heads and visages. Each face, twisted into a mask of pain and terror, emitted soul-wrenching cries of which no mortal throat was capable. The incessant cacophony of bellows, howls, and screams sent Ashtar to his knees, shaking his head, clenching his eyes closed, and putting mailed hands to the sides of his helm in a futile attempt to deny the sound.

At the clangor of plated bodies falling to the stone floor, audible in their nearness over the harsh, desperate din, Ashtar wrenched his eyes open and saw that two knights had succumbed. Even as he watched, their contorted visages appeared among the others of the creature and joined in the unholy chorus. Seeing what became of his brother knights brought uncontrollable tremors to Ashtar's body and the acidic burn of bile to the back of his throat.

The sensation of having his sanity seep away was like trying to keep sand from spilling from a clenched fist. Thoughts swirled and then were gone. His mind denied the reality of what he saw and heard. It was an illusion, a trick.

His eyes and ears couldn't be trusted. But if he could not trust his own senses, into what could he place his faith? Glorious Ra? At that moment, He seemed far away, indeed. Only the pain seemed real.

Ashtar was not aware of the form engulfed in a golden aura until the resplendent blade cut through the ethereal enemy. The brilliant yellow light seared the creature and consumed it in flame. The inhuman sounds emanating from the creature rose in crescendo, striking like hammer blows inside his skull, and sounding to Ashtar as if exquisite terror had joined the agonized cries. Then, abruptly, the cacophony ceased, and the creature was no more.

With the enemy gone, the light about Hakor's blade faded, though his holy aura remained until the spell had run its course. Training among the Knights of the Righteous Light consisted of more than martial practice, memorization of Ra's doctrine, and mastery of etiquette and protocol; it included learning all the known forms of the twice living. From such studies, Ashtar knew the type of creature they had faced was a grimm.

The only other enemy present was a simple, animate corpse, which Hakor cleaved in twain with a single, cutting blow.

The surviving knights began to regain their sensibilities — all but two, who remained lying on the ground and babbling incoherently, white foam visible around their mouths when their helms were removed.

"We will return for them when our enemy is defeated," Hakor said in his voice of command. "We cannot relax the noose now."

Ashtar was a moment before acknowledging the order. He was not pleased at leaving the two, but he understood the need to press the enemy, and questioning a commanding officer was unthinkable. "Aye, sir." With a final glance at the senseless knights, he joined in the investigation of the remainder of the floor.

A plain wooden door, opposite the brazen doors of the antechamber, led to a large, open, circular chamber. Another door at either side of the antechamber led to a hallway that ran the perimeter of the floor. At intervals, doors in the hallway led to the same central chamber. They discovered no other rooms.

The central chamber was something from the nightmares of the Warped God. It smelled of an abattoir within a tannery dropped within a cesspit. In separate piles along the wall were disembodied arms, legs, and heads; another of limbless torsos; and one of intact bodies, all in varying states of decay. Reddish-brown stains covered much of the walls and every available space of the floor, save the center, where the skeletal-hand-gripping-a-scepter symbol was set into the stone in tesserae, free from any discoloration or marring.

Ashtar heard retching from behind him. "Where are they? Where are the Necromancers?" He could not keep the frustration from his voice.

When the retching ceased, the chamber became deathly quiet.

"We missed something." Hakor's voice shattered the silence like a hammer to glass and shared Ashtar's frustration. "Search again." His tone made Ashtar fear the repercussions should they allow their enemies to escape.

Ashtar gave a throaty growl of annoyance at the situation in which they found themselves. They'd battled through hundreds, if not thousands, of the twice living, lost hundreds of knights — a significant cost that would leave the order depleted for some time — and all they had was an abandoned tower that, with all the bodies it held, was little more than a mausoleum.

The knights recommenced their search while Hakor, holy

symbol in hand, began another casting. He held the disk before him as he circuited the central chamber, then the hallway, a light shining forth from the symbol.

"Here!" Hakor called, a note of triumph in his voice.

Ashtar saw that where Hakor had shone the light upon the wall of the hallway, a rectangular section was limned in golden light.

"Find the mechanism to the door!"

They'd previously searched the whole of the level without any sign of a mechanism. No, not the whole. Ashtar returned to the central chamber and, holding his breath, scattered the pile of legs to see the wall behind. Next the torsos. He'd save the heads for last and moved toward the arms. A shudder ran through his body, a shiver at the pure evil of the place and at the stench so strong he fancied he could see it upon the air.

He was rewarded. Behind the pile of arms was a lever set into the wall. Without thinking otherwise, Ashtar pulled the lever. Distantly, through the thick wall, he heard a grating sound, like stone being dragged upon stone, then several shouts of success sounded from the knights.

By the time Ashtar reached the location of the hidden door, Hakor and the others already stood before the black aperture, like a tunnel to Duat itself.

With the uttered words "Well done," which, to Ashtar, sounded like praise of the highest order, Hakor shone the light of the disk into the passage and began to descend.

Ashtar was close behind, followed by the remaining paladins. The stairwell continued in a straight descent until terminating at a blank wall. However, the light from Hakor's symbol again revealed the outline of a door, this one accessible simply by pushing outward.

Exiting into the dying light, the knights found themselves standing atop the first tier of the tower, roughly thrice the height of a man from the ground. In full armor, they could not make the descent.

Ashtar struck a mailed fist against the stone of the tower.

"We are not outdone yet," Hakor said, as if conviction alone could make it so.

Coming from another, Ashtar might have questioned the confidence in that tone, but the words of the Lord High Commander he trusted implicitly.

"Commander Ashtar." At Ashtar's acknowledgement, Hakor continued, "I will take two knights and pursue. You will remain here and oversee the cleansing of the tower and the gathering of the knights' bodies."

Ashtar hesitated for just a moment, disagreement upon his lips. "Aye, Lord High Commander."

In the last of the light, Hakor and two others rode toward the forest — had the Necromancers fled in the other direction through the canyon, they would have been spotted by the knights who stood watch — and Ashtar saw to the undertaking of his tasks. In that part of his heart he refused to acknowledge, even to himself, Ashtar resented being kept behind, but like the knights who had been ordered to guard duty, he would fulfill his obligation.

Until a competing obligation found him.

"Commander! Commander!" a paladin shouted as he hurried toward Ashtar.

Ashtar did not know the man's name but saw by the number and color of feathers upon his bronze helm that he was of rank knight protector. "Yes, sir knight?"

The man waved a parchment about. "As I was searching one of the chambers, I found reference to another safehold of the Necromancers. We believed this was their last redoubt, but there is another, within the desert to the northeast. The Lord High Commander could be riding into a trap!" The man finally paused to breathe.

Ashtar took the parchment and doubly read its contents. His duty to obey the order of his commanding officer was clear. However, an exception existed when such an order threatened the good or the reputation of the Knights. Surely, the loss of a Lord High Commander threatened the good of the order. He smiled as if having uncovered a profound truth.

"Knight Protector, I place the disposition of the tower and of our fallen brothers under your charge. I go to warn the Lord High Commander."

"I . . . but . . . Aye, Commander!"

The man would either rise to the challenge of command, or he would forever remain of non-command rank. But that was a concern for another time.

A short time later, Ashtar was astride his warhorse and cantering toward the mouth of the canyon as quickly as the snow-blanketed ground allowed. The temperature had fallen precipitously, and he shook beneath his armor. The chill had the benefit of helping to keep him awake, however. He'd been fighting nearly continuously for two days with the merest respite and no sleep, and fatigue threatened to over-whelm him as he slumped in the saddle. Yet he could not rest. To do so could consign the Lord High Commander to death — or worse, a second life as a creature of the Necro-latrists.

Upon entering the forest, Ashtar continued without pause, though he slowed his pace, for if he hobbled his mount, he'd not hope to arrive in time to aid his commander. The canopy was thick, refusing most of the light from the night sky, though it also had the effect of lessening the covering of snow upon the ground. Under full light, he might have been able to discern the impressions through the snow; fortunately, however, he was not limited by such mundane means of tracking. With his own holy symbol of Ra, he produced a light that would lead in the direction the Lord High Commander had traversed.

* * *

With a start, Ashtar awakened and chided himself for dozing in the saddle. A glance at the holy symbol showed that he still traveled in correct direction, and the intensity of the light showed that he neared his objective.

By the time the beginnings of an orange glow appeared in the sky, he caught sight of something that left his heart in his throat. Limbs splayed, the armored bodies of the two knights who had accompanied the Lord High Commander lay unmoving in the snow.

Ashtar alighted and checked for life in the two. Neither had any sign of violence upon them, but their skin was as cold and pallid as the surrounding snow, and their faces were frozen in a grimace of final terror. Some twice-living abomination was certainly the cause of their demise.

Ashtar remounted and continued onward. After descending a slope and fording a frozen brook, he spied movement a short distance away and the flash of light of off an azure plate. Infused by the impending combat, all fatigue was burned away. Adjudging it easier to fight afoot among the trees rather than mounted, Ashtar descended and rushed forward.

He came upon the Lord High Commander standing above a heavily robed body, a gaping wound in its abdomen. Hakor made no move to pursue the two other fleeing forms, reduced to black shadows fliting among the trees under the rising sun.

"Sir, we can catch them!" Ashtar, running past Hakor, shouted while pointing his blade after the two fleeing Necromancers, who, even then, retreated out of sight. However, the Lord High Commander made no move to pursue. Nonplussed, Ashtar turned to face his commander.

Hakor was not looking in the direction the Necromancers had run but rather, heaume in hand, regarded Ashtar with an ambiguous expression lying somewhere between curiosity and uncertainty.

"Sir, I don't understand. We must stop them before they can warn —"

"Commander, do you recall the oath you took upon your elevation?" Hakor spoke with the imperious tone of command.

Ashtar's expression scrunched in confusion, his heart racing at the thought of the enemy so near yet escaping. "Sir, I don't — Yes, sir, of course!"

"If you encountered a conflict between the interests of the order and the dictates of Glorious Ra, which would take precedence?" Now, Hakor spoke in the slow articulation of a schoolmaster to a student.

Ashtar stood a moment, his breath wafting in ephemeral wisps. He was obviously being tested, though he couldn't, for the life of him, understand the purpose at such a time. Still, the answer was clear, and Ashtar spoke with firmness. "By my oath, the will of Glorious Ra is all."

Hakor nodded at the answer, though his expression was strangely calm, yet sad, as if resigned to some lamentable fate or task. "Commander, is your mount nearby?"

"Yes, sir, not far." Ashtar's face lit at the prospect of renewing the chase.

"Retrieve your mount and return with all haste."

"Yes, sir!" Ashtar moved past Hakor and did not understand the cause of the sudden pain at the base of his neck. His mind failed to register the meaning or that he had fallen to the ground. He thought he had, somehow, been punched beneath his armor until he coughed and choked on his own blood. Looking up, he tried to make sense of the vision of the Lord High Commander holding a bloody stiletto.

"I truly wish you hadn't witnessed that." To Ashtar's ears, Hakor's voice held real regret, and the Lord High Commander shook his head. "There *is* no conflict between the order and the will of Glorious Ra. They are one in the same. Without an enemy for the people to fear, what would become of our power and influence?"

Ashtar struggled to understand, to find some explanation. The knights existed only to see the will of Glorious Ra be done. The foul Necromancers must have laid some trap, tricked the Lord High Commander. The people revered the Knights of Ra and would celebrate them for eliminating the threat.

The shock and pain of the wound jumbled Ashtar's thoughts, but his sense of duty recalled for him a single fact, like a lifeline for a drowning man. He'd had a message for the Lord High Commander. The Necrolatrists had another safe-hold. If he could just relay the message, Hakor would understand, all would be set right . . . though his attempt to speak caused another coughing fit and blood to spew from his mouth.

Even as Ashtar's vision began to dim and his mouth and throat filled with the taste of liquid copper, his thoughts flew back to days of his youth. Since his first encounter with the knights, all he'd ever wanted was to join their illustrious ranks. In his mind's eye, he recalled the first time he'd seen the Knights of the Righteous Light, the majesty and pageantry of their cavalcade through his town after they'd destroyed a pack of rampaging ghouls —

A.R.R. Ash is a lifelong fan of both science fiction and fantasy, though he typically focuses his talents on writing dark, epic fantasy. His first self-published novel, The Moroi Hunters, *is available digitally and in print through www.LMPBooks.com/store. In 2020, he received a Silver Honorable Mention for the L. Ron Hubbard Writers of the Future Contest, first quarter, for his novella* Oneiromancy. Xy: Descent, *the first book of his* The First Godling *trilogy, is undergoing editing, and he continues to make progress on* The Tribe of Fangs, *a prequel novel to* The Moroi Hunters.

In other trivia, his favorite dishes are burgers and sushi (not together, though), his favorite book is Dune *by Frank Herbert, and his sense of humor is decidedly an acquired taste.*

THE MAD MAN OF BRIARS LODGE ROAD

BY L.S. KING

"I heard rumors of women who disappear around here."

At her statement, I peered more closely at my new neighbor. Iris, she called herself. Such a perfect name.

Agnes, the elderly woman from across the road, bit into a biscuit. "Three women. A concern is all it was. Local opinion is they're all runaways."

"Aye," her husband Karl said. "Just a coincidental spate. Anyway, no one has gone missing for quite some time."

I sipped my tea, not looking up. Runaways — ha! Blackmail had stopped the disappearances.

We sat in wicker chairs chatting in the front garden of her bungalow after helping Iris move in. I helped with the heavier items. I'm not the strongest man, but I can lift and tote well enough.

Iris glanced at the shabby Victorian house on the left. "Who lives there?"

I waved a hand, hoping it came across nonchalantly. "At Briars Lodge? Don't bother with him. He's a strange one."

"Briars Lodge? The road is named after his house?"

"It is. Was the first house along here, ages ago," Agnes said.

Karl laughed. "The Briars Lodge Loony!"

"Oh, you're being dramatic!" His wife waggled a finger. "He's just a loner is all, and a bit shy. I got him to wave at me once, just so's you know."

We continued to chat, but Iris kept twisting around to stare at the house.

"What's so fascinating about that place, dear?" Agnes asked.

"I love that style of old, rambling house. I've always wanted to live in one."

"Drafty and hard to heat, they are," the old woman replied.

Iris shrugged. "You're right. Still, it's a dream." Her smile took on a sharp edge for a moment, but then it passed.

* * *

IRIS CALLED to me over the fence, beckoning with a trowel. "I got him to chat a little bit yesterday."

I straightened from my work; I was preparing a new flowerbed. "Who?"

"The man who lives at Briars Lodge. He's called Tom. It's taken weeks of trying, but I've succeeded!"

I frowned. Not good. "He's mad, that one. I told you."

"He doesn't seem to be so bad." She lowered her head slightly with a coy smile. "Besides, he might invite me in some time, and I'd see the inside."

"It's . . . really best if you avoid him."

She waved her trowel. "I'm going to try to chat him up about gardening. He has his own herbs in a bed behind his house. I'll keep you updated."

How could I warn her not to get too cozy with him? My

best bet was to keep close tabs on her efforts. "Come for tea tomorrow. I'll cook. I'm known for my spaghetti Bolognese. You can tell me if you have any success."

She grinned. "Sure! I'll bring the wine."

* * *

"Tom's lived there for years. Inherited the house. It's all a bit creepy." She set down her glass. "I think you're right about him having a screw loose. He claims all you neighbors have secrets."

I snorted. "I bet he does, too."

"True. I even have one or two of my own, you know. Agnes and Karl's secrets, he says, are that they are notorious teetotalers. And a bit nosy."

That much was true. "Dark secrets, those," I replied with a chuckle.

She leaned forward with a grin. "He did warn me away from you."

I laughed. "Oh, yes?"

"Mm." She took a sip of wine. "I think he's jealous."

"Smitten, is he?"

"I think so." She tipped her head with a shy smile. "What about you?"

Cool and calm. That was how to play it. "I'm . . . getting there. But right now, I'm more concerned about you and Tom. Be careful. Please."

"Oh, don't worry about me!"

But I did worry.

* * *

Another casual meal, in her kitchen this time. Takeaway. She twirled her spoon absently in her curry, frowning. "Tom seems quite despondent. I think it's from rattling around in that big house by himself. I'm wondering if I shouldn't call social services about him. Agnes thinks I should, but Karl said to let the lad be. What do you think?"

"You mean . . . suicide? I have to agree with Karl. I don't see that happening."

"Really? Do you know him that well?"

"No, I just . . . he doesn't seem the type."

"Hm. I'll wait and try to talk to him again." Her smile seemed forced, worried.

"Please, listen. Stay away from Tom."

"It's so sweet of you to care." She patted my arm. "I will be fine."

Desperation filled me. What should I do? What could I do?

* * *

SIRENS — and they got louder. I ran outside to see emergency vehicles gathering in front of Tom's house.

Iris stood outside watching the spectacle, her face pale. "He did it. I think it was poison. He grew his own herbs. I told you! I told you!"

I wouldn't have believed Tom would do that. It just didn't fit. I stayed long enough to see the body being rolled out, face covered. Well, no more blackmail.

* * *

I JOINED Iris in Tom's back garden. She stood near his herb beds. Indeed, there were several kinds of dangerous herbs including foxglove and monkshood.

"You were so sweet to worry about me with Tom," she

115

murmured. "But I told you it would be fine. And guess what? I'm going to buy this house!"

"Are you? That's . . . fortuitous."

"Mm. I always get what I want." Her smile grew sharp, just like that first day. "I wanted this house."

I blinked. Everything clicked into place. She'd befriended Tom, told people he was suicidal. I laughed, amazed at her cleverness and audacity. "And you almost got it."

"Almost?"

I grinned, leaning over her. "He warned you, but you didn't listen." I grabbed her throat and squeezed. "But I do thank you for ridding me of my blackmailer. And now my new garden bed is ready. An iris bed."

Horror filled her eyes before they glazed and dimmed.

L.S. KING HAS BEEN a science fiction fan since she was a wee babe, cosplaying for Star Trek *conventions back in the early '70s, and has always loved writing. Editing, not so much, although it would be hard to tell by the fact that she pulled her hair out as a submissions editor and a copy editor on several magazines (the hair grew back, but grey. She's not that old — really!) and then was unceremoniously dragged, screaming, into becoming a founding editor of the online magazine* Ray Gun Revival, *now on hiatus. On the plus side, they made her Lord High Editor and gave her a Big, Red Button™ which she used to threaten to vaporize puny planets. As well as her work on* Ray Gun Revival, *L.S. was a submissions editor and a copy editor on several magazines, authored a column for new writers, and currently hosts a fiction writing support group online. Several titles in both of her series,* Deuces Wild *and* The Sword's Edge Chronicles, *are available in ebook and print. Her short stories have appeared in various publications, and the fact that several of them are now defunct has nothing to do with her. Honest.*

To read more about L.S. King and her work, visit her website at https://www.loriendil.com/.

TOUGH LOVE

BY MICHELE STUART

*D*arryl slotted three quarters into the vending machine and punched the button for the packet of salted peanuts, ignoring the call of the Snickers bar right next to it. After ten hours on the road, a shot of sugar was sounding pretty good, but he'd hate himself when he did his next blood check and saw the spike in his levels.

"You don't have to come," Lin said from behind him. He braced himself before turning around. Her head hung at an unsettling angle on her broken neck. She'd died in a car accident. She said she couldn't remember it, but he'd found an article about it on one of the Santa Fe news sites. Her car was the only one involved. She ran off a wet road and through a barricade, into a construction site, and impacted a crane at high speed. It was late at night, fortunately, he supposed. Nobody else was hurt. Seemed like she was speeding and lost control, or lost her brakes, or something. Maybe an antelope ran across the road. None of his questions about it seemed to jog her memory.

"We've been over this," he said, tearing open the plastic packet before turning to face her. "I lived with you and your mother for two years. I mean, maybe I wasn't much of a step-dad, but even if you weren't haunting me, I'd have wanted to go to your funeral."

"You were nice to me," she said, "and I don't mean to be haunting you."

He nodded, wandering aimlessly toward the edge of the concrete area and looking into the dark mass of trees behind the highway rest stop. There were only three other cars at the stop, drivers asleep in two of them. Something he should consider doing. His back was killing him. Some Tylenol would help with that, though, as would a little while standing or walking around. He could keep going.

He hadn't known he'd be making this trip two days ago. He'd been getting milk out of the fridge, on a perfectly usual morning, when he heard his girlfriend's cat hiss. He turned around and there was Melinda, standing in his kitchen in broad daylight, having trouble looking him in the eye because of the way her head was hanging. She was obviously, unquestionably, dead. He realized a heartbeat later that the broken neck made that pretty clear, along with her sudden appearance in his kitchen, but in that very first moment, he just knew. She wasn't gauzy and floating like ghosts in movies, and she didn't look like a zombie from the movies, either. Maybe it was some sort of animal instinct, or some sense he hadn't known he had, that said, "What you're looking at here is wrong."

His girlfriend, Trish, came in while he was gaping. She didn't react to the dead girl at all. She looked at the milk spreading across the kitchen floor from the jug Darryl hadn't noticed dropping. Maybe he looked white as the milk or something, because instead of lobbing a barb at him, she said, "Darryl, are you okay? Do you need to sit down?"

Darryl turned and vomited into the kitchen sink. He wasn't sure if it was shock, or fear, or that feeling of "wrongness." Trish was all worried then, and he let her help him into a kitchen chair and even let her clean up his mess. The whole time, Lin just stood there, watching. She looked solid, like he could reach out and touch her, even though Trish clearly couldn't see her. The cat could, though. Or she at least knew something was there. She wasn't even distracted by the spilled milk. She just crouched next to his elbow, on the kitchen table, hackles up and tail lashing. He rested a hand on her back. She allowed it, but didn't seem any calmer.

"Melinda died," he said.

"Melinda." It took Trish a minute, then she said, "Oh. Your ex's daughter? I'm so sorry. How? And when? Did someone just text you or something?"

He nodded, grateful for being handed the lie that he lacked the wit to come up with at that moment.

Trish sponged up the last of the milk, then sat back on her heels as it sank in. "Wouldn't she still be a kid?"

He nodded. "Eighteen."

"That's awful, Darryl." She rested a hand on his knee, then glanced at the cat, maybe looking for some way to lighten the mood.

"You freaked Trixie out."

He nodded, stroking the cat a little. "I know. Sorry."

Trish shrugged. "She'll be fine." She stood and leaned over to kiss him on the head.

"You want me to stay home today?"

She asked it with obvious reluctance, and he understood. They needed her paycheck more than ever since he'd been laid off. He was moved by the offer though. Trish could be prickly, but she was a decent person. She could probably do a lot better than a middle-aged man with a beer-belly, and now, no income.

"No. Thank you, but I'll be okay. Sorry about the mess."

She shrugged again. "Shit happens."

And here he was, accompanying Lin to her own funeral. She said he was the only one who could see her. She'd tried a few others. She'd even tried a priest. She said she wasn't even sure how she'd found her way to Darryl. After her mother had thrown him out, they hadn't been allowed to stay in contact. Darryl had wanted to, but he had no legal rights in the situation. He hadn't even been married to her mother. Lin said she'd just wanted to see him and ended up in his kitchen.

"I missed you," he blurted out, as he pulled out onto the highway again.

"I missed you too," she said. "You know she'll be there."

"Of course. She's your mother."

"She's married again. He'll be there too, I guess."

"I would hope so." He glanced sidelong at her, in the passenger's seat, and for maybe the hundredth time fought back the urge to tell her to buckle up.

"You like him?" he asked.

"He's fine, I guess. He doesn't bother me. I don't bother him."

They lapsed into silence for a while. Darryl wanted to start asking about the accident again, to see if she'd remember something, but she broke the silence by asking what he'd been doing lately.

"Fitness trainer," he said, patting his belly. She laughed. It sounded just like it had when she'd been alive, and he suddenly had to choke back a sob. She continued on like she didn't notice.

"You actually look better. Lost some weight?"

"I have. Got to, what with the diabetes. Not easy. Our neighborhood's a — what's that phrase for when you're surrounded by fast food but have to drive ten miles for an apple?"

"Food desert."

"Yeah, that's it. But I try. And I'm still in demolition. Still tearing things down. Or I was. No work lately."

"You're really not like that, you know. You've just had some bad luck. Maybe the new girl will work out better."

"Maybe," he said, and left it at that. It was kind of her to say, but she really hadn't known him that long. They'd been a rough couple of years, in some ways. He'd met Lin's mother at an AA meeting. Maybe getting involved with another group member wasn't his best move, but they'd liked each other. And, if he was being honest, he thought he could help her. Also not a great foundation for a relationship. Trish had since taught him what 'patronizing' meant.

Melinda hadn't taken to him at first, and he couldn't blame her; he knew he wasn't the first boyfriend to move in with them. But she'd warmed up to him, and he liked her a lot more than he'd expected to. At first, he hadn't really known how to be around a kid. He didn't have any of his own. What did you say to them? Turned out, she wasn't that different from how he'd been. Kind of shy. Kept to herself. Bookish, his mother would have called her. Darryl always thought she seemed kind of sad, not that he could blame her. It wasn't easy, growing up with an alcoholic parent.

Darryl had never been the reader Lin was. He was more of a movie guy, but she liked movies too. He'd take her to see second run shows and matinees when she was out of school, because they were cheaper. He tried to get her out of the house, especially when her mother was off the wagon. One time, he'd even taken her to visit his parents for the weekend. Her mom had been invited, of course, but said she had to work that weekend. The state of the house when they got home said she'd spent the time too drunk to work.

He used to worry, sometimes, that Lin's mother was rough with her. He figured they probably did have that in their past, but he never saw it confirmed while he was there.

Maybe she'd been afraid he'd step in? He liked to think that he would have.

Their last fight had been over Darryl pushing her to get back to meetings and her screaming at him that she was sick of his holier-than-thou bullshit and of him always trying to tell her how to raise her own kid. In hindsight, he had to admit the truth of that. She told him to go, and he did. It was a thing that still kept him awake some nights, wondering what he could have done. Should he have fought harder for the kid? Should he have called social services? Yeah, he always concluded. He should have. But what would they do? If they believed him, would they take Lin away? Put her into the system? She and her mother had no family that he knew of. They weren't too likely to give Lin to him. More likely, they'd think he was making shit up to get back at his ex-girl-friend. Maybe they'd even see something "wrong" in his attachment to Lin. He had all kinds of rationalizations. Valid ones, Trish assured him. Trish was definitely too good for him.

He woke with a start as the car drifted over the rumble strips on the shoulder, and he realized he'd dozed off behind the wheel.

"Time to pull over," Lin said.

"I guess so. Sorry."

"Don't worry about me. You're the one who can still die."

Darryl frowned, then cranked the air conditioning up so his shivering would keep him awake. "Is that what happened?" he asked, pulling into the next rest stop. "You fall asleep at the wheel?"

"I said I don't remember."

"Are you even trying to remember?"

"Why would I want to? Do you think you'd want to remember dying?"

"No. But you don't want to stay like this, right? You want

to figure out what's keeping you here, you said. I mean there must be someplace — I don't know — someplace else you should be?"

"You believe in an afterlife, Darryl?"

"I don't know. But I'm pretty sure if everybody who died ended up like you are now, we'd have heard more about it."

"Yeah. I think that too. Okay."

"Okay?"

"I'll try harder."

"Okay, he said. I'm going to get some sleep."

When he woke, it was still night, and he was still tired, but not as sleepy as before. He got a cup of terrible vending machine coffee, used the rest room, and got back in the car. Lin was just as she'd been, in the passenger's seat. For the first time, he reached out and rested a hand on her arm. She was solid, like a living person, but cold, and she gave off that sense of "wrongness" so strongly that he had to yank his hand away. "Sorry," he said.

"I get it."

"Being in the car doesn't bother you?" he asked, as he started it up and pulled out onto the highway.

"Why would it?"

Maybe it was time for the tough love approach, Darryl thought. Trying to be delicate about the whole thing hadn't gotten him anywhere so far.

"Because you died in one."

She didn't say anything for a minute, then, "I told you, I don't remember that."

"What do you want, Lin?"

"I told you. I want to — I don't know . . . move on. Go wherever I'm supposed to be. Not be like this."

"What's the last thing you do remember?"

"I told you."

"No, you didn't. You keep dancing around the question,

like you're doing now. What were you doing before you got in the car? Had you been drinking?"

"No! I don't drink."

"Drugs?"

"No drugs."

"Had you had a fight with somebody?"

"I'd watched a movie. Then I went out for a drive. I was just driving around, listening to music. You know? Just thinking."

"What movie? What music?"

"What does that matter?"

Darryl didn't know why it mattered. He was no shrink. He hadn't even gone to college. In group, you don't push like this. You let the person settle in and learn to trust the group, let them come to sharing on their own time. Maybe that's what he should be doing, but it felt like this was going some-where. So he pushed. "I don't know. Just tell me."

"Okay. I watched *Little Women*. The new one. And I was just listening to a radio station."

"Huh. I always listen to music on my phone."

"How do you find new music?"

"You're changing the subject. So you got in the car and you're driving around listening to the radio. Why? Why just go driving?"

"Sometimes I just do that."

"When? After you watch a movie?" Darryl wished he knew anything about the movie *Little Women*.

"No. Any time. I mean, usually at night. Because I'm at school during the day. I just want to get out of the house, you know?"

"You're still in school? College? What were you studying?"

"Computer science. That and business stuff, or maybe law, or to be a doctor — that's all anybody studies anymore. It's all about getting a good job after you graduate."

"What's wrong with that?"

"Nothing, I guess." She waved a hand, a gesture he remembered as her way of brushing a subject away.

"Do you like computer science? You used to love to read. And play guitar. Do you still play?"

"I did, a little. When mom wasn't home. She'd just yell at me to give it a rest."

Darryl could picture that, especially if Lin's mom was drinking again. "And your stepfather?"

"What about him?"

"He yell at you?"

"No. He mostly just ignored me. Which was okay by me."

"You couldn't afford to move out?"

"Nope. Not on what I could make working retail. I got loans for college, so —" Again, the wave of the hand.

"Lin, did you go driving when you were sad?"

"I suppose."

Darryl drew in a breath, and decided to just go for it. He'd been shying away from the thought for the last two days, trying not to think it. Maybe he needed a dose of that "tough love" too. Maybe he just had to deal with it.

"Lin, did you drive into the crane on purpose?"

"I don't remember!" she screamed, and disappeared.

Darryl kept driving, fighting back tears.

With the sunrise, the rolling hills of Oklahoma started to break up the monotony of the long, flat expanse of nothing that had been the drive through Arkansas. Well, nothing but bugs. Plenty of bugs, splattered all over his car. Lin reappeared in the passenger seat just as he was pulling into a gas station. He said nothing, got out and filled the tank and washed the windshield, then went inside to see if they had anything not made of processed sugar. She was still there when he got back in the car.

"I'm sorry," they said in unison.

"Where'd you go?" he asked.

"Top of the Pedernal."

"Seriously? You what, teleported there?"

"I don't know how it works. I just wanted to be away from you."

Darryl supposed he had that coming. After all, he had just asked her if she'd killed herself.

"I don't know, Darryl," she said, breaking the silence. "Did the article you read say anything about the car?"

"Like that you lost the brakes or steering or something? No. But they might not have known yet."

"I don't usually drive that fast. I don't drink, like, at all. I don't do drugs. Maybe I fell asleep behind the wheel?"

"And the car accelerated? Maybe, I guess. I don't really know how that would work."

"At least I didn't kill anybody else."

"Yeah. There is that."

"I mean, I'm not saying I haven't thought about it. Everybody thinks about it, right?"

Did they? Darryl didn't know if that was true or not. Certainly, he had. And a car often seemed like the perfect opportunity. You see a lake by the side of the highway and you think, what if I just ran the car off the road here into the water? Or off a bridge? Or into a concrete wall? Nobody else gets hurt. But what if you didn't die? Sometimes he wondered if that was what stopped him, more often than not. What if you just suffered brain damage, or lost a limb, or paralyzed yourself? You already found life just a little too hard, and you went and made it harder.

"I don't know. But I have," he said, after what was probably a longer time than he should have remained silent.

"Yeah?"

"Yeah."

"Why didn't you?"

He told her all that he'd just been thinking, then added, "Plus, my mother's still alive. Imagine what that would do to her. She'd think it was her fault, somehow. And she'd be all alone."

"Oh, I didn't know your father had passed. I'm sorry."

He nodded. "Yeah, a year after I left Santa Fe and went back to Georgia."

"I don't think Mom would blame herself."

"Course she would, Lin. She's got her faults. I mean, we all do. But she's still your mother."

She didn't say anything. He glanced over once to see if she had disappeared, but she was still there.

"You were eighteen, right?" he asked.

"Yeah."

"Damn, Lin. Things would have gotten better. You'd have moved out. Put some space between you and your mother. Met somebody. Did you have a boyfriend?" Then added, "Or a girlfriend?" belatedly reminding himself that people were open about that sort of thing now.

"No. I mean, I went on a few dates in high school. Went to few parties. But nobody special, no."

It was a little hard to tell just from her voice how she was reacting to something. All he could do was glance at her, given that he was driving, but she showed no body language at all, except for that dismissive wave of the hand. He hadn't caught her shrugging, or turning her head away — maybe because she couldn't, or shrinking down in the seat. But he thought she might have cringed, just a little, when he'd asked about that.

"Nobody you even liked?"

"I guess there were boys I liked. But it never went anywhere."

Darryl frowned. He didn't remember her having any close friends in the years he'd been around. She certainly never brought any kids home, and he totally got that. He'd rarely done that as a kid, especially during his father's drinking years. "And your stepfather?"

"Why do you keep asking about him?"

"Because he moves in and your depression skyrockets, or plummets, or whichever way you'd say it."

"We're assuming that I committed suicide now?"

"How's the idea feel to you?"

"How does it feel?" She was getting heated again. "It feels like shit! It feels like I'm a big zero! A failure! Like I couldn't hack life past the age of eighteen!"

"But does it feel wrong?"

"No! Okay? Is that what you want to hear? It doesn't feel wrong!"

It was absolutely the last thing Darryl had wanted to hear, and the thing he had most feared.

"I killed myself?" she said, like she was testing the words in her mouth. "I killed myself. I. Killed. My. Self. I stepped on the gas, drove the car through the fence, and steered it at the crane. I shut my eyes, at the end. I guess my aim was still pretty good."

Darryl didn't say anything. He felt like he should say something, but had no idea what. Maybe this was a thing she needed a minute to process on her own. Miles passed in silence, until Darryl couldn't stand it anymore. "You're still here," he said.

"Yeah. I noticed that too."

"So, that wasn't the thing."

"The thing that gets me to move on? I guess not. Maybe I'm stuck here. Maybe I'll be like this forever."

Darryl said, "Well, I mean, you're welcome to stay with me as long as you want." The words sounded so lame to him, like he was offering her a couch to sleep on. She didn't seem to think so, though.

"See?" she said. "You were always nice to me."

Darryl drew in a deep breath and said, "Okay. So. This might send you to the top of another mountain, but —"

"Pedernal's the only one I've ever climbed."

"Okay. But . . . well, I'm just going to blurt something out. Again."

When she said nothing, he pressed on. "Was your stepfather, you know, abusing you? Doing wrong things?"

"No," she said immediately, and with a conviction that sounded like truth to him. Darryl breathed out a relieved sigh.

"Mom did," Lin said.

"Wait. What?" Darryl turned his head to look at her. The car swerved into the breakdown lane, and he hastily yanked at the wheel. Then he eased it right again and rolled to a stop, his hands shaking too hard to control the vehicle.

"What are you saying, Lin?"

"Mom used to come into my room at night and — well, look, do you really want the details?" Her voice was so low, he could barely hear her, but then the words started flowing like water from a broken faucet.

"I remember now. I remember it all. Like every detail of my life. Stuff I thought I'd forgotten. I remember how she'd do — you know, the things she did. Then she'd be angry. At herself. At me. Like it was my fault, right? And I mean, it must have been because a mother wouldn't just do that, would she?"

Darryl stammered, "But, you're both —"

"Girls? Women? Yeah, I know. Women have sex with each other. I mean, usually not mothers and daughters. And you never knew!"

The last words were a shriek that no living human throat could have made. He pressed his hands over his ears and leaned his head on the steering wheel, fighting the urge to vomit.

"You said you loved me, and then she told you to go away, and you just — you just went! You left me with her!"

"I didn't know. How could I know?"

"You lived with us!"

"Lin, I admit, I thought she hit you sometimes —" He stopped. He wasn't going to do that. He wasn't going to defend himself. She had to get this out. He leaned back in the seat, his heading pounding in the aftermath of that shriek, and looked at her. "Yeah," he said. "You're right. I should have known."

Her rage left as quickly as it had come. "No. There was no reason you would have. It wasn't your fault."

But it was my responsibility, he thought. *I should have done more. And I'm always going to have to live with that.* "What do you want me to do now?" he asked. "Do you want me to go to the police?"

"No. You'd just get in trouble. It's not like you can prove it."

"Then what?"

"Hold my hand," she said. He reached out and took her hand. It was hard to hold onto. Every part of him wanted to pull away. But he held on like he would have if she were dangling from a bridge and he was trying to save her.

"I think I just wanted someone to know. I wanted somebody who loved me to know," she said.

Then she was gone. Darryl sat there and cried until a state trooper came along and asked if he'd broken down. He said he kind of had and that he was on his way to his daughter's funeral. The trooper offered condolences and didn't give him any trouble. Darryl drove on alone.

. . .

MICHELE STUART IS a native of Salem, Massachusetts. She and her husband now reside just north of Atlanta. When not at her day job or writing, her time is consumed by reading or listening to books and podcasts, playing a couple of very old online games, exercising, continuously attempting to learn Spanish, and working on TTRPG games, more or less in that order. She also thinks a lot about drawing more and playing guitar again. She has had poetry published, in years past, in the Soundings East literary journal and in the anthology Between the Leaves, *published by Barnes & Noble books. "Tough Love" was written for First Line Journal, though the first line has now been slightly altered. It has the distinction of having been both her first personal rejection and first professional fiction sale.*

VOICES IN MY HEAD

BY STEPHEN JOHNSON

The rain drizzled lazily outside, creating trails of meandering water falling in random streaks down the window. Jeremy Collins watched one droplet as it formed and traveled down its undetermined path and found comfort in the uniqueness of that single drop. His head rested on his hand as he lost himself in the endless parade of rain crawling down the window.

"What are you looking at?" a voice whispered to him with a curious and even interested tone.

Jeremy lifted his head and turned to see Beverly Glass seated next to him. She was listening to Mrs. Clark and noticed Jeremy glancing at her.

She turned with a disgusted look and sneered, "Stop looking at me!" She quickly refocused on Mrs. Clark as she began her review of the cell makeup and nucleus. Jeremy shot Beverly a nasty look and peered behind his desk to look for the genesis of the voice. He murmured under his breath as he quickly remembered he sat in the last seat in the corner with no one behind him. *Strange,* he thought, the voice I heard was not a girl's voice but that of another boy. He began

133

to dismiss the incident entirely until he heard a playful giggling all around him. The sound did not seem to be coming from his left or right or even behind him — it was all around him.

"That was funny, but I don't like her. I don't like the teacher either. Why do we have to be in here?"

Jeremy looked around in a more concerned manner, especially behind his desk. Beverly annoyingly looked over, as did several other students in the seventh grade biology class, causing Mrs. Clark to stop the lecture.

"Mr. Collins, is there something we can help you with? You are disturbing the whole class. What is it that is so important that you can't sit still?"

Jeremy shifted uncomfortably in his desk, clearly disturbed by the increased attention, and sat in silence not knowing how to respond. Mrs. Clark pressed with an impatient and intolerable tone, "Well, what is it?"

Jeremy looked down in embarrassment when he heard the voice whisper playfully, "Tell her she has a big butt."

Jeremy laughed to himself and then immediately looked up in horror as he saw Mrs. Clark's eyes widen in rage. "You think this is funny. Well, we will see how funny you think it is when you are suspended. Go to Mr. Edward's office immediately."

Jeremy frowned as he stood, gathered his books, and walked out of the classroom while the other students laughed at him. He could hear Mrs. Clark scream, "Quiet now, everyone quiet!" before she resumed her lecture over the cell membrane.

Jeremy walked slowly down the hall, looking down to the floor, passing rows of lockers, when he glanced up to see a boy standing directly in front of him. The boy stood silently, looking directly at Jeremy, his eyes never looking away or blinking. Jeremy shifted his eyes nervously and looked behind him to see if the boy may be looking for someone else, but Jeremy was the only other person in the hallway. Jeremy looked up and stopped as he approached within a few feet; the strange quiet boy made no attempt to move. Jeremy shifted to the other side of the hallway to pass the boy.

As he came to his side, the boy turned his head and spoke to Jeremy. "What are you looking at?" The sound came out in a low rasping voice that did not match the young man staring back at Jeremy.

As he passed the boy, he saw out of the corner of his eye that the stranger turned to watch him. Jeremy jerked his head back to look again and saw the young boy's eyes staring at him. Usually, that would be disturbing enough, but it wasn't just that the boy was staring at him. The boy's head had turned to follow Jeremy, but the rest of his body still faced the other end of the hallway. Jeremy's face drew taught as he witnessed the boy's head turn completely backward.

The face reflected a set of bright crimson eyes that beamed back with a cold dead stare masked with an eerily sinister smile that spread across the entire bottom of his face. The most disturbing part of the smile was the teeth. Pale and yellow with ridges on several of his bottom teeth, his mouth looked like a jagged chainsaw blade, and Jeremy noticed streams of blood flowing down both corners of his mouth.

"What are you looking at?" the boy creature screamed after Jeremy. The creature began walking backward toward Jeremy with its head facing him. It placed its left hand on the side of the lockers and produced a low wretched sound of fingernails scratching on metal as he passed each one.

Jeremy stood frozen in terror, his eyes locked with the creature's as it moved forward across the hall toward him. Jeremy felt the bile move up his throat as a smell like rotten eggs filled the hallway. He covered his mouth and nose, trying to block the hideous smell.

"What are you looking at?" The creature howled in laughter, quickening its pace, running toward him. Jeremy turned and dropped his books and ran as fast as he could down the hallway. Jeremy did not dare glance back as he reached the intersection. He continued running, racing to the right toward the exit of the school, and hit something with such force that it knocked him backward. Jeremy felt blood burst from his nose at the impact. Tears blurred his vision and pain throbbed in his nose as he fought to open his eyes, knowing the boy with the chainsaw teeth was standing right in front of him.

Jeremy opened his eyes and forced his vision to peer through the pain and watery eyes when he heard a booming voice, "Mr. Collins, what are you doing running in the hall? I expected you in my office fifteen minutes ago."

A strong arm lifted him from the floor, and suddenly he was surrounded by a hallway of children moving about to their next class, some stopping to gawk at the boy with the bloody nose and others whispering to their friends, wondering what had happened.

"Follow me, now!" Mr. Collins escorted Jeremy to his office." We called your parents, and they are on their way. While we are waiting for them, do you want to explain to me what happened in the hallway?" Mr. Edwards ushered him into a seat next to his desk and settled into his own chair across from him.

The chair made a strange creaking sound as he gently rocked back and forth, rotating a pen between his fingers. Jeremy sat silently in the seat looking absently out the window, searching for the peacefulness in the trails of the raindrops flowing down the pane. A knock on the door behind them interrupted the quiet, and both turned to see the school secretary enter with Jeremy's mother who carried a very troubled look.

"What did you do?" she fumed as she entered the room, acknowledging Mr. Edwards with a short glance before turning her attention back to her son.

Jeremy started, "Mama, I —" but he was cut off quickly.

"Go outside and get into the car. We will deal with this at home."

Jeremy sat quietly in the back of the car for the entire twenty-minute ride home, waiting for the lecture, but his mother never turned around. She simply drove home and remained surprisingly calm. When they arrived, she turned around and spoke sternly to him, "I am so disappointed in you. The principal told me what you did. What do you have to say for yourself?"

Jeremy stammered for a few seconds, considering whether to tell her about the voices in his head and the strange creature in the hallway, but he instead turned and shook his head, lowering his eyes, "I am sorry, it won't happen again."

His mother looked back at him, shaking her head, and finally muttered, "Fine, let me look at your nose." She gently checked his nose and stroked his hair. "Is everything alright, JC?"

The use of his nickname and her affection nearly caused him to cry, but he held his composure and responded, "Yes, ma'am, everything is good. I am sorry for today. Guess I just let a bad day cause me to act up." He decided to try a version of the truth that he thought could pass. "There was a boy in the hallway. He chased me and he tried to hurt me."

His mother looked at him alarmingly. "Why didn't you say something earlier?" She looked protectively at Jeremy and kissed him on the cheek. "Just go up to your room and wash up. You can help me clean the house today. I will go to the school tomorrow and talk with Mr. Edwards again. You sure you're okay?"

Jeremy forced a smile and nodded, "I am okay, promise. Can I just sit out here for a minute?"

"Sure, don't stay out here too long, though. I will cook you your favorite, hamburgers." She turned and walked into the house.

Jeremy sighed and tried to rationalize the day's events while he sat for a few minutes in the car. He spent the rest of the afternoon and early evening waiting to see the boy with the chainsaw teeth around every corner of his house, but every time he turned the corner, there was nothing but empty space. He slowly began to wonder if it was just his imagination, and by bedtime, he had almost put the thought out of his mind. Unfortunately, the boy from the school and the voices in his head were not through with him.

Jeremy was sitting in his room absently thumbing through an old Spider Man comic book when he heard something that seemed to come from his closet whisper out, "What are you looking at?"

He jerked up in bed with beads of sweat forming on his brow. He felt the drops of wet perspiration form at his forehead and travel down his cheek and past his lips. Despite his fear, he laughed softly as he thought of the rain traveling down the window, then thought himself crazy that he would even remember that.

As he drifted back to sleep, he was roused from his thoughts again by the familiar phrase from his nightmare, "What are you looking at?"

Again he sat up in his bed, trying desperately to adjust his vision to see into the darkness of the closet. From the deep void at the back, a low guttural sound emanated like a choking animal; it reached a crescendo that felt like a high pitched wail from a wounded dog. Jeremy backed against the headboard of his bed, pulled the covers up close to his nose, and held his hands over his ears to block out the relentless, deafening cry. He sat shaking for what seemed hours, until the sound stopped.

He uncovered his ears but kept the covers pulled over his body. He focused again on the back of the closet and noticed two small lights that pierced through the darkness of the open door. The lights shaded to a reddish hue and increased in brightness and diameter until two flashlights of deep crimson looked back at him. "What are you looking at?" the voice repeated in its low, watery, cough-like hoarseness.

The crimson eyes moved out of the closet and toward Jeremy as he lay in the bed, trying his best to hide under the covers, crying and shaking. Footsteps on the floor sounded as the creature moved closer to Jeremy, and he heard the familiar creak of the baseboard that he knew was just at the end of his bed. *It must be right next to me*, Jeremy thought, closing his eyes hard as tears soaked into his sheets. Finally, the footsteps stopped, and he no longer heard the hoarse uneven breathing. Feeling the creature may have left, Jeremy pulled down the covers and peeked toward the end of his bed. He opened his eyes and took a deep breath as he saw nothing at the bottom of the bed, and the closet was dark and quiet.

He relaxed and leaned back against his bed frame. He felt a soft breeze across the back of his neck. Jeremy froze as the breath turned hot and sticky and droplets ran down his back. He felt the slight indention of teeth as they punctured his skin, and Jeremy jumped to the floor. He peered back to see the young boy creature from school staring back at him. His head was still turned around, but it was the truly sinister smile that spread across his face that pierced Jeremy's soul. Mucous seeped from its nostrils and coagulated blood dripped from its chainsaw teeth as it quickened its breathing in anticipation of new prey.

"What are you looking at?" The creature uttered the

relentless phrase in slow, methodical repetition, inching forward with a smile that widened to expose the jagged sharp teeth covered in crimson and aching for another victim. Jeremy dodged around the end of his bed and ran down the stairs to the living room, looking for his parents. He screamed for them as he ran frantically all around the downstairs of the house. The stairs creaked as he heard foot-steps descending from upstairs. He knew he did not have much time as he snuck through the rooms toward his parents' bedroom and burst in to find them sleeping.

"Mama, something is chasing me. It is trying to kill me." His mother sat up nervously, half asleep. "What are you talking about?"

His dad murmured something and jumped out of bed. He ran toward the door and grabbed his gun that he kept in his drawer next to the closet. "Both of you stay in here." His father crashed out of the room and headed upstairs. Jeremy waited with his mother, clutching her while he wept in her arms until his father came back into the room.

"Nothing else in the house. Are you sure you saw some-thing, or maybe it was just a dream? I told you about those scary comics right before bedtime."

Jeremy spoke between sobs and gasps, "No, I promise this was real. It was the same boy I saw at school who chased me in the hallway."

Jeremy's father looked at him suspiciously and then to his mother. "What is he talking about?"

Jeremy suspected that his mother had not told his father about everything that happened at school, so for the next few minutes the three discussed what had transpired over the last twelve hours. After refusing to go back to his bedroom by himself, Jeremy spent the night downstairs in his parents' room, without any restful sleep. His dreams continued to return to the creature's face with the hideous smile and the crimson eyes boring into his soul. As he woke from a fitful night of sleep, all he could hear was the repetitive phrase, "What are you looking at?"

The next morning, Jeremy's parents escorted him to the doctor and the three discussed their concerns. While Jeremy tried to plead his case that what he saw was real, the doctor gave him a variety of rational explanations that disproved whatever he said. "What about the bite marks on the back of my neck?" he said in a clearly agitated voice.

The doctor looked closely at his neck and then gave a purposeful look to his parents. "There is a mark on the back of your neck, but . . ."

"What is it, Doctor?" his mother asked.

"Well, the shape and indention of these marks are not consistent with bite marks. It looks more like marks made by a set of fingernails, specifically a young boy's fingernails. Did you scratch yourself on purpose?" the doctor asked Jeremy suspiciously.

"No, I swear, it was the boy with the chainsaw teeth."

Jeremy's mother sighed and began crying while his father looked at the doctor with concern.

Jeremy found himself starting to cry and spoke softly back to the doctor. "Am I going crazy?"

No one talked much on the trip back after the experience at the doctor's, nor during the dinner they picked up from the local Mexican restaurant on their way home. Jeremy was not in a hurry to rehash anything from the day. In fact, he was not even sure if he really knew what happened. The doctor did recommend that he see a "special" doctor who treated issues like Jeremy was experiencing.

Jeremy was not excited about it; however, if it could make the creature disappear, he would do about anything. Jeremy slept in his parents' room and did not see the boy with the chainsaw teeth, nor did he see him again at school the rest of the week. Jeremy started seeing the psychiatrist a few days later and had to admit that he did feel better. He had not seen the creature since he started his treatments. He did, however, get constant visits from the boy's voice. It always had something it wanted him to do. Jeremy tried to block it out, but it seemed like it would always be waiting for him late at night. He stopped telling the doctor and his mother about it.

Instead, he kept a box buried deep in his memory. This box contained a boy who liked to whisper in his ears late at night through chainsaw teeth that oozed blood. He tried not to remember, but sometimes late at night when he was lying in bed unable to sleep, he would think of the boy and the things that he whispered for Jeremy to do. He suspected that he would never really be able to truly forget, but he had trained his mind to keep the boy locked away — back in that box.

After three months without incident, everything returned to normal; Jeremy had even gone back to sleeping in his own room. After a while the entire family forgot about the incident, and life resumed.

* * *

JEREMY EXCELLED through the following years at high school and college. He did his best to forget his past. Part of that meant he would always find excuses for not returning to his parents' home. He had not been back since he left for college. While he was at school, his father passed away, and a few months before his graduation, his dear mother lost her battle with cancer. That was the last time Jeremy had been home, and frankly, as far as he was concerned, it would be the last time he ever returned.

After college, Jeremy settled into life as everyone does. He found a job he loved as a financial planner in a promising firm. He married his college sweetheart, Becky.

Late one night after the rest of the house was quiet with Becky upstairs asleep, Jeremy was sitting alone in his living room, reading notes from meetings taken earlier in the day, when he heard a banging in the kitchen. He suspected it to be Archie, their cat, and sat finishing the page before he heard another banging noise followed by a grunt. He placed the paper on the coffee table and walked cautiously into the kitchen. On the floor he found several plates that had fallen from the table and shattered and another pot that had fallen from the stove.

"Stupid cat," he mumbled. As he knelt to pick up the broken pieces of plate, he heard a familiar guttural groan behind him. Instantly his heart sank as if he were transported back to his seventh grade self. He knew what stood behind him. He swirled around intending to see the boy from his childhood nightmares; instead, he saw a completely different creature. Before him stood a grown man, yet he could see the resemblance. It was as if the young boy with the chainsaw grin had grown into an older version of himself as Jeremy had aged.

Time had not treated this man as well as Jeremy. The face had become drawn and grayer with wrinkles and infected with open sores and blisters. The eyes were still the deep dark crimson, soulless windows he remembered. The smile widened from ear to ear, almost encompassing his entire face, fully showing the teeth that had grown sharper and longer. The boy grown into a man slithered toward him as he heard the voices return in his head, singing almost in a chorus.

Jeremy fell to his knees, covering his ears. "No, I won't listen to you. You are not real. You are only in my mind. I will put you back in the box."

The creature laughed sinisterly and kept approaching as the voices in his head built in volume and told him to do things — evil, despicable things. Jeremy took the pan and threw it across the kitchen; it bounced off the creature's head with no effect. The metal pot clanged off the side of a few teeth and echoed in a metallic savage sound as the creature continued. "What are you looking at?" the creature snarled as the voices rose inside his head.

"No, I can't do it," he screamed. He fell to the floor and grabbed his head as if he were having a massive migraine.

A voice came from behind and lights switched on as Becky ran into the kitchen. "What's wrong?" She rushed to where Jeremy was doubled up on the floor.

He raised his head quickly, trying to shield her from the chainsaw grin, but there was nothing there. Jeremy wiped the sweat and tears from his face, wondering how he could explain what had happened. Fortunately, Becky didn't ask many questions and settled for his explanation that he had awakened from a nap and was startled while sleepwalking in the kitchen. He went with her upstairs to bed and to his surprise, he fell asleep quite easily. Maybe it was the stress from the encounter that drained him or it was simply that he was exhausted, but at six in the morning he awoke refreshed and immediately thought about the previous night.

Jeremy lay in the bed staring at the ceiling until he heard a scream downstairs. He jumped up and ran to the kitchen to see his wife with her hands covering her face and pale as a ghost. Motionless in the corner of the kitchen lay the family pet, Archie. His wife stood in shock and continued muttering under her breath, "What did that? Some animal got in the house and did that to Archie!" She came out of her trance and her eyes recognized Jeremy next to her; she grabbed him and hugged him hard. "Poor Archie, poor, poor, Archie . . ." she trailed off, weeping.

After the morning's event, Jeremy sent Becky out shopping to clear her mind and give him time to clean up and dispose of Archie properly. He went out back, picked a spot away from the house in the corner of the yard, and started digging. After a few shovels, he heard the familiar grating voice rise from behind him.

"What are you looking at?'

Jeremy turned and faced the creature, screaming, "Leave me alone! Why are you doing this?"

The creature simply bared its fearful grin from ear to ear, exposing a rotting decay of flesh and jagged yellow teeth. The crimson eyes watered, and drops of blood flowed down the graying cheeks.

Jeremy dropped the shovel and fell to the ground, grabbing his head and trying to push the thoughts deep into his mind by holding his skull together. As he began to cry, he heard another noise behind him as sticks cracked underfoot. He jumped to his feet, pulled the shovel back, and reared with all his strength to end the creature once and for all.

He turned and swung the shovel with such might and strain that his teeth clenched and his eyes closed as he brought the shovel around. There was a quick sharp scream as he followed through, and the shovel swung around his back as he made contact. He opened his eyes after he exhaled a large breath of effort, then a scream rose in his throat. Becky lay on the ground, and Jeremy fell back to the earth again, this time with the creature standing over him, laughing and breathing so close he could feel the breath on his face. The voices whispered to him that it was all right, that everything would be just fine. They told him exactly what he needed to do. Jeremy cried, but this time he listened to the voices.

He finished the second hole after about an hour and waited for the voices to tell him what to do next. Jeremy nodded as he followed the directions. The creature had gone but the voices remained behind to help him. He was sure they were there to help him now — if only he had listened sooner, he would not have had to dig this hole, they said. Jeremy agreed finally, and after finishing up, he walked into the house, showered, and went to bed. The voices told him he needed to rest. Jeremy listened and did what they said, and he slept more soundly than he could ever remember.

Jeremy awoke the next day to loud knocks on his front door and shouting from the back door as well. He casually went downstairs and found several policemen waiting. As he opened the door, he was forcibly handcuffed and thrown into the back of a police car. He waited for the creature to show up, but the voices told him to be quiet and they would handle everything. Jeremy sat in the back of the police car and laughed as he listened to the thoughts in his head.

He remembered when they used to talk to him in school, and the things they whispered to him back then made him giggle louder. Jeremy felt even more relieved as he looked to his side and the chainsaw teeth man sat smiling next to him. Jeremy laughed louder and smiled broadly, nodding to him and bringing his finger to his mouth in a shushing motion to signify their secret. The policeman in the driver's seat looked stoically in the rear view mirror but said nothing. After they arrived at the station, Jeremy was transported to a special place he heard the officers call the asylum.

* * *

THREE MONTHS LATER, Jeremy sat smiling quietly in the solitary cell with his arms wrapped in the white jacket, staring absently at the wall. The voices told him to stay quiet and let them do all the talking, and he wholeheartedly obeyed. It was nice to let them take over, he thought. Things were so much simpler. He stood and walked to the mirror in the padded room and stared deeply at his reflection.

His smile broadened as he watched his reflection echo a deep hideous smile. The creature in the mirror stared back at him with the chainsaw rows of teeth and crimson eyes glaring back longingly at him. Their eyes seemed to connect, and Jeremy looked at his reflection with a deeper understanding.

The doctor called from the entrance to his room, "Mr. Collins, are you ready?"

Jeremy looked at him for a moment, then returned his gaze to the mirror. His smile widened even more, until it matched the look of the creature, and he playfully winked at the mirror whispering, "What are you looking at?"

STEPHEN JOHNSON IS A HUSBAND, father, Chihuahua dad, and retired Naval Officer, having served twenty-two years on four different ships over his career. Jumpmaster Press will publish his first novel, The Fizz Prophecy, *in 2022. His short stories appear in anthologies such as Scare Street's* Night Terrors *volumes 8 and 17, No Bad Books'* Released, *ZombieWorks Publishing's* Natural Instincts, *and Breaking Rules Europe's* Death Ship.

THE VILLAIN IN THEM

# A BASILISK AND A BITE

BY AJ SKELLY

Colin "Hunter" Abreen was my brother's best friend, the best basilisk hunter instructor at Magik Prep Academy, and definitely off limits. My treacherous heart needed more persuasion on that last part; I'd been in love with him since I was twelve. Once or twice, I'd even thought I'd seen him looking at me like I looked at him. It was enough to give me hope.

On a stupid whim I'd signed myself up for Colin's 401 Basilisk Hunter course as my senior elective. Apparently, I was a glutton for punishment. And a hopeless basilisk hunter. I'd been sent to the infirmary with fang punctures more times than anyone else. Ever. In the entire history of the class.

It didn't matter how hard I tried, how often I practiced my technique, or how desperately I wanted to excel and impress Colin. I just couldn't see the stupid, villainous creatures. But they always saw me. And then they bit me.

My pointed ears twitched; my blonde hair was pulled up and out of the way so nothing would hinder my ability to hear their soft slithering. My elf ears were more reliable than my eyesight for picking out their inconspicuous bodies in the dense underbrush of the Academy's forested park. Even using my enhanced vision goggles that protected me from the dangerous stare of the loathsome beasts, my ears were a better bet.

My fingers gripped my net and my hooked stick. I would catch this basilisk if it was the last thing I did. We'd been stalking each other in circles for the past seventy-eight increments. I was done stalking. I was ready to conquer.

A slither to the right!

No, there, in the bush!

I silently raised my net and hook, ready to scoop up the smarmy, slithery, insufferable creature. Crouching as Colin had instructed, I crept forward with the grace of a sleek-bodied water nymph.

A slight movement!

Gotcha!

I howled and dropped my net that had snared a terribly dangerous patch of wildflowers and clutched my hand. My whole arm smarted as the creature's mild venom spread needle-like tingles up to my shoulder. Glancing at the bushy fronds in front of me, I just made out the basilisk's disappearing tail.

Biting back a curse, I glanced at my hand. It wasn't a bad bite. But it was a bite. And I'd failed yet again to capture a reptilian fiend.

I ripped off my goggles and stomped toward the instructor tent set up at the opening of the woods.

Colin looked up from his desk, and I swear a smile flitted across his face as I came crashing out of the underbrush. If only that smile meant he was glad to see me and not because I required a triple dose of patience and more repeated instruction than anyone else in the class. "Again, Kaebre?"

My shoulders slumped in defeat. "Again."

"Let me see."

I held my hand out for his inspection. When he took it carefully in his large rough ones, I suppressed a shiver and hoped he didn't notice. He turned my palm over and then back to the marred skin by my knuckles. I watched his face as he examined my hand, but he kept his eyes on the bite mark.

"Come on. These are just scratches. I can patch these up myself with the first aid kit here."

He led me over to a stump where I sagged like a bag of bones. I felt like a child who wanted desperately to gain their teacher's approval. Except I wanted more than Colin's approval. I wanted him to look at me the way I had looked at him since he and my brother had let me tag along, climbing trees in the back yard together. A heavy sigh escaped my lungs.

"Cheer up, Kaebre. Basilisk hunting isn't for everyone. So long as you capture one before the term ends, you'll pass the course."

Mortification slid through me, and I clenched my teeth to keep my chin from quivering. I was humiliated. Pathetic. I was the only student in the course not to have netted a basilisk. Fresh worry for my grade slid over the humiliation.

"How did you become so good so quickly?" I asked him quietly. "You broke every basilisk-catching record within six weeks of starting the course, and now, the year after your own graduation, you're the instructor. Top universities around the country are trying to recruit you for their basilisk programs. Col, how did you do it?"

He was still a minute, his broad shoulders moving slowly as he took a breath. His shaggy thatch of bronze hair grazed over his forehead in the slight breeze. His head was bent, his fingers carefully tying off the gauze around my hand. He stilled even more; his body like chiseled marble bowed over my hand.

Slowly he tipped his head so that his blue eyes met mine. My breath caught, and my heart sped up as he locked gazes with me. His hands still engulfed mine.

"Kaebre," he started, then paused.

My eyebrows rose, encouraging him, and my fingers squeezed his lightly before I could stop them.

"I'm about to tell you something that is not common knowledge. I'd like to keep it that way."

I nodded. He was trusting me with sensitive information. Was it possible I'd worked my way up from best friend's little sister to reliable student — and maybe his friend in my own right?

He glanced around, ensuring we were alone before meeting my eyes again.

"I'm color blind. Completely."

I cocked my head, the full weight of his words slowly registering. Color blind? It was a rare genetic trait. Rare, undesired, and dangerous in a world filled with colored magic. Use the wrong color and you could kill yourself or somebody else. But how did that help him catch basilisks?

The corner of his mouth tipped at my confusion. "Their camouflage isn't camouflage to me. I see everything in black, white, and grey. Without their colors to blend in, it's easy to spot their markings between the leaves and the underbrush."

I was stunned as my thoughts caught up. "You've hid it your whole life."

He nodded. "I can't see colors, but I can see other things." He ran his thumb over my knuckles, carefully avoiding my wound, and my face flamed.

He chuckled. "I'll make a deal with you. You catch a basilisk, pass the course, and when you graduate in a month, we'll talk about the becoming shade of grey on your face right now."

He squeezed my hands as my eyes sparkled. My smile stretched across my face, but I didn't care. Not anymore. I'd already waited years for Colin to notice me. Now that I knew he had, graduation wasn't so far away.

I just had to catch a basilisk. Hidden, wretched, heinous creatures. "I will catch a basilisk if I have to do it with my teeth."

Colin laughed, a deep noise that rumbled up from his chest and set goose flesh loose over my skin.

"Look for the patterns on their skin. I can't replicate my condition for you, but I really, really want you to catch that basilisk and graduate."

He winked and my heart did summersaults.

I would be the best late-blooming basilisk hunter Magik Prep Academy had ever seen.

One more month.

AJ Skelly is an author, blogger, and lover of all things fantasy, medieval, and fairy-tale-romance. And werewolves. She has a serious soft spot for them. As an avid life-long reader and a former high school English teacher, she's always been fascinated with the written word. She lives with her husband, children, and many imaginary friends who often find their way into her stories. They all drink copious amounts of tea together and stay up reading far later than they should.

You can read more about AJ Skelly and her short stories on her website at www.ajskelly.com. She can also be found on Instagram at https://www.instagram.com/a.j.skelly/, and you can visit her Facebook author page at https://www.facebook.com/aj. skelly.71/ or join her reading group page at https://www.facebook. com/groups/4433591436652655.

THE DEMONS IN THE STARS

BY CLINT HALL

Darren knew it would be the last time he saw Melissa, so he tried his best to make her laugh. That was how he wanted her to always think of him — joyful, unafraid. He hadn't given her much else by which to remember him.

"I could be back anytime," he said, though they both knew it was a lie. "Don't forget to make the coffee."

Melissa smiled. "How many ass-cups are you making now?"

He laughed at the memory. It was a silly joke from years ago when she had mocked him for brewing way more coffee every morning than he could possibly drink.

"I don't know why you have to make ten ass cups of coffee every morning!" she had said in mock frustration.

"How much is in an *ass*-cup?" he asked her at the time. "I'm not familiar with that unit of measurement."

They stood next to a large window that looked across the galaxy. His starfighter would be ready any moment. The notification badge on his flight suit would flash, and Darren would be required to report immediately. Until then, every moment with Melissa felt stolen, filled with anticipation, gratitude, and dread. Each second could be their last together. He had a mission, and the Demons in the Stars did not leave survivors.

Darren brushed the back of his fingers along Melissa's freckled cheek. After all the time they had pushed each other toward mutual excellence in their fields, all the nights spent making love, all the wonderful adventures, all the support, this was what he would miss the most — the small moments, the jokes that no one but them would think were funny.

The left side of Darren's chest vibrated. The circular badge flashed with a red outline. His ship was ready, and the Ministry did not tolerate tardiness. It was bad enough for a Voyager to have a wife. If it hadn't been for Darren's immense value, the relationship would not have been indulged.

It was Melissa who pulled him in for their last kiss, just as she had for their first. Darren was not surprised. She was stronger than him in so many ways; it was her lead that he followed throughout their lives together, but she could not lead him into this next step, this final journey. This he had to do alone.

When they pulled apart, she did not cry. "I love you, Darren. And I believe in you."

"I love you, too." It was the truest and simplest statement he had ever spoken. If his love had been any less, he might've fled with her, away from the Ministry, away from this divine mission that would take him into the celestial hellscape. Because of his love, he turned toward the hangar.

"I hope you find him," she said as he walked away.

He stopped and regarded her over his shoulder. "I hope I don't."

* * *

THE FAINT BLUE glow of the energy barrier dominated the far wall of the hangar, separating the interior of the ship from the vacuum of space.

Darren knelt in the shadow of his starfighter, his back to the ship. The priest stood before him, offering a commission and a blessing in an ancient language. Darren did not understand the words, but he knew the message. There was no pretense about a possible return, no divine request for a safe journey. He wasn't sure he had enough fuel to make it back to the flagship, and even if he could, it wouldn't be at the same place. So little was known about the Demons in the Stars, but it was best to keep moving at all times. Worse, Darren's starfighter lacked any ability to locate this vessel. The Ministry would be able to pinpoint his location and recognize when the mission was complete, but there was no way — and no intention — to bring him home.

The priest's face was hidden in the darkness of the folds of his robe, but a strange glow emanated from beneath the skin of his hands as his words intensified. The more he spoke, the more his voice cracked and struggled, until finally the words stopped. The priest used a hand consumed in light to motion for Darren to stand.

When the holy man touched Darren's forehead, the glow penetrated his body. The light that had seemed to bring so much pain to the priest caused Darren a sense of elation. A healing fire washed through him, swirling first in his mind, then pushing down rapidly through his entire body before returning to his head and settling in his eyes.

The rites finished, the priest collapsed onto the hangar deck. Darren did not know whether the holy man survived, but it didn't matter. Everyone had their mission. When it was over, it was over.

As ordered, Darren collected his silver flight helmet from

the floor, turned, and marched to the ladder that led to the cockpit of his starfighter.

When he reached the top rung, he paused to run his fingers along the letters of his inherited call sign painted on the hull beneath the canopy. *Star Lion.*

Darren caught his reflection in the canopy an instant before it opened. His eyes glowed blue.

* * *

DARREN HAD SEEN FAR MORE galaxies in his life than blue skies. As was often the case with Voyagers, the Ministry had drafted him very young. It was a tremendous honor to be selected for the seat in which he now found himself, pushing past the edge of the universe toward what many referred to as "the celestial realm," a place wholly unknown to mankind.

With the gift of the Sight, the universe seemed more alive than ever. It was not exactly like seeing space for the first time — the stars were still the stars — but they shone brighter and were more distinct.. He could see much farther, spotting distant planets, churning nebulas, and comets streaking brilliantly through the void. It gave him both a sense of wonder and dread.

Possessing the Sight was a rarer experience than wearing a king's crown. Even if it were feasible to bestow the blessing upon every pilot in the Ministry's fleet, the experience would drive virtually all of them mad within seconds. Many before Darren had begged to receive the gift, then pleaded for release moments later. And while Darren understood why the blessing had pushed so many to their breaking points, it made him feel whole to witness such wild energy. His previous life seemed less real — his brief childhood, his relationships, his ambitions, his time at the fleet academy — all of it was like a dream, fading from his memory. All but Melissa.

Darren pushed the throttle forward, accelerating to maximum speed because he remembered her and, through her, his mission. The Demons in the Stars were waiting, perhaps watching. Even with the Sight, it would be difficult to find them.

The ship lacked faster-than-light capabilities, but none-theless, Darren had the sensation of rushing toward the dangerous unknown. A stir ran through his soul that matched the energy he had felt flow through him at the priest's touch.

As he stared into the deep reaches of space, he almost believed he could see them. His mind created lines between certain stars, forming sinister monsters so large that they stretched the limits of his imagination. The heads were those of beasts both real and fantastic — great birds, tigers, drag-ons, and gargoyles. Some appeared to rise as part of sprawling nebulas pulsating with impossible energy.

Darren felt more afraid but undeterred. He prayed that he could push his ship faster, to finally touch that which had dominated his dreams and nightmares for as long as he could remember. But each time he thought he had discovered a demon — in the moment he became absolutely certain — the stars drifted outside the perceived lines, and the monster ceased to exist.

Was none of it real? Part of him would have rather died than live in a galaxy where everything was known, without any new wonders or fresh horrors to discover.

Then he saw something.

His enhanced eyes locked onto an object far away. It drifted like an aimless fragment, perhaps the remnant of a destroyed world wandering through space in search of a new planet. As Darren's starfighter came closer, he realized it was not space debris, nor was it a demon. The starfighter's display locked on the object and identified it.

His grandfather's ship.

Darren had never met the man, but he spent many nights reading his journals, using small metal forceps to turn the pages so as not to damage them. He once considered scanning the pages to create digital facsimiles but decided against it. So few things were unique anymore; Darren liked knowing there was only a single copy in the entire universe.

His grandfather had been among the first Voyagers in the fleet and a primary reason Darren had been identified as a candidate so early in life. Darren's father had tried for many years to enter the program but was consistently rejected. The day Darren was chosen had been one of the few times he ever saw his father truly smile.

Darren drew closer to the ship. Unlike the starfighter, his grandfather's ship possessed no weapons. It was designed for exploration, for learning and discovery. It was his grandfather who first saw the Demons in the Stars, who had given them that name. Darren had listened to his grandfather's final transmission hundreds of times. His voice sounded full of disbelief and terror. "I found them . . . they're here . . . they're always here . . . the Demons in the Stars . . ."

The ship moved slowly. Though it appeared in nearly perfect condition, Darren imagined that the rear thrusters had not fired in decades. He reduced his speed drastically. He was potentially entering enemy territory.

Darren overtook his grandfather's ship easily as it drifted through the unknown, but at the same time, he was careful not to come upon it too fast. Perhaps some piece of him held onto the impossible belief that his grandfather could be alive. It was foolish, of course, but Darren was a man of dreams, and all dreams were foolish if examined closely enough.

Darren angled his starfighter to get a better look. The

vessel was in remarkable condition given its age. He had always assumed that his grandfather's ship had been destroyed by the demons, but there was no sign of damage to the hull.

When Darren peered into the canopy, what he saw terrified him to his core. His grandfather sat in the cockpit, attention forward and alert, hands on the stick. His eyes did not glow but appeared very much alive. Had Darren not recognized him, he might've guessed the man to be in his mid-forties. His short beard and flat-top haircut were gray, and his skin carried wrinkles, but he looked like the toughest pilot to ever march through the halls of the Ministry, ready to take on anything the universe could throw at him.

While it seemed implausible, Darren had long since been taught to question everything he knew about space, time, and the laws of the universe. The teachings were all over his grandfather's journal. *A flexible mind is necessary for the Voyager, for what lies beyond is madness to those unable to learn the terrible, wonderful truth.*

Darren activated the communications array in his starfighter. He paused before he spoke, without an idea of what to say or whether he should speak at all. What if it wasn't his grandfather but some clever illusion, a trick of the demons? Maybe this was why they were so hard to find. Perhaps they were shapeshifters and telepaths, capable of scanning their targets' minds and memories to choose the perfect form for drawing them in.

But Darren had to try. "Star Lion, do you read me? Over."

His grandfather showed no sign of receiving the communication.

"Grandfather, can you hear me?"

Nothing. There were no lights inside the cockpit, but that didn't mean the message wasn't getting through. Audio communication was one of the final functions to remain active before a ship completely lost power, second only to life support.

Darren jerked his attention to his display, checking for enemies. He cursed himself for getting so close and maneuvered his ship away. There were no signs of other objects anywhere on his display, but that meant nothing when tracking supernatural beings.

His display quickly forgotten, he scanned the space around him with his enhanced eyes. This would be the moment to spring a trap. If the demons could read his mind, they would see his attention had been dulled by questions, by the longing to connect with the relative who had inspired his life.

The attack didn't come, but he wasn't taking any chances. He considered firing upon his grandfather's ship. It was an easy target, and he had ammunition to spare. Maybe he would've been doing the old man a favor. Whatever happened to freeze him in that state, perhaps ending it would be a welcomed mercy, a type of release from his heir. Darren had once heard that sons did not fully become men until their fathers passed away, clearing the way for them to grow into their destiny, no longer fearful of the ogres of their childhood. Darren's own father had been dead for years — to him, at least, and that was all that mattered — but the shadow of his grandfather loomed large over his life.

In the end, he didn't fire. Perhaps what his grandfather was looking for was too important for his attention to be drawn away, even for a breath, even to acknowledge his long-lost grandson.

Darren hit the throttle and accelerated away as fast as he could.

* * *

THE FIRST TIME Darren heard tapping against the hull of his ship, he told himself it was debris, maybe the detritus of a dead planet colliding harmlessly with his starfighter. The odds were against such an occurrence in the expanse of space, but it was known to have happened. Nothing to worry about.

Until an hour later when he heard thumps.

Darren executed a barrel roll to gain full vision of everything above and below him. He saw nothing but darkness and stars. His hand reached for the switch that would end it all with an eruption of energy and the transmission of a final signal — mission complete.

Thoughts of Melissa crashed into Darren's mind. He wondered if he could use the Sight to locate her again, to find a heading back to her safe embrace.

Darren would not cower. He would not turn and run. Whatever had happened to his grandfather, the man had journeyed past the point of knowing into something more, proving himself a true Voyager. Darren would be worthy of the bloodline. He would succeed where his father had failed, though he had to be sure. He would sacrifice his life when the mission demanded, but he would not waste it.

He pushed Melissa to a safer place inside himself. If he buried her deep enough, maybe the fear would not rise again.

He covered her memory with more of his grandfather's words. *Ever forward until the end.*

* * *

HOURS PASSED in silence as Darren ventured forward. Several times he considered doubling back to the coordinates where the tapping had occurred on his hull. Had that been the demons after all? Maybe he had reached — and passed — the end of his journey but was too foolish or afraid to realize it.

Darren slammed his fist against the canopy. The outburst did little to stem his fury, and his hand throbbed in pain. He cursed himself for his inability to see the answers — the appearance of his grandfather, the tapping on his hull. They must've meant something, but he had been unable to piece them together.

When he finished abusing his own mind, body, and soul, his verbal tirade turned upon the priest. The old man must have done something wrong during the ceremony. The Sight was not as it should be, not performing the singular task for which the priest sacrificed his life.

But the Sight remained as strong as ever, revealing the brightest wonders of the universe and far away worlds where fortunate others might one day live in peace. What had once felt like a blessing, a divine birthright, now felt like shackles. Darren could see everything except that which he most needed.

And finally, when he had no one else to blame, Darren cursed the god that had led him there. The words were barely past his lips when he heard a new sound. If he had been home — his *true* home — he might have disregarded it as the wisp of the wind.

It happened again, louder this time. It was light and quick, like the sound of a barber's sure hand cutting the hair by Darren's right ear. Whatever it was, it was inside the ship.

Darren jerked his head right, seeing nothing.

The wisp sounded in his left, quiet but so pronounced that it felt tangible.

He swiped his hand across the left side of his head. Suddenly it felt like he could barely move his arms. The flight harness constricted his movements.

The wisps continued, more frequently and on both sides. The demons were with him. The sounds grew longer, less like quick breezes and more like whispers, though he couldn't tell what they said.

Darren undid the buckle on his harness, jerking side to side, waiving his hands like a madman. The cockpit seemed to close in on him, the glass canopy pushing closer even as his Sight extended further into space around him.

Something brushed through his hair, then down his back. Unseen hands crept over his skin, thousands of pinpricks across his body.

Darren's mind ran wild. He wanted to rip the ears from his head so he couldn't hear them, tear the flesh from his face so the touches would stop. It all became noise, the whispers, the anger, failure.

Ever forward until the end. The words rang in his mind with a voice he had never heard. His grandfather? Curse that man, too.

The cockpit was far too small, the demons louder, clouding his thoughts. There was something he was supposed to do when he found them. What was it again? His orders eluded him like the demons every time he reached through the noise for a memory.

Darren wanted to eject into the vacuum of space and float peacefully into oblivion. To Hell with the voyage. To Hell with the glory and the purpose. He wanted nothing more than peace. He wanted to be with her.

Melissa.

If he were to die now, his last thoughts would be of his wife, so Darren closed his eyes, breathed, and put her touch at the center of his mind. The grand adventure of his life had been at hand, but he had refused the call to chase false glories, to fill the voids left by his heritage. He could have been with her for eternity.

Darren felt hands lifting him from his seat. There was no pain, not even as he seemed to move through the shoulder straps of his harness. He kept his eyes closed, afraid of what he might see beneath him. Perhaps this was death, and if so, he didn't want to know. The hands raised him through the canopy, and Darren braced himself for the cold of space. But when he moved through the glass, a warmth enveloped his body. The hands revealed themselves. They were not the twisted, vicious things he expected. They were light of all colors, shimmering and changing with each moment. As he looked around, he saw bodies swirling with radiance, power given life, wonder given form.

These creatures were what his people had called the demons; this he knew instantly and surely. If they had only chosen to see, they would have called them angels.

He thought of Melissa. It was simple. Though worlds away, the love that bound them together not only endured but grew into something new. It was more real than a physical presence, and he dared to see himself in his truest form, stripped of the corruption that had shrouded him all his life. If the evil and the death were present, they were powerless in the face of what love had made him.

In his final moments, Darren felt closer to her than ever before.

CLINT HALL HAS BEEN WRITING stories since middle school, where he spent most of his time in English class creating comic books. Fortunately, his teacher not only allowed it, she bought every issue.

Known for stories that instill a sense of hope, wonder, and adventure, Clint's work has been published across multiple anthologies and magazines. He was recently named a double finalist for short fiction in the 2021 Realm Awards. As a tech writer, he has also authored numerous pieces for IBM and The Weather Company, including articles in partnership with The Masters, Adweek, and Aston Martin Red Bull Racing.

To read more information about Clint and his work, visit his website at https://clinthall.com/ and his author page at https://www.facebook.com/AuthorClintHall. You can follow him on Twitter at https://twitter.com/AuthorClintHall and Instagram at https://www.instagram.com/clinthall/?hl=en.

THE GHOST OF HOUSE GREY

BY ROSEMARY WILLIAMS

The house was, to Sephie's eyes, sterile. Decorated in calculatedly inoffensive shades of beige and blue, it could have been any home, anywhere. Pristine furniture, immaculate carpets, and not a speck of dust to be found. The only things that distinguished it from any other house were the family portraits on the foyer walls of a couple and their son and a little box of business cards stamped, "Heather Dawson, Realtor."

Sephie wasn't sure whether to be unsurprised or appalled that a woman who sold real estate would have a house so devoid of Boston's usual architectural charm. It certainly wasn't the sort of place one would expect to find a ghost.

She followed her host into the living room and perched cautiously upon a sofa, somewhat guilty about disturbing the slipcover's tucks of mathematical perfection. Settling her cane at her side, Sephie couldn't shake the feeling that her entire being clashed with the room's decor. Hell, when it came down to it, she clashed with herself. She'd lost count of the number of times some random stranger had told her she was "too young" to be using a cane.

It wasn't Sephie's fault her prosthetic was old and clunky and her equilibrium a bit wonky. She *was*, in fact, young to need a cane for balance, but she couldn't exactly afford something fancier. She was barely out of college.

Sephie caught Heather eying her right leg surreptitiously. *She knows I'm an amputee.* Of course she did; this woman was the elder sister of Sephie's college roommate and the reason she was there instead of a half-baked spiritualist.

That was the other reason to use a cane: best to have all tools available when you're preparing to annoy a ghost. You never know when one is going to get grouchy and knock things off shelves. The last time she'd provoked one, it had practically upended an entire library out of pique. One would think that being dead would eventually teach a dude not to be an asshole. But if two-and-a-half centuries *had* improved that man's disposition, well, she'd hate to have met him when he was alive.

Sephie cleared her throat.

Heather jerked her eyes upward with a start. "Oh! Right. Thank you so much, Stephanie, for doing this."

"It's Sephie, actually." The correction was a reflex these days.

"What?"

"My name. It's Sephie, not Stephanie. Short for Persephone." She suppressed a sigh at Heather's glassy stare. "It's Greek."

"Oh, of course! Foreign names are so trendy." Heather beamed, back into familiar territory. "My apologies. So, um, how do we do this?"

"Just tell me what's been happening in the house." Sephie would have preferred to have this conversation outside the spirit's area of influence, in a coffee shop or something, but Heather had been resistant to the idea.

"Well, it started a few months ago," said Heather, "which I

think is odd. We've lived in this house since Caleb was a baby; I thought ghosts were old, right?"

Sephie scrunched her brow. While it was possible for ghosts to move houses, it was relatively rare. More likely this was something dormant and had recently awakened. "Have you done any remodeling lately?"

The response was a shake of the head. "No, none."

Well, that is *strange.* "Okay, don't worry about it for now. Tell me more."

Heather tucked a lock of blonde hair behind her ear, revealing a glittering diamond stud. Her clothing was expensive: a mid-calf-length skirt paired with a designer blouse, and heels that made Sephie want to clutch her cane for balance.

What kind of person wears high heels all the time?

"It started out pretty mild," Heather said. "Sometimes I'd hear a giggle in the upstairs hall, but I thought it was my son. Then the pictures up there started going crooked and things would move around. We thought that was Caleb, too, so we grounded him."

Poor kid. "But it kept happening?"

"Well, sort of." Heather's face grew thoughtful. "It stopped for a bit when Caleb got into trouble, which just made us more certain it was him, but then it started again. Except then, it would only happen when he wasn't home."

"Really?" Sephie perked up with interest. *A ghost with a guilty conscience?* This boded well. Maybe this could all be solved with a nice chat.

"After a few instances, I was convinced it wasn't Caleb. But Howard, my husband, wasn't. We started getting into fights about it." Heather shifted in her chair. "And then things began disappearing. Little things, at first. Coins, a few toys. But then I noticed I was missing some jewelry."

"Has anything reappeared?"

Heather shook her head.

"What about potential motivation? Is there a pattern to the things that have gone missing? Maybe they were all left in the same place? Or shared something in common?"

"They were all shiny, I guess," said Heather. "Valuable, or things that looked like they might be. Keys, coins, plastic pirate treasure. Jewelry. Howie's Rolex. And now my wedding set has gone missing." She fluttered her hands to indicate her naked ring finger.

So, we have a ghost that thinks it's a magpie. Great. This wouldn't be simple. The key to dealing with a ghost was to understand what it wanted; more often than not, they were looking for attention, so they'd move things, make noises, and otherwise try and evoke a reaction from the living.

She needed more information. "Can I speak with your husband? I'd like to get his impressions as well."

Heather's eyes darted to the side, and she wrung her hands. "No, I'm afraid not."

Sephie raised her eyebrows.

"Howard doesn't believe in ghosts," Heather explained. "He gets angry every time I try to bring up the possibility; he thinks I'm covering for Caleb. He's out golfing right now. He'd be livid if he knew you were here."

Well, that explains a few things. Namely, why Heather had been adamant about Sephie coming to the house during such a narrow time window. "So even though you know it's not possible for Caleb to have done these things, he still thinks your son is responsible?"

Heather nodded.

What an asshole. Sephie continued to quiz Heather, ruling out the likelihood of human thieves and teasing out a few more details of the alleged ghost activity. She shouldn't have taken such a skeptical angle, but something about it felt off. Finally, she requested a moment to speak with Caleb.

As Heather led her up the stairs to the second floor, Sephie reached out with her spirit-sense, questing for a hint of a ghost's presence.

It had taken her years to hone that skill; it took a conscious effort to detect a ghost that wasn't in the room with her, and even then, she had to be paying attention or she might casually assume it was a living person for a moment. She'd once spent five minutes chatting with a kindly old man at a museum before she'd realized he was a ghost. Non-human entities, the types that were non-corporeal but not exactly *dead*, were much easier to sense and were usually more dangerous.

She detected nothing. *Well, that's odd. But at least that means it's probably not something nasty.*

The much-maligned Caleb was not, in fact, the boy of seven or eight she had expected from the descriptions of missing toys, but instead a young man of around fourteen or fifteen. Heather excused herself, leaving Sephie alone with the teenager slumped sullenly on the edge of his bed. He looked up at her with jaded eyes. "What kind of name is Sephie?"

Well, at least he didn't autocorrect to Stephanie. She shrugged, deciding to embrace the teen vibe. "A weird one. It's short for Persephone."

Caleb's expression gained some interest. "What, like from Greek mythology?"

Sephie nodded.

The teenager wrinkled his nose. "And your mom was okay with naming you that?"

Humor tugged on the corner of Sephie's mouth. "Self-awareness is not one of my mother's stronger virtues. I'm impressed; not many kids your age know their mythology."

"Oh, please," Caleb scoffed. "*Everyone* knows that one. It's in a video game."

"Huh." Sephie flashed a self-deprecating smile. "I am apparently not cool enough to be up on the trends."

"You seem cooler than my mom, anyway." The young man finally took a serious look at her. "What's with the cane?"

With the end of it, Sephie tapped at the pole of her right leg. It clunked in a distinctly metallic sound.

"Cool!" Caleb's face grew more animated, then sobered. "I mean, um, that's awful. What happened?"

The laugh crept out of Sephie's throat unbidden. "It's fine. And it was a car accident, nothing fancy."

The young man relaxed a little more, a grin forming on his face. "See, that's a terrible story. You should come up with one about getting attacked by a bear."

Sephie made a show of screwing up her face in thought. "Better make it an alligator. I grew up in Florida; it's a much more plausible story."

Caleb chuckled. "Definitely gotta go for the believability factor, yeah. When did you lose it?"

"Nine years ago," said Sephie. "I was thirteen."

A more sober expression took over the teenager. Sephie could see the thoughts working; she'd been younger than he was. He was putting himself into her shoes at that age.

He's a good kid. She cleared her throat and reset the conversation. "So, what can you tell me about your ghost?"

Caleb made a face. "My dad says there's no such thing as ghosts."

How to approach this tactfully? Stating point-blank that his father was a jerk probably wasn't wise. "Let's just say for now that maybe your dad is mistaken. Just tell me what you've experienced."

"I dunno," said Caleb. "Stuff disappears, I guess. My dad blames me."

Sephie adjusted her stance and leaned back against the

door frame. "I believe you didn't do it. I think your mom does, too."

The young man shrugged. "She *says* she believes me, but she doesn't stop Dad from grounding me. I'm *this close* to getting kicked off the Quiz Bowl team because I keep missing practices."

Sephie's estimation of Caleb shifted up a few notches. "Well, let's see if I can help prove your innocence, then." She tilted her head and raised her eyebrows, pushing sympathy and sincerity into her eyes. "The more you can tell me, the easier it'll be for me to help."

A moment of connection passed between them, and Caleb nodded. "Okay. I heard Mom, though; she told you most everything. I don't know more than she does. Except . . ." He hesitated. "Except I hear things sometimes at night. Footsteps from above. Scraping noises. Laughing. There's something *up* there, in the attic."

Sephie followed his gaze to the ceiling. "Anything else?"

Caleb chewed on his lip for a moment, then reached under his bed and pulled out a sneaker. "Well, there's this."

Examining the shoe, Sephie turned it over in her heads. It was a normal piece of athletic wear, pricey judging by the logo. It looked pristine. "What am I looking for?"

"Last week, my friend Russ and I were messing around in this old junkyard. I caught my shoe on a nail; it tore right here." Caleb pointed to a spot on the side of the shoe.

Sephie shook her head. "I don't understand. There's no damage here at all."

"Yeah, but there *was*," insisted Caleb. "I hid my shoes under my bed so my dad wouldn't yell at me. Well, couple days ago, he asked why I wasn't wearing them, so I had to go get them out, but it was like it'd never been torn."

Well, I've never seen anything like this *before.* "I think you'd better show me the attic."

She couldn't afford a fancier leg prosthetic, but Sephie had at least been able to invest in a fancy telescoping cane that had a flashlight built into the handle. If one looked hard enough, they could find a screwdriver, Swiss army knife, and a few other accouterments hidden cleverly away in its segments. She clicked the light on as Caleb pulled down the trap door and unfolded a ladder to the floor.

"Stay here, and hold this." Sephie handed him the cane. She clambered her way up the first few steps, then reached down. Her hand closed around the cane, lifted it up, and with the light shining ahead of her, she poked her head through the hole and looked around.

Despite the cool autumn air outside, the attic was warm, thanks to the cloudless day. Its limited walk space consisted of plywood laid over beams and rolls of insulation. Boxes of old toys and holiday decorations were strewn about in themed clusters that vaguely resembled order. It smelled of wood and dust.

Nothing moved or made a sound.

Gripping the floor, then a convenient beam, Sephie clambered her way fully into the attic.

Caleb followed soon after.

Sephie glared at him. "I told you to stay put."

The teenager shrugged in the face of reproach. "What if you need help?"

"I—" Sephie's protest was cut off by a small stuffed animal the size of a hacky sack bouncing off her chest. "What?" *Did I just get smacked by a flying Beanie Baby?*

Caleb picked it up off the plywood floor. "Huh. I think this used to be my grandma's."

Two more kitschy collectibles struck Sephie in the head and the arm. "What the hell?" she cried.

"Outsider! Intruder!" A very small, very male voice cried out from behind a row of cardboard boxes. Another toy came flying from the same general direction, this time a matchbox car that pinged off of Sephie's cane.

"Take cover!" Caleb grabbed her arm and pulled her into shelter behind an absurdly large Christmas tree box.

"Ye'll not take me down!" More matchbox cars thumped against the box.

Hunched over on the dusty floor of the attic, ghost wrangler and adolescent exchanged equally flabbergasted expressions. Sephie reached out with her spirit-sense to try to get an idea of what they were dealing with. What she sensed stretched credulity.

She sensed *nothing*.

"That," she said to Caleb, "is *not* a ghost." Nor was it a demon, poltergeist, or other apparition. It was nothing that her spirit-sense could detect at all, which meant it was solid. Alive.

"Are you sure? What else could it be?"

The voice from across the attic cried out again, "*Zyetz*, I'm as alive as ye! And ye'll not make me otherwise!" Several faded baby blocks came flying overhead in rapid succession.

What is that accent, anyway? It sounds like someone took Scottish and Russian, seasoned them with French, and threw the whole concoction into a blender. Sephie nodded at Caleb's first question, but she had no good answer to the second. There were options, of course, but this was *Boston*.

She stole a peek around the edge of the tree box to confirm the source of the missiles. The source stack of boxes was far too small to hide a person. Whatever he was, he had to be some kind of magical creature. But a portal refugee in Boston? It was unheard-of. The city was too well locked down when it came to magical worlds. This was, in fact, much of why the city had so many ghosts.

There were three kinds of supernatural activity in the world: spirits, magic, and eldritch horrors. A lot more people in positions of power were aware of the second two, which was how Boston had been built to suppress magical portals and keep monsters slumbering. But there was a balance to maintain, and tamping down those two types of activity had led to a wildly vibrant spirit world.

So far as Sephie knew, the city's Weird Patrol dismissed ghosts as mere superstition. It was short-sighted of them. When your job consists of keeping monsters asleep and tracking magical creatures, one would expect you to not turn your nose up at the idea of hauntings.

It annoyed her. This was why she couldn't have a normal life with Dad in the Keys. Too many ghosts in Boston and too few people who had the talent and skill to handle them.

Sephie shook her head to clear it of cobwebs. *Enough.* She had a job to do, and a teenager who needed protection right *now.* "Hey!" she called to the source of toy-shaped missiles. "I just want to talk."

"Bah!" the creature scoffed. "Likely story, from a witch! Think I can't smell it on ye?" Several more baby blocks ricocheted off of ceiling beams. "Intruder! Sneak! Witch!"

"What about me?" called Caleb. "I *live* here! This is my house, and I'm telling you to stop."

The barrage of toys paused. "*Zyetz,*" said the little voice, "that's true. And I'll free ye from that evil witch's clutches quick enough now."

"I don't need freeing!" complained Caleb.

"She's makin' ye say that!"

The young man curled his lip in disgust and lunged to his feet. "She is not!"

Sephie's first instinct was to grab Caleb and pull him back into cover, but she restrained the impulse. If this creature, whatever it was, claimed it wanted to protect him, then she couldn't allow herself to be seen as trying to control him. She needed to trust him. She caught his eye and nodded. "Be careful, Caleb."

His eyes widened, and then he stood a little taller and shot her a smile. He turned in the direction of the attacker. "You've been upsetting my parents. My mom called Sephie in to help."

There was another long silence. "Are ye sayin' that the witch has been given guest-right?"

"Um, sure," He shot an inquiring look to her, then shrugged. "I guess you could say it like that."

"Hmph." A world of annoyance lived in that single syllable. "Fine, then. I suppose I can allow a truce. For now. Come, then, Witch, let's get a look at ye. But I'm ready for yer tricks."

Cautiously, Sephie peeked around the corner of her hidey hole, then leaned on her cane to lever herself to her feet. "I don't know that I really qualify as a witch."

"I told ye, I can smell it on ye."

Sephie aimed the flashlight at the source of the voice, who stood on top of a set of stacked boxes. With flaming red hair, he stood five or six inches tall. He was outfitted in fine trousers, a waistcoat, and ornately buckled boots. Realization flashed: the fixed shoe and the missing valuables finally made sense. Her mouth dropped open. "You're a leprechaun."

The tiny man folded his arms and snorted. "Figure that out all by yerself?"

"Well, I was called in to deal with a ghost. That's generally what I do." Sephie rolled her knowledge of folklore over in her head. Mythology had been her minor in college, but her direct experience with magical creatures was limited.

What do I know about leprechauns? Everyone knew about them guarding a pot of treasure, though she was reasonably certain she could dismiss the rainbow part of the story as bunk. Making and repairing shoes didn't get much popular culture reference; she'd likely not have made the connection if it hadn't been for her studies. *I certainly never would have placed that accent as something from Irish folklore.*

The leprechaun, in the meantime, regarded her up and down with a critical eye. "Spirit-witch, eh? I'd heard Bigfolk had such things, but I'd not given the idea much regard. This world o' yers is passing strange."

Sephie frowned at him. "Speaking of this world, how did you *get* here?"

The leprechaun snorted again. "Through the usual way — ye do know about portals, *zyetz?*"

Caleb flashed her an inquiring expression, but Sephie ignored it. "Yes, but I meant specifically here to Boston. All of the magic gates here are locked down tight."

"In luxury!" declared the leprechaun. "Upon the chariot of the Hound of House Grey!"

"So, you stowed away aboard a bus. Great." Sephie rubbed at the bridge of her nose. "How am I supposed to get you home?"

"You aren't," he snapped. "I'm here by choice!"

"Can't you just take him to a city with one of those portal things and send him back that way?" asked Caleb.

Sephie shook her head. "No, it's not that simple. Portals are scattered all over the planet, and they all lead to different worlds. Even if I could find one and open it up, chances are low that it'd be his actual home. It'd be like . . . like dropping a raccoon into a rainforest. Sure, they're clever and tough, but they're not suited to the environment. The creature would die." *After wreaking havoc first.*

A sputtering noise burst from the leprechaun's lips. "*Rish!* Never! I'll not go blindly to my death!"

"I wouldn't do that —"

He stamped a tiny, booted foot. "Ye cannot make me leave! I've guest-right here!"

"The hell you do," snapped Caleb.

The faerie creature snarled. "I do! It was printed on the mat on yer doorstep, in letters as high as I am tall! Welcome, it says! Here I'm welcome, and here I stay!"

Oh, no.

Caleb's face shaded red. "You've been stealing stuff! My dad thinks it's my fault!"

The leprechaun's face matched his in color. "Stealing? *Stealing?* How dare ye! I take what's been laid out as rightful payment for my work!"

"Hey, let's just take a minute . . ." Sephie gestured placatingly at both arguers, but they ignored her.

"Payment for what?" Caleb snapped. "Sneaking into our house and living in our attic? Scaring my mom?"

"For what? I'll tell ye for what! That shoe o' yers for one! Ye can't tell me your da wouldn't've thumped ye good for that rip if he'd seen it. And as for yer mum, well, I've mended wear in a number of her shoes and clothes as well. Not t' mention the moth-eaten afghans I've fixed! D' ye have any idea how difficult it is t' weave yarn fibers in and make an invisible repair? Bloody hard! I'm an artist!"

Caleb made a move as though he were going to grab the little man.

Sephie laid a restraining hand on the teen's shoulder. "Stop it! Both of you!" Her voice echoed through the rafters of the attic, louder than she'd intended.

The three of them froze, waiting to see if Heather had heard the shout. Seconds ticked by.

Caleb let out a breath and relaxed.

Sephie took that as a cue that they were safe and seized control of the conversation. "Okay. Let's talk this out rationally. Now, um . . ." *Damn. Isn't there some sort of weird faerie thing about names?* She chose the phrasing carefully. "What should we call you?"

The leprechaun treated her to an approving grin. "Fearghan will do fine, Witch."

"Fearghan, then. And instead of 'Witch,' you can call me Sephie. Now, you said you're assuming guest-right from the welcome mat at the front door?"

"*Zyetz*," he replied. "But not assume. I *have* guest-right. It's the law."

"That's not how it works," protested Caleb. "People put out welcome mats. It's just a *thing*, it doesn't mean anything."

Fearghan wrinkled his nose. "Why do ye do it if ye don't mean it?"

"I don't know," said Caleb, shooting Sephie a helpless look.

"Humans are weird," she told Fearghan. "Our social rules are built upon the idea that we have to appear polite, even when we don't want to be."

The leprechaun snorted. "Sounds rude t' me."

He's not wrong.

"Anyway," he continued, "It matters not a whit. I received the welcome, and here I am."

"But that's not how it *works*," Caleb complained.

Silently, Sephie wished for a glass of water and a dose of ibuprofen. None appeared. "Caleb, I don't have a lot of direct experience with fae, but going by the folklore, their laws tend to be . . . twisty. A direct argument isn't going to get you anywhere."

Caleb glowered at Fearghan, which just seemed to encourage the leprechaun's cheer.

"Okay, Fearghan," said Sephie. "How did you decide which house to pick?"

"From the Carriage of the Hound of House Grey, I then hailed a ride from a similar carriage with a great yellow stripe. It dropped me down yonder road. I then wandered until I found my welcome."

"So that was it? You picked a house at random?"

Fearghan shrugged.

Caleb narrowed his eyes. "How did you get into the house, anyway? Who let you in?"

For the first time, the leprechaun's confidence wavered. "Well, nobody. I climbed up yonder trellis and into an upstairs window."

Triumph spread across the teenager's face. "So, you didn't come in through the Welcome Door?"

Sephie frowned. What game was Caleb playing?

Fearghan deflated a little more and shook his head.

"Oh, no," said Caleb in mock dismay. "Then I guess the welcome doesn't actually apply, does it?"

The leprechaun folded his arms. "Fine. Ye've made yer point. But the payment for my services was still fair!"

Sephie felt utterly bewildered by the teenager's solution. "How did you —?"

"Dealing with rules and lawyer-y non-player characters in Dungeons and Dragons," Caleb replied with a smug grin. "Sorry, Fearghan, the payment may have been fair, but you owe us *rent*."

"Oh, bollocks." Defeated, the leprechaun gloomily led the pair of humans to his nest, which he had fashioned out of a shoebox. Sephie reclaimed the family's valuables, including Heather's wedding set, as "rent." Left was some old costume jewelry, several strands of Mardi Gras beads, and a few toys.

"Are you sure you don't want to take back any of these?" Sephie asked.

Caleb shook his head. "Nah. That pirate gold was from a birthday party when I was, like, eight."

Sephie tilted her head. "But you kept it."

"Yeah. I begged for the pirate-themed party. Dad gets cranky when I get rid of things I begged for. It's okay,

Fearghan. You can keep those, though they aren't really worth anything."

Fearghan chortled. "Not worth anything. Sure, lad." He pushed his plastic treasures back together into a corner of the box. "Substance ye can't find in nature, and these Bigfolk think it's worthless. Ha! He lifted his chin and eyed Sephie. "What are ye going to do with me now?"

"I don't suppose you'd like to tell me how to get you home?" she asked.

"*Rish*," he replied. "If I wanted that, I'd not have come here in the first place."

Sephie grimaced. She couldn't leave him there, and she couldn't very well dump him out on the streets, either. He'd find new ways to sow chaos. That left one option. "Maybe we can negotiate something to our mutual benefit."

Fearghan twisted his face into a thoughtful scowl, then nodded. "*Zyetz*, on one condition."

Sephie suppressed a sigh. "What is that?"

"Show me what's wrong with yer leg."

She straightened. *Is that all?* She'd been certain it would be something weird and faerie-tricky. "Sure." She lifted up her trouser leg to display the prosthetic. "I lost the leg in an accident, years ago."

The leprechaun vaulted to the floor and inspected the leg, tapping at the metal bar. "The workmanship is shite."

"You are not wrong about that," replied Sephie.

"Well, then. Seems like maybe ye could use my skills. It ain't a bad thing, being in good with a witch." Satisfied, the tiny man leaped back up onto the stack of boxes in a feat of supernatural athletics. He hopped over the rim of the shoebox and settled inside.

He's happy with his leverage, it seems. Sephie found the lid to the box and set it loosely on top. "Come on, Caleb, let's go tell your mom that we found her alleged ghost."

The young man's face underwent a transition from surprise to perplexedness to alarm. "You . . . you're not going to *show* him to her, are you?"

"I am." Sephie shot him a smile that she hoped would be mysterious. Caleb was special, he simply didn't know it yet. *It's time to learn a few more things about magic, kid. Like what it does to most people.*

* * *

Fifteen minutes later, Sephie stood, box in hand, on the front porch of the Dawsons' house, next to a flummoxed Caleb.

"A rat," he muttered. "Mom thought Fearghan was a *rat*. And you *knew* it, somehow!"

"I suspected," Sephie replied. "I didn't know she'd see a rat specifically, but I was ready for something like that." She'd come up quickly with the explanation that the "rat" was a domestic breed and had made up a few things on the spot to account for the strange occurrences. It would even absolve Caleb of all suspicion. "Most people can't perceive magic at face value; it's some kind of protection filter that creatures from other worlds emit. But some individuals are naturally immune."

"Like kids? Is that why I can see him?" Caleb frowned. "Will I forget when I turn eighteen?"

"Not exactly, and no. It's also possible for magic-blind people to pierce past the protection if they're exposed at the right time. Children have a lower break threshold. It's possible that him being in the house cracked your filter slowly, or it might have been the moment in the attic. Regardless, it's permanent. You'll have to be careful; you can now see things your parents won't. But Boston is pretty quiet; you should be okay."

"What if I'm not?"

Sephie fished a business card out of her backpack. "Here. On the front is my contact info if you need it; on the back is the website address of a forum for magic aware people to trade information. Take care your parents don't see it and freak out, though."

Caleb accepted the card. "Nah, if they see it, I'll just tell them it's for role-playing game discussions or something. They'll never know the difference."

They bade each other goodbye, and Sephie set off for the bus stop, cane in one hand, shoebox in the other. She was also richer by a bag of chocolate chip cookies. Apparently, Heather was a stress baker.

It had taken some time to convince the woman that Sephie wouldn't accept any money for her work, such as it was. But even in a typical de-ghosting, she didn't take any sort of payment, save maybe $20 to cover bus fare and materials. There were too many charlatans out there charging thousands for their so-called services; Sephie couldn't bear to do it herself. That's what she had a day job for.

The bus stop was deserted, so she sat on the bench and set Fearghan's box on her lap. Retrieving a cookie from her backpack, she broke off a small piece of it, propped open the lid of the box, and offered the morsel to the leprechaun. He accepted it with dignity.

She took a bite of the larger piece. *These are pretty good.* "Okay, Fearghan, here's the deal. I will invite you into my home, provided you agree to my terms.

Fearghan nibbled on his treat. "Name them, Lass."

Lass? Well, that's a step up from Witch, I suppose. "That you make a good faith effort to learn, and keep learning, basic rules of human social interaction and politeness. That you acknowledge that my home is my own and that you are a guest under my roof. If you choose to do work, you will agree that your services rendered are in exchange for room and board, and that anything further must be negotiated prior to work completed. You will never assume that objects lying around are yours to take, and that you will only take payment in the aforementioned pre-negotiated terms.

He grinned up at her. "Not bad. Ye left some mighty big holes in those conditions, though."

Sephie lifted an eyebrow at him. "Well, then here's your first lesson on human interaction: relationships are built on trust, and agreements are assumed to be made in good faith. Seeking out loopholes to exploit your friends is considered the height of rudeness." *You know, like what Caleb did to you.* In the back of her mind, Sephie was aware this could be a huge mistake. But what other option did she have? There wasn't exactly a halfway house for faerie creatures to drop him at.

Fearghan considered her words. "Are we friends, then?"

Heh. Oh, I have you now. "Yes. We did, after all, just break bread together. Sugary bread, but shared nonetheless."

Fearghan rewarded her with a hearty laugh. "Ye're a clever lass, Sephie, even for a witch. I accept yer terms, and yer friendship."

A SECOND-GENERATION SCI-FI/FANTASY fan, Rosemary Williams has been on a quest for ultimate nerdity her entire life. After devouring countless genre books, movies, and TV shows, she finally achieved the mental transformation necessary to turn herself into the pinnacle of nerddom: Author Brain. She's also a costumer, crafter, convention staffer, and occasional podcaster. She resides in Olathe, KS with her husband, 1.5 dachshunds, and half a chihuahua.

HORATIO

BY KATHARINE REID

Horatio woke up in darkness, wedged between the hotel bed and the wall. He debated rolling over and going back to sleep, leaving the mystery of why he'd migrated to the floor for another time. But sleep usually meant nightmares. Plus, this was probably the only time he was going to get without Alex watching him like he was a feral dog, and he didn't want to waste it sleeping.

He got up quietly, keeping an eye on Alex in the next bed for signs of movement. The clock on the nightstand said 6:15. He hoped Alex wasn't an early riser.

He shuffled over to the bathroom, passing his hand over the light switch before he was aware that it was already on. Right. Alex insisted the light stay on all night in case there was an emergency. Alex hadn't specified what emergency required the bathroom light and Horatio had been too tired to argue.

Horatio did leave the door unlocked, in case of an actual emergency.

When he got out of the shower, Alex was sitting on the edge of his bed watching the news. A heaviness settled on

Horatio's chest. He wasn't going to be watched less out here than in his cell.

"I didn't mean to wake you," Horatio said, although he really meant that he wished Alex was still asleep.

"It's fine. Watch TV while I take a shower."

"We can wait —" Horatio started, but Alex cut him off by pushing the remote into his hand and going into the bathroom.

Horatio sat on the bed, idly flipping through channels. This early, it was mostly local news and infomercials. He didn't care about the weather in whatever town they were in, so he settled on an infomercial about some workout machine. The women demonstrating it were at least something to look at.

He thought about leaving, and not for the first time. He could probably get down to the lobby before Alex finished his shower. If he were really lucky, he might be able to get a couple of streets away, maybe get a cab before Alex could figure out where he went.

But it wasn't worth it. Alex freaked out the last time he stopped unannounced and tied his shoe, letting Alex go on across the street before he realized what happened. If Alex saw him gone — really gone, there'd be a manhunt.

Alex's phone rang. Horatio couldn't see who was calling from where he was. He got up to check, but it stopped ringing right after he stood up.

When Alex came out of the bathroom, toweling off his hair, Horatio mentioned the phone call. Alex gave him a flat, suspicious stare.

"I didn't answer it," he said.

Alex looked like he was about to start another lecture on the importance of staying away from his phone, but spared Horatio and went to check who'd called.

Alex was, Horatio guessed, several years younger than

himself. He looked like a singer in a boy band, with shaggy blond hair and a baby face that he was sure would melt tween hearts when he smiled. If he ever smiled. Mostly he just looked angry and tired.

"I have to make a call," Alex announced, sighing in frustration.

"Do you want me to cover my ears?" Horatio asked, only half-mocking.

Alex didn't bite. "It will be short." He grabbed his room key and stepped into the hallway. He flipped the bar lock, so the door didn't shut all the way.

Horatio went back to watching his infomercial. These women weren't really his type. Women who did these kinds of commercials were always hyper-focused. You couldn't take them out to dinner because they were on a low-carb, low-fat, green smoothie diet. You couldn't surprise them with a weekend vacation because you'd ruin their training schedule.

Brittney was that kind of woman, Horatio remembered.

Alex put a hand on his shoulder, breaking him out of his thoughts. "We're going to breakfast before seeing the house."

"What house?"

Alex stared like he was unimpressed with his joke.

Horatio wasn't joking; he had no idea what Alex needed him for. "No, really. You never told me what we're doing here."

"I told you in the airport."

"I probably wasn't paying attention."

Alex sighed. "There's a house that the family says is haunted. We're checking it out as ghost hunters."

"Like, an actual ghost, or . . . ?" he trailed off. *Or the other thing*, he didn't say.

"Most of the time it's nothing," Alex said. This was him

trying to be reassuring. It just made Horatio more concerned.

Horatio reminded himself that while this was his first job, it was not Alex's. Alex had a partner before, but he didn't talk about what happened with him. Horatio wanted to believe that he'd moved on or got reassigned or married or quit, but he knew it was because he was either locked in a cell, screaming about monsters, or he was dead. Horatio wasn't sure which option was better.

Horatio turned off the TV. He wanted to ask what would happen if it wasn't nothing, but he couldn't. "I'm hungry," he said instead.

HORATIO HAD SPENT many early mornings eating breakfast in a Denny's, usually after a long night of drinking and partying.

It was different now. He'd been completely sober for over a month. No more late nights drinking, no more one-night stands. If his dad could see him now, he still wouldn't approve, but maybe he'd be slightly less disappointed.

"Eat your food," Alex told him. Horatio was lost in thought again. He looked down at his partially eaten eggs Benedict. He didn't want to finish them. He had the unpleasant thought that it could be his last meal and wished he'd ordered something better.

"I . . . " *I'm not ready for this*, he started to say. "What happens if it's not a ghost?" he asked instead.

"It's not a ghost. There's no such thing as ghosts," Alex said. He was wrong about that, but Horatio didn't correct him. "It's usually carbon monoxide or pipe noises."

"But if it's . . . the other thing?"

"The most important thing is to contain it. If it's a small

anomaly, we can usually burn the path it's using. If it's bigger than that, we'll have to try a different approach."

"Oh," was all he could say. He picked up a potato with his fork but didn't eat it. He really wanted a nice, strong drink.

Alex checked the time on his phone. "We'll get there early. Maybe we can solve this and get a flight back tonight."

Horatio wished he could be that nonchalant about facing down monsters. He used to be, before he'd actually seen them.

THEY DIDN'T TALK on the drive over to the house. Horatio tried to concentrate on the radio or on the road as Alex drove, but he was scared. If there was a monster in the house, he didn't know how he would handle it. He still had nightmares about the last one he encountered, and he'd only heard its voice.

He shook his head to banish those thoughts. He refocused on the radio. Alex had it tuned to some talk show.

"We could, in fact, see a rebound in five to ten years," the radio said. Horatio vaguely recalled the story was about whales.

"And that's due to the new regulations?"

"Well, it's due in part to the new regulations, but also because I can see you sitting there."

Horatio's heart stopped. It was a mistake. He'd just misheard. *Just don't pay any attention,* he told himself.

"He's not watching you. Take the gun from his coat."

Horatio put his hands over his ears instinctively. He tried to warn Alex, but he couldn't form the words. He looked at him desperately.

Alex pulled over onto the side of the road and shut off the car. Horatio could see the gun in Alex's holster when he shifted the car into park and thought how easy it would be to grab it and shoot Alex before he even realized what was happening.

But with the radio off, it was no longer as pressing. He uncovered his ears.

"We're here," Alex said, and Horatio thought he hadn't noticed what just happened.

Alex looked so unconcerned that Horatio thought it was momentary insanity. And then he saw the house, a few houses down from where they parked.

It was on fire, except without the flames. Black smoke billowed from the windows, streaming into the neighboring yards. Layers of ash covered the once-white aluminum siding. The grass was scorched and blackened in places.

A woman ran by the house with a golden retriever on a leash. Horatio watched in horror as they were engulfed by the smoke.

Alex was staring past him, at the house, unblinking. Horatio wondered what he saw. Horatio saw smoke because in his first encounter with a monster, he'd set a bathroom on fire.

"Okay," Alex said. "This is going to be bad. We'll talk to the owners —"

"I can't. I can't do it," Horatio managed to say.

"This is the only thing you can do. We might still be able to save the family in that house."

Horatio shook his head.

"This is not going to kill you, not yet. The faster we get this done, the less likely it's going to cause permanent damage. If you don't do this, then we have to come back with a team, and then we *will* lose people."

Alex was the least reassuring person on the planet, but it did help a bit. Horatio could see the runner and her dog at the end of the street, waving to a man getting his paper.

What he saw wasn't real, he just had to remember that. He could do this.

And if he didn't, a team would mean that someone would have to be sacrificed to stop the monster from coming through. That's why they kept those too far gone in cells instead of putting them out of their misery.

"Okay," Horatio said but didn't agree.

Alex removed the gun from his belt and locked it in the glove box. Horatio eyed it, but didn't reach for it.

"It's going to know what we are when we enter the house, but these types of entities are usually arrogant. It will believe that the hold it has is unbreakable," Alex said.

"How do we break it?"

"We won't know that until we get in. But for right now, we're going to pretend that we're ghost hunters, get the family out of the house, and figure out how to banish this thing."

It was easier to focus now that there was a plan. Or maybe it was because Alex was finally telling him useful information instead of ignoring all his questions.

They got out of the car. Horatio could smell the burning house and feel the heat on his face. He wiped his sweaty hands on his pants.

"You don't need to say anything," Alex told him. "It's better if you don't." He was probably right.

The house was just down the street, but it felt like an eternity to walk. The idea of the house fire got more and more oppressive. Horatio knew it wasn't there, but he still stopped before ascending the porch steps, trying to catch his breath.

"It's going to be worse the closer we are. Act like nothing is wrong."

That's easy for you to say, Horatio thought. He remembered all those dinner parties and charity balls he was forced to attend growing up. It had become second nature to pretend that he wanted to be there, that his family was functional, and that he wasn't, usually, well past drunk. He wiped his hands again and put them casually in his pockets. His mom would be horrified at what he'd become, but she'd appreciate the effort to at least look normal.

Alex rang the doorbell. There was screaming from the other side of the door, like car brakes squealing to avoid a deer on a dark road. Horatio jumped and turned to run, but Alex grabbed his arm.

"It's children," he explained.

Horatio didn't spend a lot of time around kids, but knew they didn't sound like that. "What —" he began, but the door opened.

A woman cracked the door as if there were a pet she didn't want to escape. "Yes?" she asked.

She seemed unfazed by the blackened skin covering half her face, cracked and still oozing blood. Horatio tried to find somewhere else to look. *Act normal,* he told himself, *she's not really burned.*

"Ma'am, you called us because you think your house is experiencing some paranormal phenomenon," Alex said. It was polite, practiced.

"Oh. Oh! Thank God you're here." She opened the door wide, and Horatio saw that she had a small, diapered child on her hip and a little girl standing behind her legs. The two children did not appear burned like their mom.

"Come in, come in!" She ushered with her free hand.

"It's gotten really bad recently," she continued as they entered the foyer, and she shut the door behind them. "I mean, I didn't really believe in this stuff, but then it started happening and there's really no other explanation, is there? I mean, I guess you guys do this all the time, so you can tell us for sure, right?" She set the child in her arms down, saying, "Go play with your sister."

Horatio was so focused on the woman's ramblings that he forgot he was trying not to look at her face. He did, and then he couldn't look away. One of her eyes was milky white, and her lower eyelid had melted and fused with her cheek. Horatio thought he might throw up.

Alex introduced them, and Horatio shook hands with her, automatically recoiling from the expected feeling of charred skin. Her hand was soft and warm. She said her name was Lori.

"I'm sorry, come in!" she said, leading the way into the house. "You're here earlier than I was expecting; I'm sorry the house is a mess."

"That's fine. It won't affect our work," Alex told her.

From the outside, the smoke had been pouring out all the windows, but from the inside, it was a hot haze hanging in the air, like a roast had burned, or was still burning, in the oven. Horatio tried to suppress a cough, which only made him cough more.

"Oh, no, are you okay?" the woman asked, concerned. "Let me get you some water."

Horatio shook his head. He didn't want water; he wanted to get out before the whole place filled with smoke.

"Yes, please," Alex said.

Lori brought Horatio's water. They sat in the living room after Lori swept toys off the couch and chair and into a basket. Horatio sipped his water, trying to pretend the house wasn't filled with smoke and Lori wasn't horrifically burned. The water tasted of bitter ash, but it was just his imagination.

"It started about a month ago. Our daughter Janie said that there were monsters in her room, but she's four and the internet says that's perfectly normal for a four-year-old.

Then, things would be out of place, but with two kids, we didn't think anything of it."

Horatio wasn't looking at her. He was staring at a half-melted fire truck on the floor. He waited for her to get to the part where a voice told her to kill people, or she was having nightmares about things grabbing her from the shadows.

"But then I was getting the kids ready to go out one day, and I felt this . . . this presence brush by me. I told my husband, and he didn't laugh it off like I thought he would. He says he's seen this figure, like a girl in a white dress. And that's when we realized that the signs were all there." She sighed. "It sounds so crazy when you say it out loud like that."

Horatio looked at her in disbelief. She couldn't see that her whole house was on fire. Or that her face was melting off, and there was an entity from another dimension coming through a portal in her house intent on killing her whole family in horrible, insane ways. She thought this was a ghost, and the kind that caused a mild inconvenience.

Alex told her gently that she didn't sound crazy at all. He told her about ghosts and unfinished business, and the simple way they were going to get the ghost to the other side. "Can you show us the rest of the house?" Alex asked.

"Oh, right. Of course." Lori stood up. She brushed her hands on her pants like she was nervous. To Horatio, she just smeared more ash on her already ashy pants.

Horatio set his glass of water on the coffee table and stood up. He grabbed Alex's arm as he walked past. "I don't want to be here," he said quietly.

"I know," Alex said. He pulled his arm out of Horatio's grasp.

"Did the water help?" Lori asked, and it took Horatio a second to realize she was talking directly to him.

"Yeah. Thanks."

"He's sensitive to paranormal phenomenon," Alex explained. "He's sensing a lot of it."

She nodded understandingly. "So, there *is* a presence here?"

"We think so," Alex said.

She led them up the stairs. There were family pictures on the wall, untouched from the fire, although the wall was scorched around them. They looked like a happy, smiling family: two parents, three kids, and a cat. He didn't see a cat anywhere. If it was smart it would've left after the entity moved in. Pets always seem to sense these things before their humans.

She showed them Janie's room, where Janie and the little child were playing Barbies between the two beds, oblivious. Their dolls were twisted and melted. The girl and the child were covered in soot, but not burned like their mother was. He wondered what it meant.

"Are you getting anything from this room?" Lori asked. Both she and Alex were looking at him. What was he supposed to say?

"No." He hoped that was the right answer.

"Oh." She sounded disappointed.

"It might be better if we could spend a few hours here, try some of our tricks to get the ghost to show," Alex said. "Is there somewhere you could take the kids for a few hours?"

"Well, there's a park down the street. Is it that bad? Do we need to think about getting a hotel?"

"No, nothing like that. I'll call you when we're done."

"Oh, well, let me show you around the rest of the house." She turned to her children. "Kids, we're going to the park, go get ready."

Janie and her brother pushed past them, dashing down the stairs, screaming. It didn't sound the same as the screaming Horatio had heard at the door.

"That's the master," Lori pointed out, absently. "We haven't had any activity in there."

Horatio and Alex followed Lori down the stairs. The two kids were arguing over a toy airplane.

Lori didn't even acknowledge them. "This is the kitchen, obviously. And that's the garage. That's where my husband said he saw the girl. It's his workshop. He makes tables and stuff. Oh! Do you think that could have something to do with it? Like, from the wood he was using?"

"It's unlikely, but we'll look into it," Alex said. He sounded impatient.

"Oh, right. Kids, it's —" she was cut off by a loud banging on the door to the garage.

Horatio looked before he could stop himself.

A hand slid down the window, leaving a trail of blood.

Everything else dropped away: the kids, Lori, Alex, the rest of the house. There was just him, the darkened garage, and the bright red smear of blood on the window.

"Help me," a quiet voice said.

Horatio found himself in front of the door. The bloody handprint dripped, pooling on the casement. The garage beyond was dark, but the shapes of woodworking equipment were visible in the shadows.

"Open the door. I don't want to die in here," the quiet voice pleaded.

He put his hand on the doorknob. It jiggled from the other side.

Something slammed him into the wall, hard. It was right in front of him, grabbing at his hands, but his vision slid around the entity. He struggled against it, worming his arm around to find its body and push it off. It responded by throwing him to the floor.

He'd been in plenty of fights when he was younger, but he could always see his opponent. The entity flickered at the edges of his vision, even as it pressed its weight on top of him. Horatio felt his fist connect, and the entity howled in pain. The entity grabbed his flailing arms and pinned them to the floor. Horatio kicked his legs uselessly.

"Use it! Help me!" the voice from the door screamed at him. He had no idea what it was talking about.

"Stop struggling," the entity growled. "You're going to hurt yourself."

And suddenly, he was on Lori's kitchen floor. Alex was on top of him, holding his wrists. His cheek felt red.

Horatio took a minute to catch his breath. "I'm okay," he finally said. Alex let go of his wrists and got off cautiously. Horatio didn't get up immediately. He felt like he'd just run a marathon and his shirt was sticking to his back. He felt cold.

He didn't need to ask what had happened. The entity — the real entity — had tried to take him. Possess him or drive him mad. Alex had stopped it, although Horatio was a little unclear about how he'd been able to. He was also unclear about when it had happened. When he touched the door-knob? When he saw the hand? Was it as soon as he entered the house?

"You need to get up," Alex said. "Don't look at the door."

Horatio rolled up to his knees, away from the door, and used the wall to get himself standing.

The smoke had cleared from the house. The walls were no longer scorched, and the burning smell was gone. It didn't mean the entity was gone, only that it'd failed to take Horatio this time.

"Where's Lori? And the kids?" Horatio asked.

"They left. Before you tried to open the door."

"How long ago was that?" Horatio asked. He felt unsafe standing this close to the door, like it would reach out and grab him again. It didn't help that Alex was staring past his shoulder.

Alex shrugged. "Several minutes ago. You stood there for a while. We're going to go outside. Don't turn around. Here," Alex said, leading Horatio to the patio door and sliding it open. Horatio stepped outside, and Alex slid the door closed behind him, blocking Horatio from going back in.

Horatio breathed in the clean, outside air.

"How do we kill this thing or banish it or whatever we're supposed to do?" Horatio asked. He glanced toward the door without thinking, but it was completely blocked by the kitchen wall.

"I'll take care of that part," Alex said. "But first, tell me what you've been seeing."

"No, what does that even mean? You'll 'take care of it'?"

"It's a ritual. That only I can do." Alex withheld a lot of information, but Horatio had never seen him outright lie. He was really bad at it.

"That's the stupidest thing I've ever heard."

"I can't tell you what's going to happen," Alex admitted.

Horatio knew Alex was right. Whatever the weapon or ritual was that could get rid of the shadow entities that plagued Horatio and this house, then Horatio couldn't know about it. He was touched, tainted by them, and anything he knew would make its way back to them.

"Alright. Fine," Horatio said. He described the smoke and the heat from the outside, and the hazy air inside. He told Alex about Lori's half-melted face and the children's toys. "But the children were okay. They had ash on their faces and clothes, but they weren't burned."

Alex nodded, listening. Horatio knew he could see *something*, but it wasn't enough if he was taking the risk of bringing Horatio along.

"What did you see in the garage?"

Horatio didn't want to think about it, so he tried to

describe it as clinically as possible. "A bloody hand. And the shadow, which was you."

"I saw the hand. Lori heard it banging on the door, too. She brushed it off and then just took her kids and left. I didn't get a chance to stop her before you went for the door."

"I don't get it, why would she just brush it off?"

"The entity got to her. Probably her husband, too." Horatio knew what that meant. They were like him, influenced by the entity into seeing or not seeing what it wanted. Even if Alex could banish this entity here and now, Lori and her husband were going to go insane and end up in a facility like Horatio.

"Oh God, their kids."

"It's better if you don't think about that."

"What —" Horatio started to say, but Alex held his hand up to cut him off.

"They'll have more of a chance once this entity is gone."

Horatio was incredulous. He wanted to hit Alex for being so nonchalant. He wanted to run to the park and tell Lori to get as far away as she could, as if distance could change her circumstances. He wanted to light the house on fire, for real, and watch it burn.

"Horatio, stop."

Horatio realized that he'd been pacing and was too upset to worry about the time he might've lost.

"I know this is upsetting. You need to calm down before the entity grabs you again. You know this."

He did know this. And he knew that Alex was right. He just hated it. He picked up a child's tennis racket from the ground and hurled it into a neighbor's yard in frustration.

Alex didn't take this as a threat or a warning, just watched.

"Fine," Horatio said. "What do we need to do?" Alex took

out his phone and held it up. "I'm going into the garage, and I need you to call the police."

"Isn't the reason that we're here because no one else can do this? What are the police supposed to do?"

"There is going to be a lot here that we can't explain. The police won't be able to, either, but it'll give something for Lori to hold on to, to normalize this." Alex gestured vaguely toward the house.

"I don't understand how the police are going to do that."

Alex grabbed Horatio's arm, not in a comforting way, but in a way that held him there. "The entity has possessed someone. That's why it hasn't left the garage."

"Oh," Horatio said in understanding. He thought about the bloody handprint on the garage door window and felt a chill run through his limbs. It was one thing to hallucinate the hand; it was another to know it was real. "Who is it?"

Alex was watching Horatio, and it made him even more uncomfortable. "Her husband." Horatio remembered that Lori mentioned he'd been spending a lot of time in the garage doing woodworking. Maybe he'd sequestered himself in there, or maybe she'd locked him in to prevent the entity's influence from spreading.

"Banishing the entity is likely going to kill him." Alex said more, but it was lost in the sound of blood rushing through Horatio's ears. Lori was going to come home with the police all around her house and her dead husband in the garage. Her kids were going to lose their father. Would they see him there, before Lori rushed them away? Or would she put them off by telling them that eventually their daddy was going to come home, until one day she'd tell them the truth and break their little hearts?

The impact against the house siding jarred him out of his thoughts, and Alex's face came back into focus. Horatio thought he was going to get another lecture on not freaking out, especially when Alex was premeditating murder, but he didn't.

"I don't like this. It's just the only way," Alex said.

Horatio started to protest: there *had* to be another way, but Alex cut him off. "He's already dead. He can't be saved." He looked almost sorry.

Horatio knew Alex was right. This is what they were here for, to find and eliminate these entities. It was still hard, impossible, to reconcile that with the knowledge that someone had to die to banish the entity.

"I don't want to do this," Horatio said. Alex accepted it as if he'd agreed.

He held the phone out to Horatio. Horatio took it reluctantly, trying not to look at it. "When you call, you need to tell them the address here. Then say you're worried about Dan —"

"Who's Dan?"

"Lori's husband. Whatever you hear through the phone, make sure you say those two things."

Horatio swallowed and nodded. "The address and Dan," he repeated. He thought about the last time he'd used a phone and how the entity had made Horatio believe it was a trusted friend. It made Horatio do terrible things. "What if it gets me again?" Just holding the phone was making him smell smoke.

"I can't guarantee it won't. It should be a short enough conversation that it can't. Go to the front door when I go into the garage. Do not enter the garage, no matter what you hear."

"Call the cops. The address. Dan. Don't go into the garage."

Alex opened the sliding door back into the house. Smoke billowed through the opened door. Horatio covered his nose and mouth with his free hand and went inside. Alex followed, sliding the door shut behind them.

Horatio walked carefully, slowly, toward the front door. He didn't like the idea of Alex opening the garage, and he hated the idea of what would happen after he did.

Horatio dutifully made it to the front door. He heard the garage door open and close as Alex slipped in. There was no fanfare, no swell of evil presence. Just a puff of smoke from the hallway.

Horatio took a deep breath and choked on the smoke. He recovered, stooping lower to the ground where the air wasn't as smoky.

He swiped the emergency call button on Alex's phone and dialed 911. It rang a concerning number of times before it connected. "Hello, this is emergency services, what is your emergency?"

Horatio gave her the address, trying not to stumble over it.

"Sir, could you repeat that, please?" Horatio took a deep breath, careful of the smoke in the air. He repeated the address.

"Okay, sir, what's the emergency?"

"My friend, uh, Dan." Horatio felt the sweat prickle on his face from the growing heat in the house. "He's missing. I mean, I haven't seen him in a few days, and I'm worried."

"Alright. Where are you? Are you at his house? Are you inside?"

"Yeah."

"Okay, if you could just go to the kitchen, Sir. Tell me when you get there."

"I'm here," Horatio said, and when he looked up from trying to find the rapidly-shrinking clean air in the house, he was standing in the kitchen.

"Take a knife from the block on the counter," the dispatcher said.

He pulled the phone away from his ear, but it was already on speaker. His hand was clawed around it, and he couldn't pry his fingers off.

Relax, it's not real, he thought as he started hyperventilating, and he hit at the phone's screen clumsily, trying to end the call.

"No, I need . . . the police," Horatio said. "Dan is . . . " He didn't remember what Dan was. Had anything made it through to the real dispatcher? Had he even dialed?

The dispatcher laughed, a pleasant laugh, if a little too loud. "Alex lied to you. Dan's not in that garage."

Don't listen, don't listen. Horatio tried to get out, through the sliding door, but his steps were leaden.

"Alex didn't want you to know it was the girl."

Horatio stopped struggling toward the door. "What girl?" he asked aloud, but he saw it. Four chairs and a highchair around the kitchen table. The two beds in Janie's room. The three children in the photos.

Smoke was filling the room. He had to stop Alex. No. It was the entity that was lying.

There was a high-pitched scream from the garage. It was undistorted and very real. He looked toward the garage.

"Do you know what he's doing to her?" the dispatcher asked. "He's sawing her apart, limb by limb. The hacksaw blade is dull, but he doesn't care. There's so much blood."

"Shut up!" he screamed into the phone.

"He started with her hands."

"Stop it! Stop!" he pleaded, but it was useless. He dropped to his hands and knees. He had to get out before the smoke got him, even if he had to crawl.

"Can you imagine it? His hands grabbing her, twisting

her? The saw can't make it through the bone, so he has to smash them and wrench her apart."

The screaming in the garage continued. The neighbors were going to hear. The police were coming, and they would find him and Alex in the house with a dismembered girl. Lori would identify them.

He was standing in front of the garage door. *No no no no no*. He closed his eyes, but he couldn't stop seeing the door and the darkened garage behind it.

He grabbed the doorknob. It was intensely hot, hot enough that it pulled a layer of skin off when he snatched his hand back.

Horatio searched around desperately for something to insulate himself from the hot doorknob.

"If you hurry, you can still save the girl. Before she bleeds out. Take the knife from the block," the dispatcher said from the phone still clutched in his hand.

He wrapped his hand in his shirt, even though that wasn't enough. The kitchen. There'd be a potholder. He ran for it and started throwing the drawers open, looking. He finally found one shaped like a giraffe, slipped it on, and ran back for the garage door.

"Open the door slowly. He won't see you," the dispatcher said.

He put his gloved hand on the knob and turned.

The door flew open, and he jumped, throwing Alex's phone across the room.

It was quiet. All he could hear was the sound of his labored breathing.

He opened his eyes. Had they been closed the whole time? The smoke was gone. Alex was standing in front of him, holding the other side of the knob. He had blood on his shirt.

"We have to go," he said.

Horatio recoiled. Entities lied, but they also knew things. It's what made them dangerous. "The blood," Horatio said.

"We have to go, now," Alex repeated.

Molten rage flowed up Horatio's spine. He grabbed the front of Alex's jacket and shoved him against the wall. "Did you kill her?" he shouted at Alex.

When Alex didn't answer, Horatio shoved him again.

"No," Alex finally said.

"Don't just tell me what I want to hear!"

"You can see for yourself."

He didn't let go of Alex immediately. He wasn't sure if this was a trick or deflection. Alex wasn't even looking at his face, but at his chest, and he didn't like it.

"She survived," Alex said, patiently. Horatio hated when he talked like that.

Alex extended his arm, slowly, grabbing the edge of the garage door with his hand and pushing it open.

Horatio let go. He moved past Alex and into the garage. The light was still on; the lathe and workbench and power tools looked a lot less sinister than they did in shadow.

And Horatio saw her, her eyes closed, lying next to a stack of two-by-fours. She was small, Janie's age, give or take. Her pink dress was dirty and frayed at the hem and sleeves, and it was clear that she'd soiled herself multiple times. She'd been locked in the garage for a while before Horatio and Alex had arrived.

Her little chest rose and fell, but there was something about her that seemed lifeless, or empty. The entities were parasites, corruption of the soul, unable to be removed because you couldn't separate them from their host.

Except, somehow, Alex had.

· · ·

HORATIO GOT UP. The house looked so strange. Like every other house.

He looked at his hand. It was unburnt.

He followed Alex out of the house and back to the car. He looked around, paranoid that he'd hear police sirens and there'd be cops waiting by the car, with guns and questions.

He fumbled with the door handle trying to get it open.

"Calm down. Let me unlock the door," Alex said. He held up the key.

"They're going to know we were there. Lori's going to tell them it was us." He got in the car. He looked around again for police.

"She's going to have a lot more explaining to do than we will. They are not going to be looking at us."

Horatio could see the scenarios play out in his head, and all of them ended up with him in prison. It wouldn't matter what he told them; he'd look crazy enough they'd pin it on him anyway.

They drove back to the hotel. Horatio tried not to worry, but kept looking for lights in the rearview mirror.

KATHARINE HAS BEEN DREAMING up stories since she could talk, and writing them down since she could hold a pencil. She writes across a spectrum of genres, mostly fantasy, sci-fi, and horror. She spends her days wrangling data and her nights writing, drawing, and playing video games. She lives in Northern Virginia.

MYSTERY OF THE SOMERTON MAN

BY TRACY L. SNYDER

There are many things I'll miss when my tour of duty on Earth is over. Finding a dead body is not one of them.

Especially when it's someone I know.

I stare down at Hanza. His head rests against a concrete retaining wall, crossed feet toward the ocean. He looks comfortable, as if he had lain down on the soft sand and fallen asleep.

I touch the brim of my fedora, saluting a fallen comrade.

A memory comes of waking up next to Hanza after we'd been transferred into our human bodies, so many years ago. I admit I was jealous at how young, fit, and handsome his shell was. Not that there is anything wrong with the one they assigned to me. But Hanza always had the luck.

Until now.

A shiver races down my spine. I turn up the collar of my jacket against my neck.

The sun is well past dawn, and there is a welcome coolness to the air before the heat of summer kicks in on this first day of December. In three weeks, the good people of

Australia will crowd Somerton beach for Christmas Day picnics. But at this time, the sand is almost empty. Just a few early risers, pausing to stare.

We need to move fast.

I tap the communications chip in my throat, connecting myself to headquarters.

"Dvornak. So good to hear from you," the sibilant voice whispers in my ear. "It's been too long. We were beginning to think you'd gone native."

It's good to hear a voice spoken through reptilian vocal cords. For the first time in years, I feel the pull of home-sickness.

"How do you like being a human policeman?" Ana's voice is playful. "I hear you've been promoted to Inspector."

I cut into her banter. "Ana. Notify the director. We've got a dead agent. It's Hanza Cerny." I pause, staring at the corpse. Saying his name out loud makes it real.

A hiss echoes between my ears. "How did he die? Was it assassination? Any evidence that the Verdim have found this planet?"

The knot in my stomach rises to my throat at her words, making it hard to swallow. "No visible signs of how he died. I hope it's not the Verdim, but we need to follow up."

"I agree." Ana speaks quickly. "Get the body processed and transferred to the ship for testing as soon as possible. Do you need reinforcements?"

I shake my head, which is ridiculous. She can't see me. "We're waiting for Svoboda to show up as coroner. And I've got my new assistant. The three of us should be able to handle this."

I sever the link and glance up. Sergeant Novotny stumbles down the wooden stairs, his plain clothes perfect for his new role as a mid-level policeman. The shell they found for him is tall, dark haired, and handsome. But he wears it wrong.

Novotny fumbles a thin, leather-bound book to the ground and stops to pick it up. He shakes the pages vigorously as he walks my way, his gait stiff, elbows held out from his sides. Honestly. Even the most obtuse human will begin to suspect he is an alien.

I realize Earth is a minor planet and doesn't draw the highest talent, but the quality of this assistant is appalling. He lacks the most basic training. I make a mental note to enter an objection with my supervisor.

"Inspector Dvornak." Novotny slides to a halt in front of me, identifying himself by extending his hand with the index finger pointing up, the thumb to the side, in an exaggerated L shape.

"Yes, but make it less obvious. Like this." I also make the L but use the index finger to push my glasses up on the bridge of my nose. "That way, if the person you're speaking to is a human, they won't notice the gesture at all."

"Ah," Novotny nods. "Like spies."

"No, like humans. Our goal is to blend in."

I watch with dismay as Novotny leers at a heavy-set woman walking by. When he notices my disapproval, he moves his eyebrows up and down several times in a suggestive manner. The gesture looks odd on a human face.

"Stop it," I hiss.

He wiggles his eyebrows again. "Did you see how wide her hips are? I bet she can lay some smooth eggs."

I step close and lean in until my face is within a few inches of his. "Humans are mammals." I whisper the words, so the locals won't hear me. "They don't lay eggs; they give birth to live young. And if you want to appear to be human, you stare at women with tiny little waists. Curves on top and bottom are acceptable. But a thin waist is an absolute requirement for leering."

I push him back a step. "Now, hurry up. We need to get this body processed as quickly as possible so that it can be transferred to the ship. We need to make sure this death wasn't caused by the Verdim."

Novotny stares at me, his eyes wide. "The Verdim? Are they on this planet?" His words trip over each other. "I was told this planet is safe. It is safe, right? No Verdim."

I make a shushing motion with my hands. "Calm down. No Verdim that we know of. But we always check."

Novotny glances at the sandy beach behind him, his shoulders creeping up to his ears. "I can't stay if the Verdim are here." A note of panic creeps into his voice. "You'll have to send me back. Send me back."

"You're fine," I insist. "It's just standard precaution. We have no evidence the Verdim are here yet. And if they have encroached on this planet, you know how to identify them. Just look for that third eyelid."

"Eyelid?" Novotny's eyes glaze over.

It looks like I get to explain everything, and it's probably not his first time hearing it. "The Verdim have one trait that carries over no matter which species they imitate. They have a third eyelid under the other two that moves from side to side. Our tale-tell sign is that we need green blood to survive. Their give-away is that third eyelid."

Novotny holds his hand vertical and moves it side to side.

I nod encouragingly. "Right. You see that third eyelid blink sideways like that, and you run. Don't try to investigate, don't try to fight. Let Command handle it."

My assistant shudders so violently he nearly comes out of his clothes.

I snap my fingers in front of his face until he looks at me. "We need to process this body. Do you know what to do?"

Novotny gives himself a final shake and takes a deep breath. "Blood, labels, pockets," he recites in a sing-song voice. He gets awkwardly to his knees next to the body, lays his book on the sand, and pulls out a silver device the size of a cigarette lighter.

"Oh, look." Novotny reaches for the dead man's left collar. "One of those cylinder things. It's even partly burned."

"Don't touch it," I said. "We leave everything for the coroner. And it's called a cigarette. Nasty habit. Bad for the lungs. But since their Second World War, it seems everyone smokes them."

I pat my jacket pocket and feel the reassuring outline of my own half-empty package over my chest.

"Oooh. Everyone in the world was involved in battle at the same time?" Novotny claps his hands together like a human child saying prayers. "I'm sorry I missed that. It must have been fun."

I shake my head at the memory. "Not particularly. It was all we could do to keep this species from killing themselves off." For a moment I smell the fumes of burning petroleum and hear the screams of the dead.

I take a deep breath and let it out slowly. I feel for the sand under my shoes, the early morning sun warm on my back. I listen to the wheeling song of the sea gulls, call and response, a conversation rooted in this moment. It always works. I feel myself anchor to the present once more, the memories of war slipping back into the past. I open my eyes and look at my assistant.

"Oh, for Pete's sake. The red button. You look for the red button and push it."

Novotny holds up the silver device and points to a large red circle in the middle. "This?"

"Yes." I give an exaggerated nod. "And why is it red?" I ask a question any first-year cadet would know.

"Because." Novotny stops moving so he can think. "We're turning the blood red?"

"Exactly."

"I don't see why we have to bother." Novotny sits back on his haunches, squinting up at me. "Isn't the coroner one of us?"

"Yes," I nod. "But even Svoboda would have a hard time explaining why a corpse he was working on started leaking green blood."

I stare with rising concern as my assistant paws at the corpse. "Put it over the heart," I order. "The heart." I grab his hand and move it down to the chest. "Right here, in the middle of the upper torso, a little to the left."

He holds it without moving.

"Do you remember the secondary locations?" I ask with a sinking sensation.

"Why would I need another location? Isn't the heart the best place?"

"Imagine you are surrounded by humans and can't get access to the chest." My voice is high-pitched and cheerful, as if I am talking to a child. "You could put the transformer up here on either side of the neck," I point to the soft location of the jugular veins. "Or, if you are by the legs, you could use the femoral arteries."

Novotny's eyes widen. He stares at me in silence.

"Femoral. Down here. On the inside of his upper thigh." I take Novotny's hand and try to move it down to Hanza's thigh, but the sergeant snatches it back.

"The heart is good enough. I'll just use the heart. I know where that is."

I stare. "How did you pass human anatomy?"

"I didn't."

It's my turn to have my eyebrows go up. "You didn't pass anatomy? How did you swing a posting?"

Novotny gives me a secretive grin. "I'm special."

I run through all the ways my assistant is special. Especially ignorant. Especially arrogant. Especially dense. I watch while nothing happens. "Well, Mr. Special, did you press the button?"

Novotny finally clicks the red circle. He holds the device on Hanza's chest. A subtle change sweeps up from the neck and across the motionless face. The skin still looks dead, but there's a little more pink to the grey. A little less green. A little more human.

A little less like Hanza.

"Good," I say. "Now check his clothes. I'm sure that someone with Hanza's experience will have removed the labels so that he can't be traced, but we always check. Then go through his pockets to make sure there's nothing else that will identify him."

Novotny casually puts the blood transformer on top of his book and rummages through Hanza's clothes with both hands.

I snatch up the device. I grab the thin book as well, positioning it so that no one can see what I'm holding. I imagine the transformer being found by one of my human colleagues at the police department. I feel faint.

I stuff the transformer into the chest pocket of my suit, next to my pack of cigarettes. It occurs to me that it is resting right over my heart. What if I'm jostled, and my blood becomes an inhospitable red? My soul would be forced into the morning breeze, without any mechanism for inserting me into another shell.

I relocate the device as deep as possible into the front pocket of my trousers.

Right over my femoral artery.

A bead of sweat trickles from my right temple to the angle of my jaw. The drop lands on the leather cover of the book. I look at the title as I wipe the moisture away. I look closer.

"No labels," Novotny announces. "He slides his hands into the corpse's trouser pockets, one at a time. "I know what this is," he announces with pride as he holds up a comb. "It's used for grooming."

Novotny pulls out a soft, rectangular packet, yellow in color. He stares a moment. "This can't be right." He holds it up so I can see the lettering. "Look. It says Fruit, but I've seen fruit before. This isn't it."

"It's chewing gum."

"No, it isn't." He points at the package. "It says right here. Juicy Fruit."

"Put it back," I snap. "And what is this?" I hold up the book. "A recent translation of an ancient Persian poem? This isn't standard issue. Where did you get it?"

I fan through the pages, looking at the illustrations, the quatrains of verse. I run my hand over the inside of the back cover, feeling where the imprint of writing has been pressed into the leather. I hold the cover up to catch the morning rays of light.

"It's a Rubaiyat. Poetry of four lines." Novotny pauses. Apparently, he can't think and move at the same time. "Omar." His face splits with a wide smile. It's the first time I've seen him look non-reptilian. "Some guy named Omar wrote it. Says life is short, so we should drink alcohol instead of worrying." Novotny starts going through pockets again. "Our lives aren't as short as theirs, obviously. But I agree with the general sentiments."

"White liquid, sweet powder, avian eggs." I translate the writing inside the cover from our native language into English. I lower the book, and my voice raises to an undignified squeak. "You wrote your shopping list inside of a copy of the Rubaiyat? In Ludmillian?"

"Yeah." Novotny holds up his hand in the "L" shaped salute as he hears the name of our home planet. I don't think he knows he's doing it. The salute is a reflex. "Have you had this food called ice cream?" Novotny asks. "So cold. So tasty." His tongue flicks out over his lips at the memory. "I'm going to open shops selling ice cream when I get back home. It'll make a fortune."

I force myself to breathe. "And where will you get the ingredients?" I ask.

Novotny shrugs. "I'm sure I can source them from somewhere. I have connections," he adds in a conspiratorial tone.

"The white liquid is cream, which comes from milk," I explain.

Novotny stops, again. So he can try to think, again. It doesn't seem to be working.

"Milk comes from cows. Cows are mammals."

He stares.

I enunciate each word. "There are no mammals on Ludmill."

Understanding dawns. Novotny's eyes widen, his lips forming a horrified O. "You mean," he gasps, "ice cream is made from the secretions of mammals?"

I nod.

"But I ate five servings for breakfast." Novotny leans forward, resting his forehead on the corpse. Humans speak of turning green when they feel nauseous. But those of us from Ludmill turn *green*.

"Get up," I order.

Novotny moves his arms and legs one at a time and manages to stagger to his feet.

"Take this back where you found it." I slap the book into his chest, and he grabs it with flailing arms.

"It's just up the street," Novotny whines. He makes the mistake of rolling his eyes, as if I'm being unreasonable. "I found it in the back seat of an unlocked car just up there." He turns and points at the town of Adelaide.

"Take it back," I bark. "Before someone notices it's missing. And hurry up," I yell as he stumbles up the stairs.

Novotny bumps into a petite blonde woman at the top. He doesn't spare a glance for her, even though she has a properly trim waist.

She approaches me with her hand extended, a smile on her face. She is trailed by an orderly from the coroner's office, carrying a canvas stretcher.

My eyes look past her, searching the parking lot for Svoboda.

"Inspector Dvornak? I'm Dr. Wilson, from the coroner's office."

I ignore her outstretched hand, and push my glasses back up the bridge of my nose, my fingers carefully forming an L.

The smile fades from her face and she gives me a puzzled frown. Not one of us, then. She must be human.

"Glad to meet you." I grab her hand and give a quick shake. "I was expecting Svoboda this early in the morning. What happened? Did he sleep in?"

"I don't know." Golden curls sway as Dr. Wilson shakes her head. "Nobody can find him. Not in his office, not at home. They called me to fill in."

A tingle races to the tips of my fingers as my adrenaline levels go up a notch. Another agent gone.

"You can take the body to the morgue immediately," I say. "My assistant and I have investigated, and there's nothing remarkable about this death."

Dr. Wilson drops to her knees and starts going through Hanza's clothes herself. "What assistant?" she asks.

"This is him." I don't bother to keep the irritation out of my voice as the tall, handsome shell slides to a halt in the sand. "Dr. Wilson, this is Sergeant Novotny. Novotny," I say pointedly.

My assistant glances at me.

"Dr. Svoboda is missing." I put emphasis on the last word, hoping he can put two and two together. "I've never worked with Dr. Wilson before."

"Oh." Novotny stands motionless for a moment, then extends his hand in an exaggerated L shape and shoves it within inches of the doctor's button nose.

She looks up at the sky, trying to see what he's pointing at.

"Oh." Novotny drops his hand. He draws in a deep breath of surprise, eyes widening. "OH!"

Subtlety is not his strong suit.

Dr. Wilson looks up at Novotny, her head cocked to one side, a small smile curving her lips. "Aren't you a tall one?" She maintains eye contact and waits for a reply.

It's his turn to look puzzled. He'll need to be briefed on mating rituals, as well as everything else.

The doctor looks back down at the corpse. "This is odd," she mutters. "The labels have been removed from all his clothes. Who does that?"

"Agents," Novotny blurts.

I step on his toe as a signal to stay quiet.

"Ow."

"Yes, but agents on which side? Is he a German operative, or one of ours?"

I step harder on Novotny's foot. He gives me an angry glance, and I shake my head at him. He stays silent.

"It could be a number of things." I try to think of a few. "He might be a regular bloke trying to escape an unsavory past with the police or evade an angry wife."

"Maybe you're right," Dr. Wilson concedes, but she keeps going through pockets.

I try to hurry her along. "I think Svoboda can do this back at the morgue."

The doctor refuses to be pushed. She takes items out of Hanza's pockets, notes them in a small book, and puts them back.

Dr. Wilson slides a finger into a tiny pocket made to hold a watch fob. She pulls out a small piece of paper, unfolds it, and stares for a moment. She stands gracefully to her feet, pausing to dust sand from the knees of her stockings.

"What could this mean?" She holds out the scrap of paper. It has rough edges, as if it has been torn.

I lean close enough to see the calligraphy. "Tamam Shud," I read. "What language is that?"

"Persian," Dr. Wilson says.

I feel Novotny tense beside me.

"It's a phrase traditionally used at the end of a piece of writing," the doctor explains. "It was probably torn from a book. It means 'ended,' or 'finished.'" She gasps, realization flashing across her face. "He must have been executed. Whoever did this is letting us know the death is deliberate."

A buzzing of panic fills my brain. It's an effort to keep from gasping. It's an effort to breathe at all. "No, no," I say hurriedly, trying to get things back on track. "It was probably a suicide note, letting everyone know he had decided to choose his end."

"It could have been meant as a joke?" Novotny suggests. He draws his lips back in a reptilian grimace, shoulders raised as if to apologize for planting the cryptic phrase on the body. I bet if I had looked at the last page of the Rubaiyat I would have seen a tear.

I stomp on Novotny's foot. By now he knows better than to say ouch.

I gesture to the crowd of onlookers, which is growing by

the minute. "I think we should take the body back to the morgue. We can do an in-depth investigation there."

"Yes." Doctor Wilson stares at Hanza with a curiosity that makes me nervous. Her assistant kneels on the sand and shifts the body onto the stretcher.

The doctor lays manicured fingers on Novotny's forearm. He startles, but at least he doesn't fall.

"Would you be a dear and carry one end of the stretcher?" she asks.

My assistant glances at me, and I nod. He and the orderly pick up the stretcher and shuffle through the sand.

As the orderly starts up the stairs, Novotny doesn't know enough to raise his end to keep the stretcher level. Hanza's corpse slides, planting dead feet squarely into his stomach. My assistant squeals and belatedly raises his end. Now the feet are in Novotny's face.

"I am curious about something," Dr. Wilson says. "Dvornak, Novotny, Svoboda. Your names are Hungarian, aren't they? Do you all know each other?"

I gave her our cover story. "We are Czechoslovakian. Svoboda and I know each other. Our grandparents all immigrated to Australia about fifty years ago, and we grew up in the same community. Novotny's family came over right before the war. He's still figuring out how things work in this country."

All lies, of course. The reality is that our race made first contact with humans in Czechoslovakia hundreds of years ago, and the director spent a few months in Eastern Europe when he was starting his career. He insists that all agents on Earth use Czechoslovakian names out of nostalgia for his vanished youth.

What an idiot.

The doctor smiles up at me. She is attractive, in a human

sort of way. I'm not sure what to think of her. Is her gaze too knowing? Too sly?

Does she like me?

I have a hard time reading human females. Although, to be honest, the men I work with at the police department seem to have the same problem.

"I'd better escort the body back to the morgue and see if Svoboda shows up." Dr. Wilson walks across the sand, her hips swaying. She glances over her shoulder. "Should I tell him to contact you when I see him?"

I nod. "Yes. Thanks." My body responds to the sight of her walking away. After all the years I've spent as a human, it's still unsettling to feel the tingle spread out from my nether regions. My shell likes human women.

I take a deep breath and turn away from her. I move a few steps down the beach so I can tap on my communication chip without being noticed.

"Is the body on its way to the ship?" Ana's voice is brisk.

"We've got a problem," I say quietly. "Svoboda's disappeared. I had to work with a human coroner. There's going to be a delay."

"Svoboda's gone as well?" Ana gasps. "Two agents compromised?"

I'm happy to hear the concern in her voice. When you're posted to an unimportant world, it can be hard to get anyone's attention.

"Wait." After a pause Ana says, "The director himself wants to talk to you."

My breath escapes in a sigh of relief. The Council is aware of the situation. They'll know what to do.

There's a click inside my head. "Dvornak?" a voice booms, making the bones of my skull vibrate.

"Yes, director." My words come out in a rush. "I'm honored to have you take a personal interest in this case, sir."

A full-throated laugh rattles my ears. "Of course, I'm taking an interest. I requested you personally. Heard you're the best trainer on Earth."

"Trainer?" My headlong concern swirls into confusion.

"What do you think of your new assistant?"

I open my mouth to report that he is the biggest fool I've ever been sent, but years in service make me cautious. "He's coming along," I say. "There's a lot to learn."

"Capital. Capital." I imagine the director clapping me on the back with a scale-covered hand. "I knew he'd do well. My nephew, you know. My sister's eldest. He reminds me of myself at that age."

That explains the incompetence.

"Train him well. Keep the boy safe, but let him get a little experience with the locals. You know." The director laughs again. "The kind of experience that makes for a good story in council chambers."

I've heard the stories the director tells. Just thinking of them makes me blush.

"But sir. We have a situation down here. Svoboda's missing now, as well. That means we've lost two —"

"Yes, yes," the director breaks in. "I've assigned a supervisor to look into it."

My stomach sinks. The supervisors I know are worthless. They sit around the office on their long, green tails, swapping gossip.

"But sir," I try again, a note of desperation in my voice.

"Yes, yes," the director booms. "Of course, there will be a bonus for you, maybe even a promotion, if you work things right. I'm going to make my nephew head of your division when he gets done with his tour." Another peal of laughter splits my skull. "How do you like that? You're training your own boss."

I take what I know of Novotny and extrapolate into the future. My life stretches out like a desert before me.

A slurping noise sets my teeth on edge. "Food's here, so I won't keep you. Work hard, Dvornak. Keep my nephew safe, and I'll look in from time to time."

Another click, and my head fills with silence. Blessed, blessed silence. I turn and make my way to the parking lot. I drag my feet from step to step, as if Earth's gravity has doubled. There will be no help from Command. It's just me, trying to figure out how Hanza died, where Svoboda is, if the Verdim have found Earth. And now I'm saddled with the nincompoop-in-training.

I feel a headache bloom behind my eyes. I look up to see Novotny standing next to Dr. Wilson. He's smiling, so excited he's nearly vibrating off the pavement.

"I'll drive behind the van and follow it to the coroner's office," the doctor calls over to me. "Can I borrow your assistant? I could use his help unloading the body."

Novotny gives me several excited nods. If he was my assistant, I'd say no. But as my future boss . . . "Sure," I say. "I'll meet up with you later."

They turn and walk toward a cream-colored Morris Minor. Novotny puts an arm around the doctor's shoulders. She nestles in, coordinating their strides so she can walk pressed to his side. Novotny's hand slides down Dr. Wilson's spine until it rests on her lower back. At home his hand would have been on the sensitive place at the base of her tail.

It seems the gesture translates across species.

Novotny grins over his shoulder at me and waggles his eyebrows up and down. He will get plenty of stories to tell in council chambers.

I watch as Novotny folds his long limbs into the passenger seat of the tiny, rounded automobile. The doctor climbs into the driver's seat, and the engine coughs to life.

The coroner's van passes within feet of me, my murdered colleague in the back. I call out a farewell to Hanza with my mind, but his soul dissipated hours ago.

Dr. Wilson drives by, Novotny grinning happily from the passenger seat. As they pull even with me the doctor gives a direct stare and smiles. It's a small smile, a self-satisfied smile. The way my cat looks as she grooms away the last feathers from her morning hunt.

Dr. Wilson guns the tiny motor. As she turns away, I see a third eyelid slide sideways across her eyes. An electric shock of recognition jolts through me, rooting my feet to the asphalt.

The Verdim are here.

Tamam Shud

TRACY L. SNYDER is an award-winning author from Oregon, wife of one man, mother of two sons, and servant of a cat. Her passion is writing tales of Science Fiction and Fantasy. She feels the ultimate compliment of her writing is a snort of laughter. Tracy has had several short stories published in anthologies and a digital magazine.

During the day she is a Certified Lymphedema Therapist, helping people recover from injury and illness. When not healing people with words or touch, Tracy paddles on a competitive dragon boat team named The Unsinkables.

To read more about Tracy and her work, visit her website at https://tracylsnyder.com and her author page at https://www. facebook.com/TracyLSnyderauthor/. You can follow her on Twitter @tracysnyder111 and Instagram at tracylynnsnyder.

A NEW SHIFTER IN THE HOOD

BY KEVIN A. DAVIS

Sane people don't walk 22nd Avenue in this part of Fort Lauderdale — not in this fog at this time of night with the shifters howling. The dense mist blanketed the stucco houses and dulled any other noise, including the cars that crawled along the asphalt and my own footsteps on the sidewalk. Only the distant howls made it through.

The gray hue of city lights against the night sky couldn't fight the haze; the moon had risen to my left, but I couldn't see it from where I walked. I'd left my car in the relative safety of a crappy burger joint at the edge of the hood and strolled in a sweaty tank top and a Marlins cap. I ate my burger, spitting out the pickles I'd told them I didn't want, leaving a sour green trail in the wake of fog. The residents of the houses I passed knew better than to venture out on a night like tonight. They left it to those less wary or stupid, like me — and the shifters.

Locals might chance a quick smoke outside their apartment or dance out to toss a bag at their dumpster, but they remained hidden in mist. I passed the occasional whiff of burning tobacco and deeper, pungent smoke. The sharp stench of dumpsters lingered longer.

I saw no one. Still, I felt eyes on me; the shifters knew I had crossed into their domain. The unwary visitor rarely made it this far in. But, you had to take chances to make it in life.

Our family business had started generations ago, and my mother had trained me at an early age to work the delicate and dangerous trafficking between the cryptids. She traded with groups in southern Europe, while I handled South Florida.

I stepped over the broken concrete beside a weathered fence that no one dared tag. Nature had worked on this wood, stained and warped it, but no paint had ever touched it. A Spanish-style, pink stucco house rose behind it, easily surveying the surrounding neighborhood. This was Isabella's house and territory.

I followed the sidewalk as it curved around the tip of the triangular property, discarding my wadded-up burger bag toward the opposite side of the street. Golden eyes glinted through the mist ahead of me, unblinking; a throaty growl came from their direction. I hadn't expected them to be changed into their non-human form. It happened on occasion. However, as a fence between cryptids, the shifters let me pass into their dominion; I brought information or objects they couldn't trade for directly. They knew my scent and would let me through unless bloodlust took them.

"Hola," I said, coming to a stop. "I'm here to see Isabella." I brushed my greasy fingers across the thighs of my sweatpants.

A shifter stepped forward through the fog, a gray shape with arms so long they nearly touched the ground and fur that had turned silver in the weather. Its toenails scratched against concrete with each step. Canine ears stood high on his head, and his golden eyes reflected what little light the mist allowed.

"Isabella," a voice drawled from the yard to my right, "is unavailable."

The fog was too thick to see through, but I recognized the voice of Sofia. A chill crawled up my sweaty neck. Avoiding a telling swallow, I spoke as evenly as my throat allowed. "Could you tell her Carl is here to see her?" I had to play it out without alerting anyone to my fear. However, in that one moment, I guessed that all the shifters would have noticed it.

Sofia laughed. "Come, see — Isabella."

The shifter in front of me backed into the dirt and grass swale bordering the street, permitting me to pass. Eddies of mist swirled around it. I heard the clicking of nails behind and to my left in fog too thick to make out shapes. Running would not be an option.

Taking a deep breath to calm the dread of what I would find, I strolled forward, wiping the last taste of burger from my lips. "Thanks." I tried to sound relaxed, no matter what I smelled like.

A white mailbox tilted back on a pole already absurdly short. A young elm with yellow and green leaves marked the end of the swale. The fog swallowed everything else. Following the chain-link fence to the driveway, I stepped to the side of a rivulet of blood meandering into the street, as if avoiding an errant oil spill. I snorted at the smell of fresh death.

Isabella, in her human form, lay torn apart on the concrete. Her clothes had been shredded into her bloody flesh. She'd never been allowed to shift before they'd killed her. Bones showed through her right arm crossed under her chin. Her green eyes stood out even in the dim light, staring into the mist, while her gray hair seemed to blend into the concrete drive. The other body, a silhouette crumpled closer to the steps of the house and almost overshadowed by the dark red door, would be her mate, Rodrigo.

My pulse raced. I'd been too late. Did Sofia know of my little errand? This was going to be tricky. I held my breath.

Naked, Sofia stepped out of the fog to my right, likely having just shifted back from her wereform. Bare feet remained on the grass instead of joining me on the driveway. The blood on her arms and face still glistened.

Sofia's dark brown hair rested over her shoulders, its matted tips leaving ruddy streaks on light brown skin. Her blood-stained face held a sly smirk, and her green eyes watched my expression with a piercing coolness. She'd arrived a few years ago and had quickly become a sharp candidate favored to lead the pack as Isabella grew older.

This carnage had happened recently. *Perhaps minutes ago.* Possibly while I'd been walking into their neighborhood. *I didn't hear a thing.* Shifters in wereform could work very quickly. Considering the heightened level of emotions that had to be stirring through the pack, I'd been lucky to have survived this far. However, I wasn't getting my hopes up. "You are the new First — Primera." I feigned the shock, but the fear oozing out of my pores was real. *Stay calm,* I told myself.

Sofia had been the reason I'd come to deal with Isabella. We had both determined that a Fae had infiltrated the shifters. The signs were there: beer going bad, missing jewelry, and the odd flowers growing through the asphalt and concrete. Sofia had been our most likely candidate, though it rarely happened that Fae used glamour to mimic and penetrate a pack, so we had to be sure. I'd procured the tool we needed, and it lay in the bottom of my pocket, a quick death sentence if Sofia suspected. This was one of the more awkward situations I'd gotten myself into lately, to put it mildly.

Adjusting to interpreting her as Fae, I noted her hands loose at her hips, indicating concern or nervousness. Still worried about her new position? Other shifters may attempt to test the new leader — it happened. I didn't want to be standing nearby if that occurred. What had moved Sofia to act this night after waiting for three years? Fae lived for hundreds of years. Patience was their norm.

The pack would kill her together if they knew she were Fae. Three things truly threaten a Fae's life: iron, cremation, and being eaten. None of those methods was really my problem; I just needed to get out alive.

Sofia tilted her head. "Well, Carl, what business did you have with Isabella tonight?"

Good question. Just bringing a ring that would disrupt the glamour on the wearer, talisman to out a Fae. *Something you might kill me over in a blink of an eye.* Isabella could have simply required that her people put it on, and when Sofia refused, it would have been the end of her. Now, it was a death sentence for *me* if Sofia discovered what I carried. Then again, she could be exactly what she claimed. Somehow, I doubted that.

My muscles stiff with tension, I shrugged as if we were chatting at the local bodega. "Things have been slow for me this month. I was hoping to drum up some business." I nodded toward Isabella's body. "Perhaps, I should let you settle in. I can drop by at a more convenient time."

Sofia didn't relax. She didn't seem to buy my story. I wouldn't have; it had been weak. I needed a quick plan.

"Perhaps we should turn you." Sofia offered a cruel smile, showing her teeth.

Disturbing, but also a relief. I sighed, draining some of my anxiety. Sofia didn't know any specifics of my dealings with Isabella, or perhaps that we suspected a Fae at all. If she had, she wouldn't want that knowledge alive in *any* form, human or shifter. Whatever the situation was, I needed to be out of it.

The moon glowed through the fog. "The East Bay Vampires would have an issue with that; they've already claimed my blood." I grimaced lightly. "Besides, I'm sure I'll be more useful to you as a fence. I have no qualms with changes in leadership. Happens all the time in my line of work." I tried not to sound desperate.

Shapes formed as the mist thinned. Ten or more shifters stood inside the small yard and on the far end of the driveway by the garage. The one still behind me, my original escort, was likely Sofia's mate, Albert. I rarely saw them in wereform, but I recognized him in the clearing mist by the large black tufts under his ears.

I'd lied; I did worry when leadership changed. Sometimes new regimes wanted to wipe the slate clean and hire new people — start fresh. Always a good time to keep out of the way. More so, with Fae. Shifters were far more practical. Well, when they hadn't shifted.

Taking a deep breath, I geared into salesman mode. I flicked the index fingers of both hands toward the sky and put on a beaming smile. "Give me a task. Nothing too small or too big." With a wink, I pointed at Sofia. "New client. I'll wave all commissions."

The other shifters remained in the depths of the fog, but as the wind swirled, I could see their shapes fade in and out. I didn't dare turn from Sofia, but I could be sure there were others on the street behind me. Isabella's pack, now Sofia's, held about thirty shifters. They were the second largest in South Florida, but hardly my strongest client. I just wanted out alive, and human.

Sofia studied me, possibly trying to decide what to believe about my visit. I didn't come often, and rarely to drum up business. Vampires had the real money for traders like me. She'd only been in the pack for the past three years, during which I'd seen her a dozen times. Claiming to be without a pack, she'd arrived as a transplant from South America. Was she buying my act? Being a recent rogue had been part of the reason Isabella and I had suspected her.

"There is nothing I can imagine needing from you." Sofia spoke with a finality that chilled my blood. Her gaze moved to Albert behind me. Hell. I felt him approach. Her hands had moved up from her sides, a Fae movement indicating relaxation. She no longer viewed me as a threat, but she might kill me just to be sure.

"New rogue in town," I said, a bit too quickly. It could be excused — everyone wanted to live. But, as a Fae, she would be loath to accept a gift, even of information.

"Bernardo." Sofia smirked. "I've heard." She rubbed her right forearm, a solid Fae indication of sensing a powerful position and pleased with themselves.

Where had she heard about Bernardo? Could she be working with the other Fae? Isabella and I had thought perhaps this a personal rebellion against Fae culture, not a cryptid war. Had we been wrong? There hadn't been a Fae attack since the Salem massacre. My grandfather had been killed in that one.

I needed something to prove my worth. "Mimi is working on him. Recruiting him. Catalan stock, he's very strong." I took a breath, trying to calm myself. My speech had become stilted, short, and staccato. Panicked. Not a good stance with shifters, or Fae.

Sofia shrugged. "We've known this. She can have him."

The shifters had started to move positions, as if restless. They hadn't shifted back. I didn't know many of Isabella's pack, and fewer in shifted form. If they did have designs on leadership, it would happen soon, possibly while I was there.

If she killed me, discarded a useful tool of the old regime, would that stave off any attempts at rivals standing up to her? Otherwise, it made no sense for her to get rid of me, if she didn't think I was a threat.

I couldn't be sure Sofia was Fae, but every instinct told me that Isabella and I had been right. Part of it could be the slight mannerisms, ones that I recognized from the times I had dealt with the Fae. They only cared about talismans, and pretty ones at that.

How could I possibly get Sofia to put on the ring — with witnesses? Fae would not take gifts.

However, Fae could take spoils; a new leader owned all the possessions of the vanquished. Fae liked trinkets far more than shifters.

I held my breath as I reached into my pocket and took out the gold ring. A small uncut emerald sat in a crude setting, nothing much to look at. I tilted it in hazy moonlight, wishing the edges sparkled more. Albert would rip my head off if Sofia called for it.

"I'd almost forgotten. Isabella paid for this a while back. I'll not be called a thief." With what I hoped was a nonchalant flip, I tossed the ring onto Isabella's corpse. It stuck in one of the bloody trenches slashed into her stomach. The moonlight caught the edge of it and glinted.

Sofia straightened. Her fingers splayed out, pointing toward the ground. A Fae ready to work their power with the earth. "What is that?"

I felt her mate's breath at my neck. Shifters in wereform could be a bit — proactive. Sweat oozed out my pores, and I cursed every drop.

I held up my hands. "Nothing. A talisman she'd requested. An illuminator. Rare, but hardly important or powerful."

Sofia relaxed. "Explain."

I assumed my best sales posture. Legs spaced evenly with my shoulders, head slightly forward, and hands gesturing at neck height. My stomach in knots, I wanted to wretch up that burger. "Simple enough. The wearer will be able to see silver, even iron, at about twenty to thirty feet. Through clothes if close enough, say half that. So, a hidden silver bullet or knife would shine out like a beacon with this illuminator, even hidden in a pocket."

I smiled excitedly as I reached in my pocket and pulled out my set of keys. One, old and slightly rusted and smelling of oil, stood out as larger than the rest. In truth, it was iron and opened a chest that especially Fae and most cryptid would avoid. "This is old, raw, blood iron. I don't have anything silver, but I'd not walk in here with something like that, would I?" I dropped the keys back into the pocket of my sweats and waited with innocent expectation. "From here, it'll look like I've got a candle in my pants." Not my best sales pitch.

I waited as Sofia looked from my pants back to the ring I'd tossed on Isabella's corpse. Her hands had drifted up to chest high, fingers pinched to thumb — a Fae expression of curiosity or desire.

Albert hadn't moved, his hot breath close. He needed a mint.

Sofia stepped forward and picked the ring off Isabella's intestines. In a trait which would fit both a Fae and shifter, she sniffed the metal. Her fingers were slightly larger than Isabella's. I hoped she wouldn't notice that the ring would fit her better than the supposed client. Glancing at my pocket, her eyes seemed to gleam. Fae liked magic, talismans, shiny jewelry, and hated metals — silver and especially iron. For good reason.

I held my breath.

She put on the ring.

Her glamour vanished. Eight wooden horns rose up from the crown of her head. Sofia had cloven hooves. Long, delicate fingers spread out, one bearing the ring. Large ears pinned back against the side of her head. Glowing white eyes squinted at my pants — perhaps surprised that she found no glow there.

I blinked. I hadn't been sure.

The shifters around us exploded in howls.

Albert snarled, grabbing my arms with sharp claws that sunk deep into my muscle. His teeth nipped into my right shoulder before he threw me across the driveway.

I skidded on concrete, barely feeling the skin scrape off under my left shoulder. A maelstrom of howls and snarling filled the yard and driveway.

Bluish lightning flickered from the tips of Sofia's fingertips, dancing into concrete and grass alike. The scent of cinnamon and pine blossomed in the air. The driveway cracked open, and a root spiked through six inches of concrete to pierce Albert's chest. His growl turned into an anguished howl.

Branches from the small elm extended like snakes, stabbing two snarling shapes. Against the gray sky, they squirmed, skewered. The fog seemed to thicken and swirl. The moon faded. Howls and rustling branches roared in front of me. Isabella and Rodrigo's blood tainted the concrete around me with a sour metallic scent. I crawled on my back away from the frenzy.

The mist only allowed me to see clumsy shapes and movement. Another root drove through the concrete and stabbed into the fog behind Sofia, setting off an unseen yelp.

But it was not enough. One of the shifters made it to Sofia. A swipe of their paw slammed her forward, toward me. The root that had Albert pinned at its tip stabbed that shifter, who went down beside Isabella's corpse.

A heavy foot crushed onto my chest as one of the shifters ran over me. They tore into Sofia's neck. A second shifter dove on top of her, then a third. The limbs and roots wilted. Parts of Sofia flew in wet chunks into the curling mist. Shagging, growling forms dove on them, for vengeance or flesh.

I crawled away, hoping they would ignore me. I startled and cried out when one of the shifters stopped beside me. With a wolfish smile, it joined in Sofia's feast.

There would be more violence this night. The pack would need a new leader. Some of the shapes that Sofia's magic had skewered still moved. Albert was not one of them. If they hadn't been killed outright, they would heal. It wouldn't be in time to vie for leadership, but alive is alive.

On the far side of the grass, I survived the madness somehow, if not a little worse for the evening. Isabella and I had resolved her greatest concern. Despite her death, her pack was safe, if not smaller — and soon to be someone else's. Perhaps the new First would be appreciative of my efforts. *I'll settle for crawling out of here alive.*

Exhausted and in pain, I laid my head back, listening to the growls and tearing flesh. As improbable as it seemed, I felt hungry. The mist thinned, letting in the light from the city around us.

A human face appeared overhead, blocking the gray city haze. Naked, she had shifted back despite the carnage going on. She smiled, and her matted hair draped toward me. An odd, welcoming smile.

I felt the burn in my shoulder — where Albert had bitten me. My blood boiled inside my veins, and my heart quickened. I'd been turned.

Damn, the East Bay Vampires were going to be pissed.

KEVIN A. DAVIS writes and publishes in the contemporary fantasy, urban fantasy, and fantasy genres.

His origin story for the urban fantasy AngelSong series, Shat-

tered Blood, *went on sale in December of 2021, while the remaining five books are in a rapid release beginning in 2022. Other short stories of Kevin A. Davis have been or are scheduled to be published in these anthologies:* Strangely Funny VIII, Natural Instincts, Grandpa's Space Diner, Neither Beginnings or Endings, *and* Miscellany Volume I. *He won three Honorable Mentions and a Silver Honorable Mention in the Writers of the Future contest, Volume 38.*

The Khimmer Chronicles is his in-progress urban fantasy series. Set in pre-COVID Tallahassee, Kevin A Davis has been spending time hanging around the College Town area as well as the Railroad Square district where a fantastic group of artists work and his imaginary protagonist will collect friends. Depending on editing timeliness, the new series should begin release in the summer of 2022.

To read more about Kevin A. Davis and his work, visit his website at www.KevinArthurDavis.com, and you can download a free ebook of Shattered Blood *at https://dl. bookfunnel.com/lasx0yv2sr*

SOLO MISSION

BY MELVA GIFFORD

Apprentice Melossa stood in the shade of a huge oak tree, a slight breeze tugging at her braided hair. The late afternoon sun cast shadows across the floor of the forest. The rich aroma of underbrush permeated the air. Before her was an encampment within a small clearing. Her target, a young child, was screaming at the top of her lungs.

The girl's parents had offered Melossa the title of their meager farm if she could rescue their child. The father mentioned the thieves also stole their cow only when Melossa asked if the kidnappers taken anything else. She had used the cow's fresh droppings to trace the cow and thus find the kidnappers.

Her heart beat so fiercely her chest hurt. *This is fear, even though I'm a shade walker.* This was her first solo mission; she couldn't mess it up. She'd better think things through before she acted. Master Dorask had warned her of her tendency to act rashly. Her mentor would want a report after she finished. *Maybe combatting thieves shouldn't be my first task.* Too late. The parents were desperate.

"Why can't I get the brat to shut up?" a woman from the camp complained.

A man, his tone hard, answered. "We only wanted the cow. Why did you grab the brat?"

"She was such a delightful kid, giggling at us while playing in the yard. I want such a kid."

The man laughed, "Well, there you go. That fruit spoiled quickly. Stop shaking it; that will just make it yell louder. Feed it or spank it. Wait — give it to me. I'll shut it up."

"I don't want it killed, Tinsel."

"I'll only do a short cut across the throat, enough to silence it, make it mute. You'll never hear it complain or talk back to you when it gets older."

The woman's voice held resignation. "Oh, all right."

Melossa transported by shade walking and stood behind the trees next to the camp. She had better hurry and grab the girl before the kidnappers harmed her. The walker in her studied the camp, noting a row of trunk shadows stretching across the uneven ground.

What are your obstacles? Master Dorask would ask.

Two humans. I have surprise on my side, and I could quickly transport to a shade away from camp if necessary. That's why I'm here in the late afternoon.

What else?

No one else was in the camp but the couple and child. The thieves chose a thick area of the forest. They built a small fire to avoid detection. Only the scream of a child could lure fellow travelers to them. If she did not act quickly, the girl's scream would be permanently silenced.

Calm, my pounding heart.

With a clear idea of distances, she reached down to grab a wineskin hanging from her belt, next to a wooden plate. She drew in a slow breath. She hated confrontations and was glad that she would soon be gone.

Master Dorask had laughed about the wineskin. *"You expect that to protect you?"*

"I only need to temporarily blind my opponents long enough to do what I must."

"Idiot girl. You'd better learn to aim it."

What is there to aim? She'd point the nozzle and squeeze. Her uncle, acting as her mentor, was coarse in his instruction, complaints, and compliments. She'd come to love the crotchety old man as a father during his five years of tutorship. *I know what I am doing.*

The cow, tied to a tree at the side of the camp, turned to her and gave a loud moo. Too bad she couldn't retrieve the cow. The only way to do that would be to make it airborne by convincing it to jump with all its feet in the air. That was a stretch of her persuasion skills.

Maybe I could transport a horse with me if it was trained to jump. Her thoughts immediately touched upon an image of a small platoon of mounted shade walker soldiers suddenly appearing into the thick of a battle. They would enter, make strategic attacks, and disappear again before their enemies could retaliate.

Otherwise, Melossa could only transport the weight of things she could carry.

A money purse rested on the ground next to Tinsel. *Counting his treasure, most likely. I'll get the child home, pop back, and grab the purse. That should compensate the farmer for the loss of his cow. Maybe it'll teach these thieves the cost of their actions.*

The shade walker blinked slowly and was instantly beside the woman. Wineskin ready, Melossa pressed the sides and aimed it at the woman's face. The vinegar spat sharply to the left, missing her opponent's face completely. *What's wrong with the nozzle?*

The woman's gaze widened as she screamed.

Melossa twisted the skin and shoved it forward, nearly hitting the other's nose, and squeezed again.

Her opponent cried out, raising her hands and coughing at the liquid in her eyes and mouth.

The girl flew from the woman's hands. Melossa grabbed the child, stepped back into the shadow of a log, and tripped. The child fell beside her.

Tinsel bellowed an alarm and got his own dose of vinegar.

The kidnapper lunged toward her, but having been blinded, missed.

Melossa grabbed the child and rolled to her back, clutching the girl to her belly. She slammed her hand into the shade of a tree trunk and disappeared. Her surroundings instantly changed, and she lay on the ground of the homestead. Panting, she slowly regained her feet. The scream of the child drew her parents from their cabin, and shrills of joy accompanied the unification of family.

As soon as the mother grabbed her child, Melossa stepped into her shadow and disappeared.

The camp was in an uproar. The thief and kidnapper, still blinded, were groping about. Melossa crept behind Tinsel and silently reached down for the purse. She placed her foot into the shade of a rock he'd been sitting on. "Mend your ways," she said, blinked again, and disappeared.

The family was still hugging and kissing when Melossa stepped beside them. She laughed at their antics. The weight of the purse was significant. *Gold?* She opened it, and her gaze widened. *From whom had the thieves stolen this prize?*

"Master Melossa." The farmer stepped solemnly before her. "We promised you the title of our farm."

She nodded. "You did. You need not pay your debt. Just remain an honorable man." She handed him the purse of gold. "Buy a new cow and pay off your debts. Buy twice the seed for next year and expand your farm. Give the remainder to the town orphanage."

The farmer opened his mouth upon noting the weight of the purse. He bowed deeply, eyes shimmering with moisture. "Yes, Master."

The shade walker grinned. *I'd better report to Master Dorask.* Honor required her to admit to the misalignment of wineskin nozzles and watching her step when feeling panicked. He'd never let her live either of them down. Her uncle had a vicious sense of humor. *Lesson learned.*

She unhooked the wooden plate from her belt, tilting it until the bright sunlight caused a round shadow on the ground next to her. She stepped into it and disappeared.

MELVA GIFFORD HAS BEEN WRITING since her youth. She has fiction and nonfiction shorts published in various publications and websites. She won first place for her young adult book, Operation Middle School Madness, *at the 2016 Utah Arts council. Her story "Forfeit" was featured in the January 2021 issue of* Cricket. *She's won five honorable mentions from the international contest* Writers of the Future. *Melva's fiction touches upon many realms including Children, Mainstream, Science Fiction and Fantasy, and Romance. She has also published a nonfiction text,* I Know You THINK This is a Toaster: Promoting Family Values Through Object Lessons. *Her currently published works include* Pocket Troubles *and* Operation Middle School Madness, *available on her website: melvagifford.com.*

Melva is also a storyteller. She is a Utah Story Guild member, Timp Tellers member, contributor to USG's Tale swapper newsletter, and toastmaster's member. Melva has performed on the PBS radio program Story Mine, Story Crossroads, WUS story-telling festival, Pioneer Days, *and* Ellis Island *(Orem event). Her repertoire includes patriotic camps, community fairs, Provo Park, and church. She has told stories at Orem's Library's Liars Competition, Pioneer park, family reunions, Orem deaf school, family parties, and the Springville Art Museum.*

WE CALL IT A WIN

BY MIKE JACK STOUMBOS

The alarms blared relentlessly, but their noise hardly compared to the screams of both Human and Teek crew echoing through the hull, screeches of shredding metals and polymers, rushes of air blocked by slamming bulkheads, and frantic barks from command speakers. The din would turn to silence once the warship was torn apart.

Lieutenant Victoria Hass slammed against a wall when vector forces shifted around her. She shoved herself back to standing and continued to sprint, while her wrist monitor tried to warn her of too many dangers. Her flight suit's underlay would assist with minor pressure or heat loss but wouldn't be of any help if she were blasted into space. She had to reach an escape pod.

As she rounded a corner, a fear response in her blood and nerves sent the wrist monitor into overdrive. Glowing haloes, clusters of visual distortions, had invaded the deck — all spherical, completely silent, unbelievably destructive.

Hass dove toward the pod, passing within a few meters of a halo and feeling its static pull. The door opened, and Hass tumbled into her lifeboat; she'd treat bruises later. Then she heard, "Wait!"

The pleading crewman was seconds away, only a few more steps. But just before he crossed the threshold, a halo enveloped his torso, leaving his face to cry in agony until the alien energy strangled his voice.

Hass reached out her hand to take his — instinct and conditioning overtaking sense — and the distorted ring of light stretched across their arms as well. Her wrist device exploded, sending instant pain before her hand went numb. Hass saw sudden blue and white striations racing up her arm and tried to wrench away. Her scream joined the others —

* * *

Her eyes opened.

Hass lay on her side, in her bunk, in a dimly lit room. She held her breath and tensed, then relaxed her core. When she finally exhaled, Hass felt her heart begin to slow to its trained resting rate. The memory grew less acute, into the familiar dull terror of the last few months. The prickling of her missing right hand remained the most aggravating souvenir.

No alarms sounded here. This ship, the *TSS Albatross*, had not been breached. Hass had to tell herself she was safe even though she knew, at any moment, those haloes could phase through the walls and consume her crew. Again she held her breath, tensed, then released.

She fastened her prosthetic just below the elbow only after she'd dressed, then used her left hand to adjust her collar stripes in the mirror. Her hair, previously short, was now buzzed to less than a centimeter, practical for infrequent showers, and the designation marked her as captain of a deep-space warship. As such, Hass had a responsibility to the flagging morale, which included minimizing any sign she'd wrestled with nightmares. She was unwilling to inspire anyone else's jitters or cold feet.

The corridors were already alive with the crew, especially standby pilots doing what they could to keep their nerves sharp without exhausting themselves before a launch call. They knew that orders happened quickly and without advance notice. This kept them alive. In fact, they'd done so well compared to the rest of the fleet, many wore patches to acknowledge their current captain, reading, "Hass' Tross."

Human crew snapped quick salutes as she passed. Most onboard Teek — their exoskeletal allies — mimicked the gesture or made a thrumming sound, their thoraxes vibrating respectfully.

Hass said nothing and tried not to think too loudly, just in case.

"Captain," said a comms officer who was anything but calm, "received casualty report from the *Dinamis*, orbiting Syedi-3."

"Thank you, Lieutenant," she said, without audibly gritting her teeth. She avoided estimating death tolls in the offensive around Syedi's third moon or thinking how the traditional, by-the-book crew of the *TSS Dinamis* were setting themselves up for slaughter. "I'll look after my briefing." She offered an encouraging smile, knowing she would gladly trade places with the younger, less-damaged lieutenant, who only had to see a few such reports and was responsible for none of them. Not that he had it easy, sporting bags under his eyes and pale skin from lack of sleep, sun, or regular nutrition. Mostly, Hass knew, such pallor came from sustained fear.

Fear was so commonplace that most crew could barely function without taking regulators. Everyone had maintained a state of high-strung numbness for weeks at least, months for some. Regardless, it was too long a time to drift through space, around a besieged alien planet, waiting for the *go* order that might get them killed.

How could they *not* be afraid, facing an enemy who appeared through solid matter or into empty space, who anticipated tactics, who always moved faster? Though the Humans were quite different physically than their four-foot-tall insect allies, they were united by this very rational fear against the most *alien* alien either of them had ever known.

The Teek she passed chittered louder than usual, aware something big was happening, even if they wouldn't speak it directly.

Hass swiped her wrist at a high-security door's lock, which, in addition to its real designation, had a marker-scrawled *ThinkTank* label. Behind the door, rerunning notes across the touch-screen conference table, stood Teller and Jane-One, neither of whom had left the ThinkTank in days, for fear of tipping off the other crew.

"Morning, Captain," said Teller, a slender, dark-skinned ensign whose various trainings would have labeled him a doctor if the Transnational Space Force, or TSF, had accredited programs. Teller's lack of hygiene was countered by the Teek beside him, who, due to natural chemical secretions, always smelled like fresh laundry and ozone.

Jane-One raised her brick-red head, her lateral mandibles flexing in a gesture resembling a yawning mantis. The wings hanging from her back were unobstructed by a uniform and twitched while she spoke, skipping the social niceties. "Covert confirmation from all hive-queens: use all available force. The planet is lost." Jane-One's voice was mechanically precise and consistent, more like a buzzing robot than a sentient insect.

"Good," said Hass. "How many are we waiting for?"

"Um . . ." Teller glanced at Jane-One, who offered no gesture of assurance. "We might not be able to wait for all of them. At least two hives on the surface are fully compromised. Wayne has overrun —"

"Waiting is bad," interrupted Jane-One. "The planet Syedi is lost. All active queens agree. We must strike Wayne before they absorb the plan."

The Teek's blunt remark produced at least a few seconds of silence. It was true: despite the efforts of the recently-formed alliance, the planet Syedi, home to millions of Teek, now served as a playground and veritable buffet for the incorporeal invaders called *Wayne*. Hass didn't like the convenient code-word for the enemy, chosen because the Teek term translated to *wall-less* for their ability to pass through solid objects. Whatever they were called, no Human word could sum up the ruthlessly destructive force of this enemy.

Hass allowed herself one short groan. It was the kind of groan that acknowledged she shouldn't be commanding a hybrid ship with four-foot-tall hive-mind insects, who looked like *they* should be the enemy of humanity. At this point in their alliance, both species should have been struggling to overcome their language and cultural barriers, not desperately defending the fates of solar systems against an incomparable foe.

"Okay," she said, tapping her fist against the table — a habitual segue that now produced a metallic clink. "It's now or never. We'll have the admiral on the line in a minute. Where's Chandan?"

"He's escorting the scramble pilot in from the *Charlemagne*."

"Good," said Hass. "Better to do the briefing all at once."

All three nodded, even the Teek who was newer to Human gestures. They understood the hazards of too much planning or coordinating just like they knew the dangers of using space-folds for faster-than-light travel when any Wayne were in scanning range.

"Do you think he'll agree?" wondered Teller, clearly asking about the admiral.

"Yes," she said, which was more of a hope than a lie.

The door opened to two more figures, the fourth and fifth parties needed for the operation.

"Captain," said the Human, striding in. Lieutenant Nick Chandan fit the classic action-figure physique and posture, including jet-black hair in a jarhead cut. He proudly sported a scorpion tattoo above the wrist, alongside the official TSF Marines logo. Chandan too should have been suffering from lack of sleep, but he was fueled by anticipation and more than a few stims. Gesturing behind himself, he said, "Every-one, this is Jane, on loan from our sister ship."

Their fifth was a different kind of Teek with four arms and no wings. She wore a modified TSF flight suit and carried her own oxygen canister and helmet. And, like many Teek, she called herself *Jane*, not only the first Human name ever attributed to a Teek but also one of the easiest for them to pronounce.

"I guess that makes her Jane-Two," said Chandan.

Teller cut in, "Nope, Jane-Two fixed the captain's pros-thetic, so she'd be Jane-Three."

"Greetings, Jane-Three," said Jane-One, completely unfazed by the name and number debate.

"Someday, you'll have to pick surnames," said Captain Hass, in a manner she hoped didn't offend. She had met some dozen Teek named Jane, more than a few of whom served on the *Albatross*. She was also well-aware that the non-queen Teek didn't have a biological sex and only elected to use *she* when working with Humans; even the word *Teek* was an approximation of a word that couldn't be said without independent mandibles, but all of that was better than the haloes. "Glad to have you aboard, Jane-Three."

"It is very nice to meet you, Captain Victoria Hass of the *Albatross*, a-k-a Hass' Tross," said Jane-Three, which might as well have been piped out of an ancient typewriter.

"Jane here's the best independent-minded pilot in their ranks," assured Chandan.

"So I've heard. We're going to need that." Picking up the momentum in the room, she added, "Teller, patch into comms. Do we have the admiral's signal?"

"On standby. Ready when you are."

"No time like the present," she said, more to herself than anyone else. The five of them, three Humans and two Teek, in a little dark room, with a collection of highly sensitive documents, looked more like an anarchist cell planning a coup than a studied military operation. Ever since they'd learned of the enemy's powers of either telepathy or preemption, such tightly-focused planning had become essential, even if it resembled guerrilla warfare in space. If they played this right, everything would change.

Hass caught a glance at her own appearance in a dark screen's reflection and instinctively straightened her uniform. "Have the comms monitor ready to modulate or scramble at any sign of interference." They didn't know which of their signals Wayne understood, but no one took chances anymore.

For that reason, the image was poor quality and the sound choppy when the slipspace signal first came. Amazing how even the newest long-distance technology could still feel obsolete and imperfect. Even so, Admiral David Gomez populated the screen effectively enough to show his rank insignias and perturbed expression. Both Gomez's gut and balding pattern could have been easily medically corrected, so it was a statement to display them in this decade. "Captain Victoria Hass. As requested, I am alone." He had a habit of speaking with a sneer, and it was no secret that he didn't like being kept out of the fight; in many ways, he was stranded outside of the system as effectively as others were kept within. "Glad to see you're done keeping me on hold. Are you about to launch another assault?"

"Admiral Gomez," she replied, and actually had to clear her throat, which she hoped wouldn't undermine her authority. "I need authorization for something unprecedented."

The muscles at the admiral's temples visibly pulsed as he clenched. "Everything in this war is unprecedented, Hass. What's the plan this time?"

"We're going to trigger a space-fold; actually, about a dozen," she began, and even with the slight delay in the call, she saw Gomez raise his eyebrows before she concluded, "in the atmosphere of the planet Syedi."

"Are you crazy, Hass? I mean, can you even do that?" His incredulity was understandable; space-fold technology already seemed to defy known physics, and space-folds could *only* be safely maintained in a vacuum, far enough away from planetary interference — but they weren't looking for stability.

"Um, actually, yes, Sir," she said.

Jane-Three, another new addition to the cone of information, reacted to this revelation as well, asking, "Is this theoretical?"

The captain cued Teller, whose expertise was more than just theoretical. "We've observed the phenomenon twice in actuality. Once on accident," he said, setting up one of their recordings, like a lawyer presenting exhibits. A spaceship filled his screen, which would be mirrored for the admiral.

The warship in the recording stood out bright against the black of space and an even deeper black of the space-fold it had opened. Its nose angled partially in, frozen in a moment of entering the wormhole. The shape and decals were well-known to Hass. Even trying not to think about her narrow escape sent tingles to her missing hand.

"This is the *TSS Boudica*, right as she opened the fold," Teller explained, "in a feed captured by a rear guard fighter and directly sent to the *Dinamis*." He cued the feed forward, and in a second a tiny speck of light emerged and created a short lens flare. "Right here is the first visible instance of Wayne. They came in through the edges of the fold, like they were waiting in slipspace."

Soon, the ship was covered with tiny haloes that, from such an extreme distance, looked like bubbles of water. Innocuous, until after they'd rushed into the hull and started creating breaches from within.

"Ensign, we've seen this before," said the admiral. "Hell, this footage is why we're not able to get your asses out of there. The folds are death warrants; they draw in too many Wayne before you can even set a destination."

"True, Sir," said Teller, "but bear with me." He made some quick adjustments to the feed before continuing. "Here is where the ship cycled out of control."

The viewer's angle shifted as the fighter pilot tried to react, but Hass noticed a few silvery blips — escape pods — abandoning ship. After so many rewatches, she was pretty sure she knew which one was hers.

"This is where the fold generator bugged." He paused and clicked for his preset highlights to appear. There was clearly a twisted, warped section on the underbelly of the ship and a purplish spot that should not have existed. "A new fold started in the ship's grav systems, *in* solid matter, not a klick out in front. Here, we see catastrophic system failure, crumpling of multiple decks. From an outside scan, it looks like any attached Wayne were destroyed."

The admiral leaned back a little, but his lips stayed tightly shut.

"Well, after finding this out, I — We," amended Teller, with a look to the captain to make sure he was still on-track, "wanted to see if it was duplicatable. So we dropped a smaller fold generator on a moon."

"You dropped a generator?" asked the admiral.

"Yes, Sir. It was a portable — um —" Teller snapped his fingers a few times, trying to conjure the words. "The generators we took out of the Teek fighters. After space-folds were ruled a no-go, it was better to reduce the mass, so we yanked the generators. One we dropped on the moon Syedi-8 — no population — by a pilot who didn't know what they were dropping. Later, we remotely triggered the beginning of a fold, just a very tiny one. Once more, Wayne came instantly, like they knew it would be there. Even though it was small, they were still drawn to the field's energy. But the field quickly collapsed, and they were susceptible — Wayne, that is — to damage."

Teller probably would have kept monologuing, but the admiral cut him off. "Wait a second — you hurt them with a space-fold? I thought they fed on it."

"Well, no, Sir, it was from the instability in solid matter," said Teller, flailing a little. "See, normally, mechanical assault can't hurt them, but in combination —"

"Admiral, every test and simulation we've run shows these forces, from an in-matter fold, are deadly to anything, even the enemy," said Hass completely assuredly. "Wayne can survive in space, but they can't survive the collapse of matter in a space-fold."

"You're serious," he observed, or maybe asked. Then, he did what they feared. Admiral Gomez resolutely shook his head. "This isn't going to work. It's too rash, and it's too risky. You'd need a whole fleet to coordinate this kind of thing."

Hass knew from experience that coordinating with the full fleet was a bad decision, that Wayne somehow knew their maneuvers and showed up, and that the only reason her missions had been surviving was because they kept the planning secret and saved orders to the last second. She had to tell him that. "Sir —"

"No seasoned officer would suggest it, Hass. If Captain Wu were still —" he said, then abruptly cut himself off, realizing he was losing composure. "You're really going to sacrifice — *destroy* a planet, hoping to take a few of theirs?"

Everyone erupted at once, forgetting the chain of command for the sake of urgency. Hass, Teller, and Chandan all tried to assure the admiral of their certainty in different ways. Both Teek said the same thing: "The planet is already lost."

Jane-One knew there was no hope left for Syedi and had the go-ahead from many hive-queens, some who still had children on the surface. Hass reminded herself that Teek didn't always think in terms of children, or siblings, but she recognized this biological fact.

Jane-Three, who was hearing the plan along with the admiral, was already on board and willing to extrapolate. They couldn't do any more real harm to the terrain, and they'd provide some mercy to the Teek corpses, or soon-to-be corpses — the disconnected Teek were unable to interact, for all thought-waves were consumed by a relentless enemy. Many had been stripped of their minds completely and lay twitching, unable to control any actions, until their autonomic systems eventually shut down. To a Human like Hass, this fate sounded worse than death.

The admiral was listening, his fingers steepled before

him. Even from a great distance, he too knew they were losing the war, and so entertained even drastic measures.

"Admiral," began Lieutenant Chandan, planting firmly at attention. "If I may. Even in our worst encounters with the enemy, we are still showing that anything they are willing to consume can be modified to hurt them. Electric fields are candy, but at the right frequency, they form a shield, a net, or even a bullet to Wayne. They adjust quickly, especially if there is a swarm to disseminate the information — like a computer or something wired in series. But if we catch them off-guard, it can stun some. Do it on a big enough scale, and there won't be any buddies to swarm in and fix them."

"You're talking electromagnetic pulses?" asked the admiral. "I thought we tried that. It did as much damage to us as them. They always recovered while our tech was down."

"Yes, Sir," Chandan agreed, "and that is why we are proposing a massive EMP blast, coordinated across the planet, just *after* the space-folds have been triggered."

Captain Hass watched the admiral's face closely. His eyes widened, then narrowed. He understood. Once they started the folds, they didn't need the generators — folds triggered in atmosphere would soon collapse, even without any devices to continue the process. Once stunned, Wayne would have no time to react.

The proposed plan — though crazy — was plausible, even likely to succeed. Monumental gains, but with heavy costs.

"What kind of losses are you projecting?" asked the admiral.

Jane-One was prepared to field this question. "We have accepted the planet will be rendered uninhabitable. The forces to destroy Wayne will also kill remaining Teek on the surface. This is an acceptable loss for first duty," she concluded. Teek liked to say that. *First duty*, to the safety of the queen and continued existence of their own hive. Sacrifice was interesting in that context.

The admiral, however, had another concern which hadn't been addressed. "And the pilots?"

"That's where Jane-Three comes in," said Hass, which Jane-Three answered with a quickly snapped salute — both right hands simultaneously.

"Admiral," stated Jane-Three, much like a computer learning to repeat.

"Oh, yes, Jane of the *Charlemagne*," acknowledged the admiral, "currently joining Hass' Tross." The second showed a little more disdain.

Hass hadn't chosen *Albatross*, or the personalized nickname; she had simply been the only ranking officer on deck when a new captain was needed.

Jane-One jumped in with, "Jane-Three develops illogical flight-paths and attack patterns," which was meant as a compliment. Most Teek stayed connected to each other and their queen, which made their very coordinated movements too easy for Wayne to counter. Jane-Three was an anomaly; she developed and issued unique flightpaths, effectively allowing Teek pilots to individually do what Humans did naturally.

"I'm aware," said the admiral, "but that doesn't answer the question. How will the pilots fare?"

"Well . . ." Hass wanted to say, *better than they have with any other captain.* "The pilots have not been informed yet, and even when they launch, they won't know what they're carrying. Individual orders will come in pieces, to drop the devices as far from each other as possible, then to bug out immediately after the drop, so they're not in the radius of any collapsing fields."

Gomez started tapping his thumb on the desk. "Casualty projections?"

"Sir," she began, ready to recite what she had planned, "with the randomized scramble orders, our casualties have been minimal, and most —"

"Christ!" sneered the admiral, somehow stretching exclamation to three syllables. Her eyes must have given her away. "Don't evade me, Hass. This could be a suicide mission, and even if it works, you're saddling them with an extermination order. They'll be dropping nukes and won't even know what they're flying or dying for."

"Sir, we kept this on a need-to-know basis, because when we do full debriefs with everyone, *all* of them die and accomplish *nothing*. The more organized we are, the more Wayne anticipates our moves. I don't know if they catch our comms, our brainwaves, or can predict the future, but when we operate like this, most of my pilots come back. Some losses are better than full losses," she insisted, recalling the casualty report she still had to read, deaths from the *Dinamis*, most likely total again. Most likely futile again.

"Do you have any idea what level of destructive force you'll set off? Do you even know what a safe distance looks like?"

"No, Admiral."

"Dammit, Hass! You're sending our boys out there to die like pawns on a chessboard."

Hass swallowed. "I am giving orders to our men and *women* and *Teek*, Sir. And I understand the responsibility and risk."

"Do you, Hass? You're not trained for this." It was no secret that Admiral Gomez didn't like battlefield promotions. He had told Hass, on several occasions, that she wouldn't have been made a captain if there had been any replacements on-hand.

"Everything is unprecedented, Sir," she said, trying not to

shake, trying not to blink as she echoed his words back to him. "I'm here; I'm who they've got. I need your go-ahead."

"It's gonna haunt you, Hass." He'd said that one before too. Usually, when he spoke to her, it sounded like scolding from an angry parent to a petulant child who wants to grow up too fast. This time, seeing concern and even sympathy in his eyes, Hass had the feeling that she had actually grown up. She also had not heard an objection. "Understood, Sir."

Gomez made a gesture, half-hearted at first, a wave of the back of his hand. Then he said, "Green light."

* * *

DOZENS OF PILOTS launched in a series of short waves. They wove erratically, not always at top speed. Some flew off-course to moons; others pretended to rendezvous with other ships. The *Charlemagne* and the *Dinamis* both scrambled alert fighters and sent out their own waves, which were supplied with more of Jane-Three's seemingly random patterns.

The haloes appeared in blips along the wakes of ships and throughout the atmosphere of Syedi. Evidence of Wayne appeared even where they couldn't be seen — phantoms pulling fighters off track, slowing them down, fritzing their systems.

But still the fighters flew on, down below the cloud layer and then back up, in zig-zags, while bursts and pops from the ground below signaled the beginning of the folds.

The cascading bursts of light and sudden patches of unnatural darkness occurred quickly. Spontaneous vacuums and cracks in the fabric of the universe, openings of worm-holes without destinations. Then, waves of volatile energy were so violent, even Wayne couldn't contend.

From high orbit, Hass watched the planet fracture, sending out shockwaves that overtook the nearest fighters.

The crews of the warships surged away, then bolstered shields and braced for multiple impacts.

Even long after the shockwaves had concluded, scans of the split planet's surface revealed no surviving Teek. And no Wayne.

* * *

THE INCOMING CALL was marked *urgent*.

Hass recognized the ID, but took her time to sit down at the new desk before she answered. She was tired but had no reason to be on edge.

"Captain Hass!" exclaimed Teller as soon as his image populated, the expression more anxious than excited. "I'm on secure transmission. Are you alone?"

Hass couldn't tell what level of concern she should feel for the sensationalizing scientist. "I am, Teller. Are you okay?"

He was shaking his head and half-gasping between statements. "We didn't — Captain, it didn't work."

She leaned forward on her right elbow, the stub of her forearm stopping just before the keyboard. "What are you talking about?"

"The bomb didn't really kill them, Captain. They're still out there. All of the Wallless — somewhere in space!"

As her own adrenaline started pumping, Hass worked to quiet her clenched jaw but did nothing to temper the sudden phantom ache where her hand should be. Her words were sympathetic, her tone strained. "Teller, listen to me, we've all had nightmares about the hostiles returning —"

"No, Captain, I'm serious. I reviewed the footage from the feeds on the surface — I've triple-checked it. They were live-emitting until the millisecond they were compromised." His eyes grew wider. If they were any more reflective, the whole scene could've played out in his terrified irises. "You know how we were worried they could predict our moves, read our minds? Well, they must have figured it out, because if you watch —" He cleared his throat, then corrected. "When *I* watched them, knowing what to look for, I saw what really happened. We littered that atmosphere with bombs, and when we were finally ready, we triggered the cascade, and it *looked* like it worked. But when slowed to a microsecond, they all disappeared just before."

Hass remained still. She held her breath, clenched and then relaxed her core muscles.

As if thinking she hadn't understood, Teller tried again, "They didn't go *with* the explosion, they slipped away into an unknown dimension *before* we could do it. They knew what was going to happen to the planet, so they just stepped away."

She slowly exhaled, letting her heart find a more balanced rhythm.

Because she hadn't answered, he demanded, "Captain, what do we do now?"

Captain Victoria Hass no longer served on the warship known as the *Albatross*. She was afforded the luxury of a daily shower and the ability to sleep without sedatives. Being part of the post-war Teek relief efforts still kept her busy and responsible for a crew, but certainly not in the same way the war had.

Even Teller was a junior-lieutenant, as well as a credentialed doctor, who hadn't needed to call her in months. Much had changed since they'd destroyed planet Syedi and ended the war.

"Teller," she said, carefully, evenly. "Have you or anyone else seen signs that Wayne has returned?"

"But," he began, then had to admit, "No."

"No. Not one sighting. If you're right, maybe we didn't really destroy them. Maybe they saw what we were capable of doing, what we were willing to do, and they ran away." She counted her heartbeats, pacing herself back to calm, even while a threat might linger somewhere in the cracks of space. The Human-Teek alliance had demonstrated the gall to detonate a planet to ensure victory. Maybe that was enough.

"So what do we do now?"

Hass understood the ramifications better than Teller realized. Given her service record and obvious camaraderie with the Teek, her influence was only growing. Soon, she too might wear the rank of admiral and be a guiding force of humanity's reach toward the stars.

"We call it a win," she said. "That's what we do now. And we keep growing, building, learning. We make sure that if those bastards ever do come back, we're ready to finish what we started."

"Yes, Captain," said Teller. "Understood."

The call ended with an electronic chime. The edges of the screen formed one quick halo before fading to black.

MIKE JACK STOUMBOS is a speculative fiction author, disguised as a believably normal schoolteacher living with his wife and their parrot. He is a first-place winner of the 2021 Writers of the Future Contest and the author of the space opera novel The Signal Out Of Space, *book 1 of This Fine Crew, published by Chris Kennedy Publishing in 2021. Mike Jack's short stories have appeared in several anthologies, including* Street Magic *from Camden Park Press,* Galactic Stew *from Zombies Need Brains LLC, and* Dragon Writers *alongside David Farland and Brandon Sanderson. You can find him at www.MikeJackStoumbos.com or on Twitter @MJStoumbos.*

ACKNOWLEDGMENTS

Hidden Villains would not have been possible without Editor-in-Chief Robyn Huss, who had the final decision on the best submitted stories she could bring to the anthology and made them even better. A fantastic editor, she manages to find the right way to frame the narration while keeping the author's voice. She worked with every author to bring out their best, then organized and compiled the final manuscript. Thank you.

With tens of thousands of words to review in the submissions, Inkd Publishing would like to thank Kevin Davis, April Davis and Heather Lewis for helping Robyn read through all those stories. They brought the best to you.

Vivid Covers did an amazing job with the design and artwork. Even if you're not looking for a cover, check out their website at designcovers.com.

If you enjoyed the stories in Hidden Villains, then you'll be happy to know that Robyn has agreed to help with another production next year. Same Team, Same Time, Next Year.

Please visit us at InkdPub.com or Facebook.